The Saint and The Scribe

Andrea Sherko

Cover image:	Hildegard-reading-and-writing - Public domain dedication image - PICRYL - Public Domain Media Search Engine Public Domain Search
Cover design :	Antoinette Pellegrini
Layout:	Antoinette Pellegrini We Inspire Now Books

We Inspire Now Books
PO BOX 133 Greensborough,
Victoria Australia 3088
www.weinspirenowbooks.com

Dedication

In memory of my lovely Mum.
Thank you for everything.

Contents

A Note To The Reader

Hildegard was born in 1098 in Bermersheim, Germany, the tenth child of Hildebert and Mechthild. From an early age, it became clear that Hildegard was 'special': she later wrote that she received visions from God from the age of three, and that she 'saw' things that others present did not.

There is considerable uncertainty surrounding Hildegard's childhood, but it seems that her parents entrusted her to the care and guidance of a young noblewoman, Jutta of Sponheim (1092-1136), when Hildegard was eight years old. The two women then entered the Benedictine monastery at Disibodenberg in 1112, when Jutta was 20 and Hildegard was 14, and established a thriving community of women within the otherwise all-male monastery.

During her long life, Hildegard achieved a great many things. When Jutta died in 1136, Hildegard was elected leader of their community, and went on to establish new convents in Rupertsberg (in 1150) and Eibingen (in 1165). She was a prolific writer on a wide range of subjects, including theology, botany, medicine and natural history. She was also a gifted musician, and composed numerous antiphons, hymns and chants for liturgical use.

After her death in 1179, several attempts were made to have Hildegard canonised by the Catholic Church, but it was only in 2012, over 800 years after her death, that she was finally recognised as the saint that she undoubtedly was.

I first became interested in Hildegard through her music. As a church musician myself, I was drawn to the beauty of her plainchant, which has a quality that seems to me to be almost 'other-worldly'. I later decided to write a book about her life to learn more about her, and as an attempt to organise and synthesise the often conflicting dates, places and events that comprise the life of this brilliant woman.

I could not have written this book without the wealth of information contained in the marvellous works of scholarship listed below as 'Further Reading'. I would particularly like to acknowledge the work of Anna Silvas in this regard. Using this information, I have, wherever possible, included factual persons, places and dates, and have attempted to create a logical chronology of events.

The majority of characters in this book are based on real people. Some characters are, of course, invented by me to fill in some 'gaps'. These fictional characters include the following:

- Brother Tobias (infirmarian at Disibodenberg)

- Brother Stefan (cellarer at Disibodenberg)

- Brothers Hans and Jurgen (armariuses at Disibodenberg)

- Sister Birgitta (women's infirmarian at Disibodenberg, Rupertsberg and Eibingen)

- Hilda (Volmar's sister)

- Sisters Gertrude and Ilse (nuns at Rupertsberg)

- Sister Mathilde (infirmarian at Rupertsberg after Sister Birgitta's move to Eibingen) and

- Father Georg (visiting priest at Rupertsberg)

All other people in the book, including abbotts, bishops, archbishops, leaders of religious communities, popes and emperors are real people who featured, to a greater or lesser extent, in Hildegard's life story.

One consequence of this is that some names belong to more than one character. There are, for instance, two Juttas (the anchoress and her servant), two Berthas (the nuns' maid and the sister of Frederick Barbarossa), and even two Hildegards! I would, of course, have given fictional characters different names, but I wanted to give real people their real names, hence the duplications. Apologies for any confusion this might cause!

There is also one character based on a real person whose name is not mentioned in the literature, that is, 'the philosopher'. Rather than invent a fictional name for a real person, I have chosen to refer to him by title only.

Little seems to be known about Hildegard's life in the period between her taking of vows (1114) and her assumption of leadership of the women's community at Disibodenberg after Lady Jutta's death (1136). In this part of the book, I have sought to lay the 'groundwork' for subsequent aspects of Hildegard's life, such as her keen interest in natural medicine and her beautiful musical creations, as well as her lifelong struggles with poor health.

The romantic aspect of the relationship between Hildegard and Volmar is entirely of my own creation. I have read nothing to suggest that they were anything other than friends and colleagues, and I have sought to depict Volmar's feelings for Hildegard in a dignified and respectful manner. Little seems to be known about Volmar as a person, and I was hoping to 'bring him to life' a little. It is, I believe, quite easy to imagine that a man who spent so many years with Hildegard would have such strong feelings for her. She was a truly amazing woman!

I have included a glossary of terms at the end of the book which you may find helpful.

You are welcome to write to me at andrea@persuasivewords.net. I would be pleased to hear from other Hildegard enthusiasts. We have much over which to enthuse!

Thank you for reading my book.

Andrea Sherko

Map

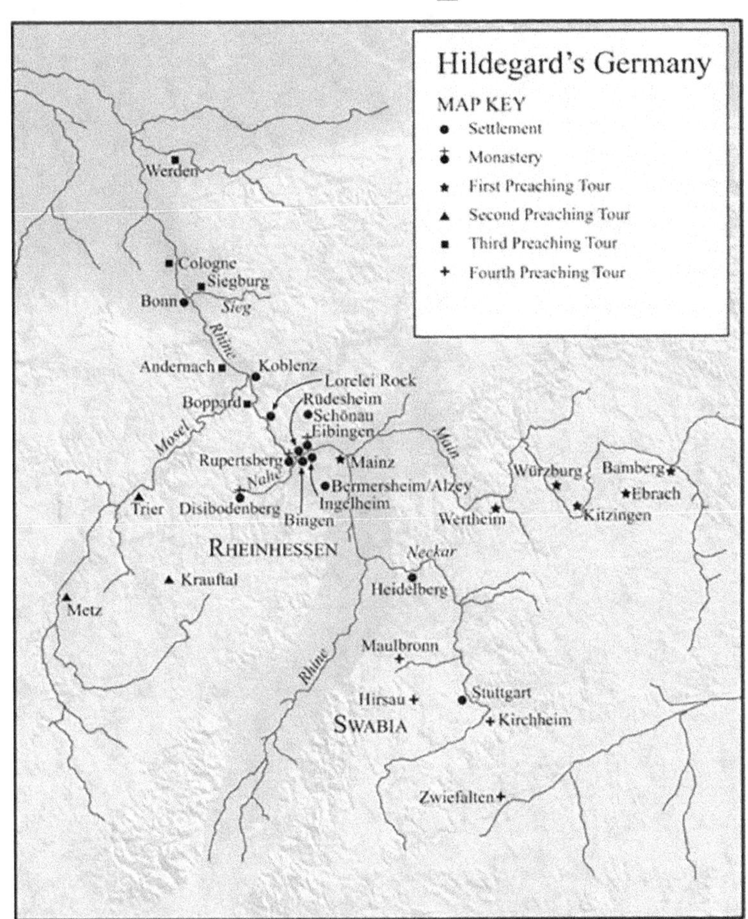

File:Hildegard map.jpg - Wikimedia Commons

Source	Own work. Map used in Hildegard of Bingen: A Spiritual Reader by Carmen Butcher, published by Paraclete Press , 2006 http://www.paracletepress.com.
Author	Sean Butcher & Carmen Butcher http://www.carmenbutcher.com
Permission	Creative Commons CC-BY-SA-2.

Prologue

Rupertsberg Abbey, near Bingen, Germany

February 1173

I lay my head back on the pillow and closed my eyes, exhausted from my efforts. Try as I might, I could not speak a word. This time was even worse than the last.

Hildegard took my hand in both of hers, and we sat in silence for a while.

"Volmar," she said quietly.

I opened my eyes. She smiled.

"It is time for me to go," she said.

Then she did something she had never done before. She leaned forward and kissed me gently on my forehead.

"Sleep peacefully, dear friend," she said, then got up and left the infirmary quietly.

I looked around the dimly lit room. Sister Mathilde moved quietly from bed to bed, checking to see that everyone was as comfortable as possible. The pungent smells of human sickness and herbal remedies filled my nostrils. The candles were burning low. Soon, all would be darkness, but I was not quite ready to yield to sleep. I closed my eyes and allowed my mind to wander.

PART ONE

*Disibodenberg Monastery,
near Mainz, Germany*

Chapter 1

February 1109

I remembered with vivid clarity how my life of service to God first began. I had not thought about this part of my life for years and years, but there I was, on that cold, grey morning long ago.

The journey had seemed a long one. I was seated behind my father on his favourite rouncey, my hands gripping the back of the saddle. The rain had stopped some time ago, but the branches of the beech trees, heavy-laden with rainwater, dripped on us constantly. I was cold, wet, hungry and tired. Then we came around a bend, and my father stopped the horse. I looked up and gasped. Before us, high on its hill, stood the monastery in all its dark majesty. My spirits soared.

Even at first sight and from some distance, I knew that this was where I was meant to be.

Chapter 2

I was fifteen years old when I entered the monastery. Like many of the boys who arrived at the same time, I had always known that I was destined for a life in the Church. Unlike most of them, I wished for no other life.

For the first year, we novices lived apart from the community of brothers. In the novices' centre, we ate, slept, and studied. Our lessons included reading and writing in German and Latin, the study of Holy Scripture, and reading and singing the music of the Divine Office. Our meals were simple and sparse; the bigger boys often complained that they were still hungry after a meal was finished, but only when they could not be overheard by one of the brothers. We all slept together in one dormitory, and I often heard younger boys crying themselves to sleep.

I was fortunate that I adapted quickly to our strict, regulated lifestyle. For those boys that did not, punishment came swiftly, in the form of beatings or deprivation of food. There were times when I felt that the punishment was unjust, but I was not permitted to intervene in any way.

It would be about five years before I could expect to make my final solemn vows, but at the end of my first year, I and the other boys who had lasted that long made our first vows before the community of brothers. From that day onwards, we became part of the community and performed most of the tasks that they did.

I loved the camaraderie in this community, where the old taught the young, and the young helped the old. I also loved the rhythm of daily life: the Offices, study, reading and eating, and even came to like the periods of manual labour required from all who were able. The contemplative aspects of this life enabled us to rest our bodies, while the labour rested our minds and strengthened our bodies. Everything was structured, balanced, and orderly.

After my first few days in the full community, I felt certain about my choice of vocation. I was, however, under no illusions: I knew that this would be a challenging life, but I also expected it to be a rewarding one. Consequently, I looked forward to my future with varying degrees of both anticipation and apprehension.

Chapter 3

The monastery was a hive of building activity when I arrived and for many years afterward. Although an ancient site, the Benedictines had only founded the current monastery in 1108, so there was much work to be done to bring the site to an acceptable standard and size.

Mostly, I took little notice of the work. I became accustomed to the sights, sounds and inconvenience. Silence was, at least, observed during the daylight Offices and there was, of course, no work done at night.

In early October 1112, a small, house-like structure was begun on the northeast edge of the herb garden. I often worked in that garden, so was able to watch it being built. I did wonder briefly about its intended purpose. It was quite unlike the rest of the building works, and was set apart from the main complex. I did not wonder for long. Its purpose became apparent a few weeks later.

Towards the end of October, when I was on kitchen duty, I took food and drink to the visitors staying in the guest house. We usually had a few visitors staying there, but the servings of food and drink were uncommonly large on this particular evening.

When I arrived at the guest house, I saw that the dining hall was quite full. Sitting together at one of the tables were three women. One was about 30 years old, another was a younger woman, while the third was a young girl, no more than 14 years old. When I looked at this girl, she seemed to me to be the most beautiful human being that I had ever seen. She sat with her back to the fire, so that the bright light surrounded her like an aura. I gazed at her for far longer than was appropriate, and was only brought back to my senses by the older woman shifting impatiently in her seat.

The girl had smiled shyly in response to my gaze, but her smile vanished quickly when the younger of the two women tapped her hand lightly. I served the food and drink quickly, and moved to serve at another table.

I did not sleep well that night. For the first time, I was still wide awake when the bell rang for Matins. The rest of the night was no better. I could not stop thinking about the girl I had seen in the guest house. I did not know her name, or if I would ever see her again, but I knew with certainty that I would love her until the day I died.

The next day was All Saints' Day, an important day in the Church calendar. It also proved to be a significant day for me. While working in the herb garden between Terce and Sext, I was astonished to see a large procession approaching from the direction of the old church. Taperers led the way, followed by Abbott Burchard and the senior brothers. Last in line came three women, wearing veils over their faces. My heart skipped a beat when I realised that these were the women I had served the previous evening.

The procession stopped at the small house next to the herb garden. The monks parted to make way for the women, who stopped in front of the abbott. Psalms and canticles were sung, prayers said, and then, to my further amazement, the words of the funeral rite were intoned by the abbott, as the three women entered the house. The door was then closed and boarded up. There appeared to be no other openings apart from a small window on the north side of the house.

I was standing in the garden, open-mouthed. As the procession made its way back toward the church, Abbott Burchard saw me.

"Get back to your work, boy!" he snapped. I did not need to be told twice.

A short time later, Brother Tobias, the monastery's infirmarian, came to join me in the herb garden. Unlike the abbott, he seemed amused by my consternation.

"Well, what did you make of all that, young Volmar?" he asked, smiling.

"I have no idea *what* to make of it," I replied, flustered. "What was it all about?"

"Two of the women are from noble families. The other, older woman is a servant. The older of the two noble women, Jutta, has devoted her life to God as an anchoress, meaning that she will stay in that building for life."

"Her whole life? In that small house?" The thought horrified me.

"Yes, that is correct," said Brother Tobias, laughing. "Do not look so appalled. She made the decision willingly, even happily, it seems."

"What about the other two?" I asked. "Are they also locked up for life?" *Please, God, no!*

"The servant, also named Jutta, will stay with her mistress," he told me. "As for Hildegard, well, she is just a girl, really. She is the anchoress' companion and also an oblate. She has not yet made any vows, but I think she intends to be a nun, not an anchoress."

Thank goodness for that, I thought. I certainly understood the desire to remove oneself from the secular world – that is what I had wanted when I entered the monastery – but to be confined permanently to one small room seemed to be a step too far. I said as much to Brother Tobias.

"Do not let the abbott hear you say that, lad. He is very happy with the arrangement. Having an anchoress of such social standing – Jutta's brother is the Count of

Sponheim, you know – is bound to bring prestige to our community, not to mention the sizeable dowries both of the noble women brought with them," he said, chuckling.

My thoughts were swirling. I had thought I would never again see the nameless angel from the guest house. Now, I knew her name – Hildegard – and I knew that she was staying here permanently, albeit locked in that tiny prison. I was not sure whether to laugh or cry. I waited until I lay in my bed that night and chose the latter.

Chapter 4

For the next year or so, I only saw the women when I was on kitchen duty, and was required to take them their meals. I passed their food and drink to Jutta, the servant, through the small window. While doing so, I always tried to see beyond the servant, to catch a glimpse of the other occupants. I sometimes saw Lady Jutta, the anchoress, in prayer, either standing, kneeling, or prostrate on the hard floor, but I rarely saw Hildegard. She was usually beyond what I could see through such a narrow opening. When I did see her, I returned to the kitchen with a lightness of heart and step. When I did not see her, I returned to the kitchen more slowly, feeling disappointed and frustrated.

In the spring of 1114, I made my final solemn vows, and entered even more fully into the life of the community. I was now invited to attend Chapter meetings, where the business of the monastery was discussed on a daily basis. I also became more involved in the work of the scriptorium, where I copied precious manuscripts to add to our library and to distribute to the libraries of other monasteries. This was work I loved doing and for which, if I say it myself, I quickly developed aptitude.

In the autumn of that year, Hildegard emerged from the anchorage to make her solemn vows before Bishop Otto of Bamberg. The ceremony took place in the small, ancient chapel, and was attended by all the brothers. This was the first time, apart from the occasional glimpse through the window, that I had seen her since her enclosure. I was relieved to see that she seemed quite happy, although she was quite pale and thinner than I remembered. She had also grown quite tall. Her pallor was easily explained. The occupants of the small house received no sunlight, apart from any that managed to gain entrance through the narrow window. Her thinness was, however, another matter. I was sure they were *given* enough to eat, but I had noticed quite a bit was left over. I knew that Lady Jutta ate sparingly, but I hoped that this self-deprivation was not also being forced upon Hildegard.

Not long after the ceremony, the subject of the women's anchorage was raised in a Chapter meeting. Abbott Burchard had died the previous year, but his successor, Abbott Adilhun, was equally keen to support the women in their spiritual endeavours.

Lady Jutta's devotion to God and constant self-chastening had quickly become known to all the brothers. Many of them went to her for advice and counsel on both spiritual and personal matters. Her piety, wisdom, and maturity were extraordinary for one so young. I later discovered that she was only two years older than I, although she always seemed much older. Many of the brothers told me of predictions made by Jutta that subsequently proved to be accurate, with the result that her warnings were usually obeyed and her advice usually followed.

Now, at the Chapter meeting, it became apparent that word of Lady Jutta's wisdom and abilities had spread beyond the walls of the monastery. After the reading of that day's chapter from the Rule of St Benedict, and the abbott's sermon, the abbott made the following announcement.

"We have received many requests, both in person and in writing, from people of all ranks, and both local and distant, for access to the Lady Jutta. Her wisdom and piety have attracted much interest, and I believe that this is to be encouraged. The current arrangement is clearly not suitable for her to receive and counsel visitors, so I am proposing that the doors be unboarded, so that visitors and members of our community can come and go more easily."

The abbott had clearly not finished speaking, but a sudden murmuring among the brothers caused him to pause.

As the newest and youngest member of the Chapter, I said nothing, although I was as surprised as everyone else present appeared to be.

The abbott raised his hand for silence. "There is more," he continued. "I have received letters from three noblemen of this region, offering their daughters for the service of God under the tutelage of the Lady Jutta. I am of the opinion that we should accept these offers, and expand the current anchorage into a larger women's community." Much louder murmurings greeted this announcement, and seemed to express both excitement and some disapproval.

"This is an excellent opportunity for our community to enhance its service to God by providing a centre for worship, and the study of Holy Scripture," said Brother Cuno.

"We must be selective as to whom we accept, of course," said Brother Stefan, the monastery's cellarer.

"Of course," the abbott agreed.

I was reminded of my conversation with Brother Tobias in the herb garden on the day that the three women were enclosed. Enlarging the women's community by accepting the daughters of noblemen as oblates would certainly contribute to the monastery's coffers. I quickly dismissed this thought as cynical and unworthy.

"Will it not be rather *distracting*, having all these women so close to us?" asked one of the older brothers.

"Only to those who are easily distracted," replied the abbott tartly. Some of the brothers smirked at this, but quickly rearranged their faces into expressions of appropriate humility.

"Well, then," the abbott continued, "if there are no *real* objections, I will make the necessary arrangements. That

is all." The abbott rose, signalling the end of the meeting. We
all got up and left the Chapter House without another word.

Chapter 5

A few weeks later, work began on the expansion of the anchorage. I could observe the work's progress on the days when I was working in the herb garden. First, the boards were removed from the door, then the whole back wall was removed in order to extend the side walls.

The women had relocated to the guest house while the work was being done. Lady Jutta was not happy about leaving the anchorage, but accepted that her devotions could not continue amidst the noise and dust of the building works.

One evening when I was on kitchen duty, I took their food to the guest house. They were the only people there. It was winter, and the number of travellers always reduced at that time of the year.

Hildegard greeted me with a smile. I smiled in return and felt my face grow warm.

"I see the building works are nearly finished," I said as I served the soup, bread, and ale, my hands trembling slightly. "You should be able to move back in soon."

Lady Jutta nodded. "I am keen to resume my devotions in a more suitable place," she said, "and to welcome the new oblates, of course."

"It will be lovely to expand our group," Hildegard said. "I am looking forward to lively discussions of Holy Scripture."

"The oblates will need to be *taught* the Scriptures before they can discuss them," Lady Jutta observed.

"Then I look forward to assisting their learning," Hildegard replied. "It will be to the benefit of all of us."

When I returned later to collect the empty dishes, I was unsurprised to discover that they were not all empty. Lady Jutta, in particular, had eaten very little.

The building works were completed by January 1115. The women were able to move back in and resume their routines, although these routines were likely to alter considerably once the new oblates arrived in spring.

I did not see the oblates arrive, but I knew that they must have done so when I was given a much larger portion of food and drink to take to the anchorage one evening in mid-March. As I had always done, I approached the narrow, north-facing window with the meal.

"You can use the door now, Brother," said Jutta, the servant, with a broad smile. "It is so nice to have fresh air and sunshine after such a long time in darkness."

I agreed that this must be so, then went around to the door and entered the anchorage for the first time. It still seemed small to me. *It must have been like a dungeon before its expansion,* I thought. Lady Jutta was on her knees in the far corner, reciting verses from the Psalter. Hildegard was reading aloud from the Bible in her lap. Seated around her were three young girls, all about 14 years of age.

Hildegard looked up as I entered. "Thank you, Brother Volmar," she said, closing the Bible and smiling at me. "Your visits are always most welcome."

I smiled in return and nodded. "My pleasure, my lady," I said, then set the food and drink on the small table and departed. I wondered briefly whether it was my visit or the meal that was welcome, but as I walked back to the kitchen, I realised that Hildegard had called me by name. She had never done that before, and my face grew warm with pleasure at the thought.

Not long afterwards, on a sunny but crisp April morning, I was summoned to Abbott Adilhun's chamber. As I entered the room, the abbott, seated behind his desk, looked up from the parchment he had been reading.

"Good morning, Father Abbott," I said with a bow of my head.

"Good morning, Brother Volmar." He indicated a chair and nodded at me to be seated. "I have a special task for you to undertake," he said once I had pulled the chair closer to him and sat down. I waited for him to continue.

"As you know, the women's community is expanding. We have already admitted three new oblates, and there are likely to be more in the near future."

I nodded.

"Hildegard and the oblates receive some instruction from Lady Jutta, but her time is largely spent on her devotions, and responding to requests for advice and counsel. She does instruct all her charges on matters of devotion and self-discipline, but I believe that they also require education in other matters – Scripture, literacy, music, and so on. Hildegard does what she can with the younger girls, but she herself has much to learn." He paused, looking at me intently. I had no idea where this was all leading.

"I want you to become magister and teacher of the women's community."

I was stunned. My mouth opened and closed like a fish out of water – I did not know what to say. Me? Lead and teach the women?

"I know you are still very young," the abbott continued, "but you are our most gifted scholar and scribe, and it would be of great assistance to Lady Jutta if you could help her to teach and train the novices and oblates that are here now and are sure to come in future."

I finally found my voice. "It would be an honour and a privilege, Father, but surely I am quite without the ability for so great a task."

"Your humility is, of course, quite seemly and does you credit," the abbott replied. "However, I would not assign this important work to you if I did not believe that you were equal to the task. You are to begin tomorrow afternoon, after Sext. That is all."

The abbott returned his attention to the parchment he had been reading, and I knew better than to stay having been dismissed. I left the chamber in a confusion of excitement and fear. Tomorrow! I did not have long to prepare myself.

That evening, after Compline, I remained in the oratory and prayed for God's help and guidance. I was still there when the brothers returned for Matins, several hours later, but felt no closer to any feelings of confidence in my ability to meet this challenge.

The following afternoon, I arrived at the door of the anchorage. I had slept little, but my anxiety banished any weariness. Despite my uncertainty, I was keen to begin this new calling. I had never thought of myself as a teacher, but I was determined to pass on my love of learning to these and other young minds.

It was a warm, sunny day in April, so the door was open. Hildegard looked up and saw me in the doorway, hesitating. She smiled.

"Brother Volmar! Do come in. We are all very keen to begin," she said.

I smiled and I felt my shoulders slacken. I had not realised how tense I had been.

The three young oblates, sitting at the table with Hildegard, did not look quite as keen as Hildegard had suggested, but they smiled shyly as I sat opposite them. Lady Jutta was in the far corner, deep in prayer.

In the short time I had been given to prepare myself, I had thought about how I should begin such a wide-ranging course of tuition. I had decided that, before I could instruct the four young women on any topic, I needed to determine the current state of their knowledge and literacy.

I began by asking some simple questions on key themes in the Scriptures, both Old and New. Hildegard was clearly quite familiar with these, and demonstrated a range of knowledge that surprised me. The oblates showed familiarity with only the better-known parts of the New Testament – the Christmas and Easter stories primarily – but seemed to know very little about the Old Testament.

I then moved on to the Rule of St Benedict, according to which everyone in our community was required to conduct themselves. Unsurprisingly, Hildegard was familiar with most of the basic rules, having lived in the anchorage for more than two years. The oblates, however, did not appear to be at all familiar with the Rule, judging from their puzzled expressions.

When it came to reading and writing, all four were fluent in German, but only Hildegard knew any Latin. I assumed she had learned this from her recitation of the Psalms with Lady Jutta, but her aptitude for more advanced Latin was apparent. I decided not to burden the young oblates with Latin at this stage. They would have more than enough to learn without complicating matters with a foreign language.

I also decided to instruct Hildegard separately from the younger girls, in order to tailor the teaching to suit everyone's needs and abilities. Beginning the following afternoon, my approach was to assign a reading task to the oblates, to be discussed when they had finished reading.

While they were occupied with that, I could turn my attention to Hildegard.

In the first few weeks, I felt anxious and self-conscious when sitting separately with Hildegard. I hoped she was unaware of my awkwardness, and she never gave any indication of discomfort or amusement. My anxiety waned and, eventually, left me entirely, as I focussed on the task of teaching.

My initial impression of Hildegard's knowledge of Scripture proved to be correct. She was quite familiar with the Old Testament, particularly the Psalms and the Wisdom books, and showed a particular interest in the Gospel of John in the New Testament. She also displayed a depth of understanding that went far beyond mere rote learning. I could see from the start that Hildegard had a formidable intellect that was likely to exceed that possessed by most people she would ever encounter. I hoped that this would not prove to be a problem for her.

One afternoon towards the end of winter, I arrived at the usual time to begin the afternoon's lessons. I knocked on the door and was surprised when Jutta, the servant, opened it. It was usually Hildegard who greeted me. As I entered, I saw Hildegard lying on her bed with her eyes closed.

I approached the bed, uncertain whether she was asleep or merely resting. She opened her eyes slowly at the sound of my footsteps. Her face was pale and drawn.

"Are you unwell, Sister?" I asked. "Should I fetch Brother Tobias?"

She shook her head slightly. "No, thank you, Brother. It is just one of my headaches. It will pass soon." She closed her eyes again.

Lady Jutta, who had been praying nearby, had, most unusually, stopped her prayers and was watching and listening to us. She looked as if she were about to say something to me, but she glanced at the oblates who were also watching, and returned to her devotions.

"Very well," I said to Hildegard. "You rest. I hope you feel better soon." She smiled but did not open her eyes or speak.

I continued to go to the anchorage each afternoon, hoping that Hildegard would be well enough to return to her lessons. For the next few days, I spent the afternoon with the oblates while Hildegard either lay or sat on her bed. Finally, after a week or so, she seemed much better, and was out of bed, talking and smiling. She still looked quite pale, and did not move around the house with her usual vigour, but she was keen to resume her learning.

I quickly became accustomed to these bouts of ill health that plagued Hildegard quite frequently. They usually passed quickly, often lasting just a few days, and I soon realised that her learning schedule needed to make allowance for her physical infirmity. In spite of these setbacks, her progress in those early years was nothing short of miraculous.

Chapter 6

The year 1117 was filled with signs and wonders.

It all began on 3 January, when an enormous earthquake struck twice: first in Germany, and then in Italy. Italy was hit hard. We later heard that the town of Verona was almost completely destroyed.

Here, at the monastery, everyone was frightened but unharmed. Thankfully, there was also no damage to our buildings or grounds. People from the local villages came rushing to our gates, convinced that the Day of Judgment was upon us. Assembling everyone in the courtyard, Abbott Adilhun led prayers until the panic subsided. We then gave thanks to God for his protection and deliverance.

Then in mid-June, there was an eclipse of the moon. The brightly lit, full moon suddenly began to darken, to the amazement and horror of those who witnessed the event. We brothers were returning to our beds after Matins and Lauds when this occurred, and saw it very clearly. The complete and sudden darkness caused a few brothers to stumble, and several were so alarmed that they cried to God for mercy.

This event was not as alarming to the villagers as the earthquake had been. Most people slept through it and were unaware that anything unusual had occurred. Those who had seen it came to the monastery in the following days, asking to speak to Lady Jutta for words of consolation and explanation. She was generous with her time, and assuaged the fears of these simple folk.

To everyone's amazement, on 11 December in the same year there was another lunar eclipse. This caused more consternation than the first, due to the apparent frequency of these strange events. Once again, the monastery in general, and Lady Jutta in particular, were called upon to provide care and support.

As Christians, we knew that God, the creator of all things in Heaven and Earth, seen and unseen, also *causes* all things to happen. God does not cause a thing to happen without a reason. Everything is part of His divine, eternal plan. These recent eclipses must, therefore, be part of this eternal plan, but this did not mean that they were not disconcerting.

There was much discussion about the meaning of these events as they occurred throughout that strange year. Were they sent as messages from God, warnings of some sort?

In the anchorage classroom, we discussed these matters in some depth. The young oblates were convinced that the earthquake was a clear sign of God's displeasure, and that the lunar eclipses, or "blood" moons as they called them, were omens of impending doom. I kept my opinions to myself, interested to hear what Hildegard might have to say. She had listened carefully to the others, who were now, as I was, looking at Hildegard, waiting for her thoughts.

Hildegard sat quietly for a few minutes, then began to speak.

"It is written in the Gospel of Luke that 'there will be signs in the sun, the moon and the stars,' but these signs are meant as a *service* to humanity, not as a threat. They do, indeed, foretell lamentable and dangerous times, but only to give us the opportunity to mend our ways before it is too late. The radiance and splendour of the moon were dimmed so that human hearts might be stirred into action, to serve God better by following the teaching of the Apostles."

When she had finished speaking, we all remained silent for some time. I noticed that Lady Jutta was watching, and had listened to Hildegard's words. She smiled, then returned to her devotions.

After a few minutes, I broke the silence. "That was well said, Sister Hildegard, and gives us all much to reflect upon. We all can and should do better in our endeavours to serve God."

Privately, I was amazed at Hildegard's response. Her understanding of Scripture and her intelligent interpretation of worldly events were remarkable in one so young. It was becoming clear that all of us, not just the younger members of this community, would have much to learn from her wisdom.

Chapter 7

From the moment the anchorage was first opened up to admit the new oblates, Hildegard had spent as much time outdoors as her duties and the weather permitted. I sometimes saw her in the kitchen garden or the orchard, but it was the herb garden that most captured her interest. On the days when I was working in that garden, I would see her roaming along the neat rows of herbs, including fennel, mint, sage and rosemary. She would touch the plants to feel their texture and bend low to absorb their pungent smells. She would ask me questions about the plants – what were their names, what were they used for, were any of them poisonous? – and so on. I had to admit that my knowledge in this area was rather limited.

"I know their names but little more," I told her on one occasion. "Brother Tobias, on the other hand ..." I had raised my voice to attract his attention. He looked up from the far end of the garden and smiled. "Brother Tobias," I continued, "knows *every*thing about the herbs. I am sure he would be happy to tell you all that you wish to know."

Hildegard had smiled happily and gone to where Brother Tobias was working. I could not hear what was said, but I could see him pointing at the various beds and picking pieces for Hildegard to keep.

From that day on, Hildegard spent a lot of time with Brother Tobias, helping him with weeding and planting, and listening intently to his replies to her questions.

One afternoon, when it was time for her Latin lesson, Hildegard came in from the herb garden, tired but happy.

"Brother Tobias is so knowledgeable about herbs and healing," she said. "Someone should record all this knowledge for future gardeners and infirmarians. I will start writing down what he tells me."

"A good idea," I said. Her enthusiasm for this new project made me smile. I wondered how she would find time for it in her already busy schedule of devotions and study, but I knew that she would. "I will arrange for more parchment and ink to be supplied to you."

It was, indeed, a good idea. Nobody knew more than Brother Tobias about this important topic, but he was not a young man, and this knowledge would be lost if not recorded before his death. I had no doubt that Hildegard, with her keen mind and love of nature, would be the best person to do this important work.

Chapter 8

By the year 1120, the first of the oblates had taken final vows, and there were two new oblates beginning their religious journeys. I was busier than ever with teaching people at various levels of knowledge and aptitude, although Hildegard helped with many of the basic lessons. Lady Jutta's workload had also increased, as she had immediately added the newcomers to her lessons on the importance of devotion and self-abasement.

Lady Jutta's schedule was, indeed, punishing. I had observed her now for several years, but was still surprised when Hildegard told me that the Lady recited the entire Psalter every day. We brothers take a whole week to chant from Psalm 1 to 150! She also prayed every day for the living and the dead, both known to her and unknown. She performed these devotions either standing in one place or kneeling on the hard floor, and refused to wear shoes, even in the depths of winter.

As if this were not sufficient, she also inflicted relentless torments and wounds on her body by wearing a hairshirt and an iron chain. I, of course, never saw these things for myself, but Hildegard had told me out of genuine concern for Lady Jutta's wellbeing.

One winter morning, when Lady Jutta and Hildegard had been at the monastery for eight years, matters came to a head. The Lady's self-mortifications became more than her frail body could withstand, and she was struck down by serious illness.

I was working in the scriptorium, copying Boethius' 'Consolation of Philosophy', when Brother Tobias came rushing in, at a faster rate than I thought him capable of.

“Brother Volmar!” he said, in hushed but urgent tones. “Please come quickly. Lady Jutta is very ill, and Hildegard is asking for you.”

I dropped my quill and hurried to the anchorage with Brother Tobias.

“Have you examined the Lady?” I asked him as we ran.

“I have,” he gasped. “She is in a state of complete exhaustion and is rambling nonsense. I do not know what I can do for her.”

We arrived at the anchorage and entered the dimly lit space. Lady Jutta was lying on her bed, writhing and muttering. I had never seen her lying down before. It seemed a strange sight.

Hildegard was sitting next to the bed, holding Lady Jutta’s hand. “Oh, Volmar,” she said. “I am glad you are here. I do not know what to do. The Lady was reciting the Lord’s Prayer and just, well, crumpled to the floor. We managed to lift her onto her bed, but I have not been able to get any sense from her.”

I sat on the other side of the bed. Lady Jutta seemed to be semi-conscious, but was incoherent. “My Lady, can you hear me? It is Brother Volmar.” I received no response. I feared that her passing might be imminent.

“We must inform the abbott,” I said.

“I will go,” said Brother Tobias, and left quickly.

Hildegard and I looked at each other over Lady Jutta’s writhing body. Hildegard was wide-eyed with alarm.

“I have never seen her like this before,” she said.

"She pushes herself far too hard," I replied. "It is a wonder that this has not happened earlier."

After a few minutes, Brother Tobias returned with Abbott Adilhun. The abbott approached Lady Jutta's bed and stopped short. His face displayed the alarm that we all felt.

"My dear child," he began. "This self-torment is just too extreme. You must rest and eat meat in order to regain your strength."

Under the Rule, only the sick are permitted to eat the meat of 'four-footed' animals. Once they have recovered, they are then obliged to refrain from doing so, as are all other able-bodied brothers and sisters.

Lady Jutta's thrashing and mumbling had subsided by now, and she humbly begged to be excused from the abbott's direction. She had not eaten meat, fowl or fish for the entire time she had been enclosed, and did not want to break this fast.

Before the abbott could respond, a large water bird, occasionally heard but rarely seen in this region, came and settled on the narrow window ledge above Lady Jutta's bed. This took everyone by surprise, and put a stop to the argument for the time being.

"Very well," said the abbott. "We will see how you are feeling tomorrow." He then glanced at the bird, which was sitting quietly in the window, shook his head and left the house.

"We should let the Lady rest now," I said. "It is nearly time for Vespers anyway. I will come back tomorrow to see how she is faring."

The next morning, I went straight to the anchorage after Prime. The bird was still sitting in the window, seemingly watching over Lady Jutta, who was sleeping peacefully.

"She had a quiet night," Hildegard told me. "She seems much calmer now."

News of the bird had spread around the monastery. Many of the brothers came to see it. The bird did not seek safety by flying away, but as if it were tame, just looked back at those who came to look at it.

I went to tell the abbott about Lady Jutta's current condition. I also mentioned the bird. When he heard this, he sighed deeply, dissolved into tears and said, "God has sent this bird as His messenger. I have failed to look after His child, as was my duty. I will hear no more arguments – Lady Jutta is to be given meat to eat, and must rest until her health is restored."

I went back to the anchorage and told Lady Jutta and Hildegard of the abbott's command. Lady Jutta humbly yielded, and I arranged with Brother Johann, the kitchener, that she was to be given meat until further notice.

The bird, its 'mission' accomplished, flew away that night and was never seen again.

Chapter 9

It took Lady Jutta several weeks of rest and good food to return to reasonable health. During this time, Hildegard, as the next most senior member of the women's community, took on many of Lady Jutta's tasks as leader of the community. Thus, as well as continuing her own devotions and studies, Hildegard had to deal with the kitchener, the cellarer, the chamberlain, and the armarius, to ensure that the community had all of their material needs met.

The armarius, Brother Hans, caused the most trouble, Hildegard complained to me privately. He regularly refused to supply all the parchments, inks and quills that she requested.

"You do not require so much," Brother Hans had told her.

"I *do* require what I have asked for," Hildegard had replied. "I need to write down what Brother Tobias teaches me in order to have a complete record of herbs and their healing properties. This is important information. We also need parchment and ink for all of us to improve our writing in both German and Latin."

Brother Hans had finally yielded to her requests, but grudgingly.

Meeting the intellectual and spiritual needs of the women was, perhaps, an even more challenging task for Hildegard. She took over the spiritual direction of the oblates and younger nuns, and, as needed, provided counsel and advice to all of the women. I continued my afternoon teaching sessions, and assisted Hildegard with other tasks as much as I could when my monastic duties allowed, but it was a very heavy workload for one person.

Lady Jutta was able, from her sick bed, to observe all that Hildegard did as the temporary leader of the community.

"She seems to be coping very well," she said to me one afternoon, while Hildegard was reading the Old Testament with the younger women. "I have no doubt she will be the ideal candidate to succeed me when my time here is finished."

This latter remark took me by surprise. Lady Jutta was much recovered and was still a young woman. "Surely, lady, that is many years from now, decades even," I responded.

She smiled briefly. "We shall see," was all that she said. I wondered if she knew more than she was telling, but decided not to press the matter.

After about two months, Lady Jutta gradually began to resume her activities. The first thing she recommenced was, unsurprisingly, her devotions and prayers. After that, she took back the spiritual direction of the new oblates, but allowed Hildegard to continue in this role with the younger nuns. Finally, she resumed her dealings with the various monastery personnel, but allowed Hildegard to assist her with these duties. Thus, with a slight re-ordering of responsibilities, the women's community settled down into a comfortable and productive routine.

Chapter 10

For the next few years, the seasons, both liturgical and natural, passed peacefully. Life was quite settled in both the men's and women's communities, apart from the occasional squabble that will inevitably arise where people live and work together without respite.

By the spring of 1124, Hildegard was showing considerable talent in all things spiritual and academic, and was also becoming highly proficient as a teacher and as a healer. Just when I thought she could fit nothing more into her busy schedule, she expressed a wish to expand the range of her reading.

"I will always love the Bible above all other books," she said, "but perhaps I could also read other works?"

"This is a good idea," I began, "but I am concerned that you are trying to do too much."

Hildegard laughed. "There is so much that I want to do, Brother. I must learn as much as possible to equip me for God's work."

I knew better than to argue – Hildegard was a most determined young woman. I laughed, too. "Very well," I said. "I will see what I can find for you in the library."

Later that afternoon, I went to the monastery's library, which had an excellent variety of books. Brother Hans looked up briefly from a parchment, raised a hand in greeting, then returned to his work. I was often in the library, so he knew that I did not require his assistance.

I stood and thought for a moment. What should I select for Hildegard? Given her knowledge of Holy Scripture, she was probably ready for some of the Church Fathers – Justin Martyr, Tertullian and Origen were some of the better-known of these. The Latin would be beyond Hildegard's current competence, but I could help her with that and perhaps translate some of the more important writings for her. Then I remembered she had shown interest in the copy of Boethius I had been reading. Perhaps some philosophy as well as theology?

I left the library about half an hour later with my arms full of books. I would let Hildegard decide where she wished to begin.

Hildegard leapt upon the volumes, and would have read them all at once in her eagerness, but we narrowed it down to one book of theology to begin with, and would progress from there at a pace in keeping with her abilities, while also accommodating her many other duties.

I was always amazed at how much Hildegard could do in the same number of hours each day that God granted to us all, but surely she had now reached her limit. As was often the case, I was soon proved to be wrong about this.

Chapter 11

The winter of 1125 was particularly harsh. The snow piled up against the walls of the monastery's buildings, and paths, when swept clear, became icy and treacherous.

Brother Tobias was in great demand that winter, both within and beyond the monastery's walls. He was often called away to one of the nearby villages to treat various winter ailments, which left the monks and nuns temporarily without an infirmarian. He had often expressed his concern to me that he had no 'deputy' at the monastery who could care for its inhabitants in his absence, and the need for such a person soon became apparent.

One freezing afternoon in January, a young oblate named Birgitta was hurrying down the anchorage's steps to fetch some water when she slipped, fell, landed awkwardly on one foot, and cried out in pain. I was approaching the anchorage just then and saw her fall. I rushed to her as Lady Jutta and Hildegard appeared in the doorway, alerted by the cry. Both gasped when they saw what had happened. Hildegard took one look at the oblate's ankle and said, "I will fetch Brother Tobias."

"Brother Tobias is not here," I replied. "He has gone to Odernheim to deal with an outbreak of the sweating sickness."

Hildegard thought for a moment, then said to me, "Can you get her inside?" I nodded. "I will be back as quickly as I can." She raced off in the direction of Brother Tobias' work room, while I carried the distressed girl into the anchorage and laid her on the nearest bed.

Hildegard returned after a few minutes, carrying an odd assortment of items: the roots of a plant, a sponge, a mortar and a pestle. "I need hot water," she said.

One of the young nuns made her way carefully down the steps, then ran to the nearby well. When she returned, Hildegard directed her to heat some of the water over the open fire in the corner of the house. While waiting for the water to heat, Hildegard put the plant root and remaining water into the mortar, and began to pulp the root. I had no idea what she was doing, but she seemed calm and in control of the situation.

When the water was hot enough, Hildegard soaked the sponge in it, wrung out the excess, and handed it to me.

"Hold this just below her nose," she said. "It will keep her still while I apply the binding."

I did as she instructed. Birgitta had been writhing in pain, but, after a few minutes of inhaling the contents of the sponge, she relaxed and even seemed to go to sleep.

Once Birgitta had stopped moving, Hildegard got to work on the ankle. The angle it lay at certainly indicated that a bone was broken. Hildegard straightened the ankle to its proper position, which caused Birgitta to groan and grimace but not to fully awaken. Hildegard then began to apply the pulped root around Birgitta's ankle.

"What are these things you are using?" I finally asked.

Hildegard smiled briefly. "Brother Tobias and I were talking about broken bones just the other day, luckily, so I knew what to use," she said. The sponge contains a mixture of opium, mandrake, hemlock and henbane, which is activated by the hot water. These herbs will put *any*one to sleep," she laughed. "I needed her to keep still while I was binding her ankle with the comfrey root. It will set hard and keep the ankle in place while the bone heals."

"Brilliant!" Lady Jutta said unexpectedly, startling us all. "Thanks be to God indeed for Brother Tobias' knowledge and teaching, and for your capabilities."

Hildegard's face reddened slightly in response to this rare compliment from Lady Jutta.

Two days later, when he had returned from Odernheim, Brother Tobias came to visit Birgitta, and to inspect Hildegard's handiwork.

"The binding of the ankle is very good," he said. "What are you using for relief of pain?"

"Willowbark," Hildegard replied, "mixed in a little wine."

"Good," said Brother Tobias. "This is all very satisfactory. I doubt I could have done better myself," he said, beaming at Hildegard. Once again, Hildegard blushed at such praise.

The following afternoon, Abbott Adilhun appeared in the doorway of the anchorage. Brother Tobias was close behind him.

"How fares the young girl?" the abbott asked Hildegard.

"She is doing well, I think," Hildegard replied.

The abbott smiled at Birgitta, who was trying to get up from the bed.

"No, no, child," the abbott said. "You stay where you are. Just rest and recover. You are obviously in good hands."

The abbott turned to address Lady Jutta, who had come over when the abbott arrived.

"Which brings me to the main reason for my visit," he said. "Brother Tobias has been saying for some time that he needs help with his duties as infirmarian, and it seems we have a skilled person right here in the women's community. What I am proposing, with your permission, Lady Jutta, and your agreement, Sister Hildegard, is that Sister Hildegard should become the official infirmarian of the women's community."

Lady Jutta raised her eyebrows, taken aback. Hildegard beamed. "I would be honoured to take on this role," she said, looking to Lady Jutta for approval.

"I have no objection, Father," Lady Jutta said. "Hildegard has already been dealing with minor ailments among the women for some time and, of course, dealt admirably with Birgitta's injury. Yes, I think it is fitting that she should be properly recognised for this work."

"Excellent," said the abbott. "Then it is settled. I do think it is more appropriate for a woman to be dealing with the women's physical..." He searched for the right word. "...*needs*. Brother Tobias is also going to train one of the boy novices to assist him with the men. It is too much for one person, now that we are a double monastery."

Brother Tobias had been silent throughout, but was smiling broadly. He seemed happy with the new arrangements. I, also, had said nothing, not wishing to dampen the occasion, but I did have grave concerns for Hildegard's wellbeing, given her ever-increasing workload.

The abbott smiled at the women. "I bid you all good day," he said, then turned and left the anchorage, followed by Brother Tobias.

Birgitta's ankle healed well and quickly. I commented on the improvement in her mobility one afternoon a few weeks after her accident.

"I do not know how Sister Hildegard fixed my ankle so well," she responded, "but I am very grateful that she did.

She is so clever! I would like to learn how to do what she did with those plants."

"I am sure that Hildegard would be happy to teach you," I said, looking at Hildegard, who was seated nearby.

Hildegard smiled and looked up from her writing. "Of course," she said. "I would be very glad to have an assistant, and I very much want to share this knowledge of plants and healing. It is an important skill, and the more who know of it, the better."

After that, I often saw Hildegard and Birgitta together in the herb garden, deep in discussion and dirt. Sometimes Brother Tobias would join the two women, and the discussions became even more animated. Seeing the three of them together, happily discussing the plants and their uses, made me feel confident that the bodily needs of both the men and the women of Disibodenberg were in safe hands.

Chapter 12

The next couple of years were quite settled at the monastery, until the sudden death of Abbott Adilhun in June, 1128. We were all greatly saddened by his passing. He had been our abbott for 15 years, and was admired and loved by all who knew him.

The election of a new abbott was delayed, due to the absence of Archbishop Adalbert of Mainz. This lacuna caused some members of the community some distress. Jutta seemed to be particularly affected. She had had a very close relationship with Abbott Adilhun and I knew that she missed him sorely. We were all greatly relieved when, towards the end of that year, Abbott Fulcard was elected as our new leader.

Lady Jutta's health, which was not assisted by this period of grief and uncertainty, was beginning to decline again. She had recovered well from her serious illness eight years earlier, but it had not taken her long to return to her harshly ascetic routine. She was only 36 years old, but looked much older. The years of self-discipline and chastisement were clearly taking their toll, and I held grave fears that her future life would not be a long one.

Chapter 13

The beginning of the 1130s was accompanied by a feeling of optimism and wellbeing at the Disibodenberg monastery. Life had settled into a comfortable and productive routine under Abbott Fulcard. Like his predecessor, the abbott had endeavoured to make and maintain a good relationship with Lady Jutta and her community of women, and ensured that their needs were met to the same extent as the men's.

News from beyond the monastery's walls was, however, less heartening. Travellers staying in the monastery's guest house often brought news from distant places, but one particular tale that arrived in 1130 was much closer to home, in a spiritual, if not geographical, sense.

We had, of course, heard that Pope Honorius II had died in February that year, but it seemed that there had been a major dispute surrounding the election of his successor. We were told by an itinerant monk, who had it on 'good' authority, that Innocent II had been elected by a minority of the cardinals, and consecrated with unseemly haste the day after Honorius' death. The other cardinals, predictably, objected to this, claimed that the election of Innocent was invalid, and duly chose their own candidate, who was consecrated as Anacletus II. I could scarcely believe my ears – two popes? How could this work, either in theory or practice?

Needless to say, it worked in neither respect. At the time we first heard the sorry story, the supporters of Anacletus had driven Innocent out of Rome, and Anacletus was now in control.

When I told the women in the anchorage all that I had heard, there was shock, grief and outrage.

"This is appalling!" said Hildegard. "Do these men not realise that their first duty is to serve God, not other men, and certainly not themselves!"

"It seems that politics has intruded upon Church affairs," said Lady Jutta, in more measured tones.

"I agree with you both," I said, "and feel quite certain that we have not yet heard the end of this matter."

Later that year, we heard that Innocent had made his way to France, where the influence of Bernard of Clairvaux had ensured Innocent's acceptance as the 'true' pope by both clergy and court. Bernard had, apparently, been travelling far and wide to muster support for Innocent, and had managed to persuade both French and Italian royalty that they should side with Innocent.

Much later, we heard that, in May of 1135, Innocent had convened the Council of Pisa, which was attended by an unusually large number of archbishops, bishops and abbotts from all parts of Europe and England. This Council declared Anacletus and his supporters to be excommunicated, thereby confirming Innocent's legitimacy.

"Thanks be to God," said Hildegard. "Surely this will be an end of such unseemly squabbles in the Church.

I murmured in agreement, but did not, in truth, share her optimism.

Chapter 14

The year 1136 was significant for both the men's and women's communities at the monastery.

The women's community had continued to grow, and now numbered 15 in total, including Lady Jutta, Hildegard, nuns and oblates. I continued to teach in the afternoons according to the needs and abilities of the younger women, ably assisted by Hildegard. Lady Jutta also instructed new oblates in the ways of devotion and self-discipline.

One afternoon in early spring, I was met at the anchorage door by Lady Jutta. This was an unusual occurrence – I was much more likely to be met by Hildegard or Birgitta. The Lady suggested that she and I go for a walk in the garden. This was also a surprise, and subsequently proved to be the first and only time we did so.

"There are important matters I must discuss with you, Brother Volmar, before it is too late," she told me.

I frowned. "What do you mean, 'too late'?"

"I shall die this year, so must unburden myself of a long-held secret," she replied.

"How can you know that you will die this year?" I asked. "You are still a young woman. Surely you have many years ahead of you."

She smiled. "You have always been so kind, Brother, but I know that my time is drawing to a close because it was foretold, on the evening before my enclosure."

"Foretold? By whom? How can you be sure they were correct?"

"The night before my enclosure, I was staying with Hildegard and my maid in the guest house," she began.

I had not forgotten that night. It was the first time I had seen Hildegard. "Yes, I remember," I said. "I served you your meal."

Lady Jutta nodded. "Also staying at the guest house at that time was an old woman, a widow, named Trutwib," she continued. "On the morning of my enclosure – it was All Saints' Day, as I recall – she told me that she had seen an apparition as she was returning to the guest house after Lauds. This, understandably, frightened her greatly, and she was about to flee when she heard the apparition proclaim the following:

'You must know that the Lady Jutta, who today is to be enclosed in this place, shall happily spend twenty-four years here, and in the twenty-fifth year, pass happily from this world. I must also tell you that, in a short while from today, you yourself are to die.' "Having said these things, the apparition vanished," Lady Jutta said.

"The venerable old woman was, of course, utterly terrified by this vision," she continued, "but she was just as anxious about my passing as her own, and though she hesitated for a few days, she then came to the anchorage window and told me what she had seen and heard. A few days after that, as had been foretold to her, she died. Her death authenticated for me the words of the apparition."

"I am now in my twenty-fifth year of enclosure," Lady Jutta said, after a period of silence, "so that is why I am certain that my time in this life is drawing to a close. I believe that the apparition was a messenger, sent to me by God through the agency of the old widow."

I have never doubted that, for God, all things are possible, but this tale troubled me. Perhaps it was mere coincidence that Trutwib had died shortly after delivering the apparition's message to Lady Jutta. She was, after all, an old woman. Coincidence or not, message from God or not, I could see that Lady Jutta had convinced herself that the prediction of her death would, indeed, prove to be true.

"It is not my place to gainsay a messenger from God," I began, choosing my words carefully, "but I do hope that this prediction proves to be false."

Lady Jutta smiled. She reached over and squeezed my hand. Neither of us spoke for a moment. I was quite stunned by what she had told me and was uncertain what else to say.

"Which brings me to the matter I must confide," she said.

I raised my eyebrows. There was more?

"This matter involves Hildegard, so you must promise me that you will not speak of this to anyone without her permission," she began. "It might be best not to speak even to her about it, unless she raises the subject. I am unsure whether I should be telling you, but it is something of which you should be aware, I believe."

"Lady Jutta, what is it?" I asked. "Is she ill?" I was greatly alarmed by the Lady's procrastination.

"Well, yes *and* no," she replied, which did nothing to ease my confusion. "As you know, she suffers from bouts of poor health, but I do not believe that the problem is a physical one." She paused again. "I believe that it is a spiritual matter."

"Spiritual?" I asked. "What do you mean?

"I have known Hildegard since she was eight years old, when her parents entrusted her into my care. I remember when she first came to stay with me, she told me about things she had seen that other people had been unable to see, and about other things that she had predicted. When she was about five years old, she saw a pregnant cow, and told her nurse that the calf would be white with dark spots on its back and feet, quite an unusual pattern for a calf. When the calf was born, it did, indeed, look exactly as Hildegard had predicted. There were other incidents, too, where she knew what was to happen before it *did* happen."

We walked on a bit further before she continued.

"Her parents were very worried about how 'different' their youngest child seemed to be, and this prompted their decision to offer her to God for a life of holy service. She stayed with me from the age of eight, until we both entered the anchorage when she was fourteen and I was twenty."

"How was she able to see the invisible and predict the unknowable?" I asked.

"I believe, and she also believes, that God 'speaks' through her. Who else could see and know such things before they happen?" Lady Jutta responded.

"Is this still happening?" I asked, alarmed and yet fascinated.

"I think so, although she will no longer discuss it with me. She seemed to become quite self-conscious about it, when she was old enough to realise that other people did not see as she did, and she has not mentioned it at all since we came to the monastery."

There was silence for some time, while I tried to comprehend what I had just been told. Could it be true? Was God really 'speaking' to people through Hildegard? I did not doubt Lady Jutta's or Hildegard's honesty, but I had never come across anything like the report I had just received.

"So you think it is this ..." I searched for a suitable word. "...*ability* that causes her episodes of poor health?" I finally asked.

"For as long as I have known Hildegard, the 'visions' and poor health have been contemporaneous, and I do not believe that this is mere coincidence."

We had reached the end of the orchard and were standing under an apple tree. The scent of apple blossom was fragrant and sweet – a reminder of life's renewal after winter. We turned to retrace our steps.

"Anyway," Lady Jutta continued, "as Hildegard's teacher, I thought you should be told."

"Thank you, Lady," I replied. "I do appreciate your confiding in me about this matter. I will not say anything to anyone about it, including Hildegard."

Lady Jutta nodded, then headed back to the anchorage. I remained where I was, as rooted to the ground as the apple trees. Apparitions? Premonitions? Visions? Was I dreaming, perhaps?

After a few minutes, some light rain began to fall, bringing me back to the present. I hurried back to the anchorage and conducted the afternoon's lessons as if my world had not just been turned upside down.

Chapter 15

My conversation with Lady Jutta occupied most of my thoughts, day and night, for some time afterwards. I hoped most ardently that the prediction of her imminent death would prove to be false, although her health certainly seemed to be failing at a rapid rate.

The revelation about Hildegard, on the other hand, was the most wondrous news. If what Lady Jutta believed to be true was, in fact, the case, we were even more blessed than I already considered us to be to have Hildegard in our community.

I had promised the Lady that I would not broach the subject with Hildegard, and I was determined to keep my promise. Hildegard and I spoke about many things – spiritual, theological, practical and personal – and I felt sure that she would tell me about her visions in her own time, when she felt ready to do so.

The months passed. Spring turned into summer, with its warm, long days and short nights. Autumn had just begun to nip at our ankles when Lady Jutta took to her bed, for what proved to be the last time.

We did our best to keep her comfortable. The fire was kept alight, day and night, and at least one sister sat at the Lady's bedside at all times. Often, when her duties permitted, it was Hildegard maintaining the vigil. She and Lady Jutta did not speak much. Mostly, Hildegard held the Lady's hand and prayed.

On 9 November and without warning, Abbott Fulcard died. This was totally unexpected and caused much consternation in both communities. Monks and nuns were all keen to avoid a delay of the sort that had followed the previous abbott's passing, so an election for a new abbott was organised hastily. In mid-November, Brother Cuno was elected unopposed as the new abbott of Disibodenberg monastery.

Lady Jutta's health continued to worsen. On 2 December, a violent fever came upon her. After nearly three weeks, she seemed to recover, enough at least to speak words of comfort to her charges. She then asked for Holy Communion, which was given to her by the new abbott. When this was done, she counselled all who were present to give themselves to prayers and psalmody.

In the early hours of the following day, 22 December, she indicated that the brothers should be called. When we had prayed the litanies over her, she made the sign of the Cross, and passed peacefully from this world.

Lady Jutta's funeral was attended by scores of people, of both sexes and from various ages, classes and professions. She had been greatly revered by the people in nearby towns, as well as by the whole of our monastic community. Although a sad and solemn occasion, it was also an opportunity for us all to come together and give thanks to God for Lady Jutta's wonderful life of service and devotion.

As was typical of her humility, she had asked to be buried in a place where she might daily be walked upon by passers-by. In keeping with this request, she was laid to rest in the floor of our Chapter House, although there were many of us who felt that she deserved a more dignified resting place.

Chapter 16

For the first time in its short history, the women's community at Disibodenberg Monastery needed a new leader. This would be their first election: Lady Jutta, as anchoress, had been the *de facto* leader of the fledgling community in its first days, but now that she was gone, a successor needed to be chosen by the community itself.

It came as no surprise when Hildegard was elected as the new *magistra* – a complex role combining prioress, administrator and spiritual mother.

"It was unanimous," Sister Birgitta told me afterwards. "Hildegard was the obvious choice, really."

I agreed. Hildegard had matured so much since I had first come to teach at the anchorage. Apart from her evident academic progress, she had also grown both spiritually and in personal confidence, and had already shown her ability to lead the community during Lady Jutta's illnesses. I felt certain, however, that hers would be a very different style of leadership. I knew that Hildegard had often been distressed at Lady Jutta's self-castigation and excessive discipline, and I expected to see some changes in the routine and practices of the women's community.

Some changes were apparent from the outset. When Lady Jutta was *magistra*, the nuns and oblates were expected to observe her practices of fasting and prayer, and to emulate them. Now, under Hildegard, excessively long sessions of prayer and worship stopped at once. Instead, the women said the Offices at the same time as the men always did.

Hildegard was not, however, entirely happy with this arrangement.

"The Offices really should be *sung*, not said," she said to me one afternoon shortly after her election. "Ever since I first came here, I have loved listening to the brothers chanting the Offices – the music adds so much to the prayerfulness of the devotions. I really believe that it is through music that the soul truly expresses its yearning for God."

"I agree," I replied. "I love the music. It takes me quite beyond my mortal self."

"Can you teach us the music?" she asked. "I want all of the women to learn the chants."

"Yes, of course," I replied automatically. On later reflection, I realised that this would be no small task. Teaching all of the women to read the rather confusing musical notation would be a very time-consuming process.

I decided that it would be more efficient to teach Hildegard to read the notation, so that she could then read the chants and sing them for the other women to learn by ear. I suggested this approach to Hildegard a few days later.

"That sounds sensible," she replied after a moment's thought. "Some of the sisters already have enough trouble reading Latin without introducing an additional complication. With your assistance, I will learn to read the notation and start introducing the chants into our daily worship."

Hildegard beamed at me, which made me smile in return. She was clearly excited about this new challenge, and I had no doubt she would master this new skill with her usual ease and speed.

Other changes in the women's routine also became apparent. Hildegard encouraged, even required, the women to eat well and to rest more. The combined result of these changes was, in quite a short time, a happier and healthier group of women.

Hildegard explained these changes to me shortly after their implementation.

"I never shared Lady Jutta's view of the human body as the 'tomb of the soul', as something unclean, to be purged and punished," she said. "After all, God created us in His image – how can that be a bad thing? No, I see the human body as the earthly temple of the Holy Spirit, which lives on Earth in and through us, and all of God's creation. If that is so, we must look after our bodies as we also must care for the rest of creation."

Conversations with Hildegard always gave me much to think about, and this one was no exception. While I, also, had never shared Lady Jutta's ascetic views, I had never thought of the human body as an almost sacred thing, to be cared for as a 'temple'. It was an unusual approach, but one that I could readily agree with.

The men's community was also beginning the year with a new leader. Abbott Cuno was our fourth, and youngest leader, and also had very firm views on how the monastery should be run.

Things had become quite relaxed in the men's community under Abbott Fulcard, and our new abbott wasted no time in addressing this. Chapter meetings were brisk and business-like, and tardiness to any of the Offices was not tolerated under any circumstances.

The building program at the monastery also seemed to have slowed in recent years. It was close to completion, but some work was still required on our new church. Abbott Cuno also ensured that the remaining building works proceeded at a much brisker pace.

It was apparent from the outset that our new abbott was not someone who tolerated fools or slackards, and the brothers learned quickly that it was advisable to be neither. To some members of our community, this came as a surprise. To those of us who knew the man better, it was entirely to be expected.

Chapter 17

Towards the end of 1137, the women's community suffered another bereavement.

On a cool autumn afternoon, as I was walking to the women's house for lessons, I was horrified to see a body in a shroud being carried out of the house by two of the younger lay brothers. I froze in mid-step and stopped breathing. *Please, God – not Hildegard!*

My breathing restarted when I saw Hildegard appear in the doorway behind the second lay brother. I exhaled with relief. *Thank you, God.* I then felt a pang of guilt for feeling so relieved. *Some*body had died, which was no cause for celebration. I did not wish this person dead, but I was very glad that it was not Hildegard.

"Who ..?" was all I could say.

Hildegard came to meet me, tears in her eyes. "It is dear Jutta, our beloved servant. She seems to have died peacefully in her sleep. I know that she has been very sad since her mistress died, but I was not aware that she was unwell."

"This *is* a surprise," I agreed. "She was a devoted servant and will be greatly missed." I rested my hand briefly on Hildegard's arm. "I will ensure that all matters are attended to with due diligence and respect."

Hildegard managed a weak smile. "Thank you, Brother. I trust you to do what is proper." She then turned back towards the women's house, where several young nuns were standing outside the door crying. "Come, dear sisters," she said. "We will pray for Jutta's soul."

Jutta's body was laid before the altar in the chapel, and both sisters and brothers held vigil and prayed all that night. Jutta was laid to rest the next day in the monastery's cemetery. Her interment was attended by all the women and most of the men of Disibodenberg, as was appropriate for the faithful servant to our holy lady Jutta.

"I am the only one left," Hildegard said to me, as we walked away from the cemetery.

I raised my eyebrows, then realised what she meant. "The last of the original three, you mean," I said.

Hildegard nodded.

The women's community was, indeed, undergoing great change. What had begun 24 years earlier as an enclosed anchorage was now an open, growing community and centre for learning. I observed to Hildegard that I thought these changes to be very positive.

She nodded again and smiled. "You are quite right. Nothing remains the same for ever, and this community of women has great potential. I will do my best to nurture and guide it wisely."

"It could not be in better hands," I said.

Chapter 18

The year 1138 began on a positive note. In mid-February, as a direct result of Abbott Cuno's urgings, three altars in our new church were dedicated by the Bishop of Dessau. While there was still work to be completed, these dedications were greeted with joy, and it seemed that there was, finally, an end in sight to the noise and disruption.

The year proceeded smoothly in both men's and women's communities. Towards the end of the year, however, I noticed a change in Hildegard's demeanour. She was coping well with the demands of her new role, but I could see that something was troubling her. She had become quite short-tempered – quite unlike her usual self – and seemed to be having more 'sick' days than previously.

I never liked to press Hildegard on any personal matter, and generally did not. This time, however, I decided that I needed to enquire, although I was fairly sure that I knew the source of her illness and anxiety, given what Lady Jutta had told me.

"Is everything alright, Hildegard? You seem quite anxious at the moment." It was an unusually mild afternoon in late November. We were strolling in the flower garden, and this seemed like a good time to broach the subject, away from other ears.

Hildegard was bending down, picking some late-blooming flowers. Without looking up, she said, "Everything is fine. I just feel tired – there is always so much to do."

That was true enough. "You know I am here to help you, in whatever way I can," I said, watching her closely.

She stopped picking, straightened her back with some effort, and smiled at me.

"I know that, Volmar," she said. "You already do so much for me, for us. We could not manage without you."

I smiled and said nothing more. I was a little disappointed that she had changed the "me" to "us", but knew that she was right to include the other women. I also knew that there was nothing to be gained by further questioning this day.

Although Hildegard was clearly not yet ready to confide in me, I looked for ways to ease her workload, in an attempt to reduce her anxiety.

"Perhaps it is time for you to relinquish your role as infirmarian of the women's community," I suggested a few days later. "Sister Birgitta has learned much from you and Brother Tobias. I am sure that she could take on this role now."

Sister Birgitta was sitting nearby and looked up from her needlework with an eager smile. "I would love to be infirmarian," she said. "I *have* learned much and have had quite a bit of practical experience, too."

"You can always ask Hildegard or refer to her notes if there is anything you are unsure of," I said, indicating a large pile of parchments on a shelf.

Birgitta looked askance at the pile. Hildegard had been recording information, observations and outcomes since she first became interested in the subject of herbs and healing, nearly 20 years earlier. While Hildegard probably knew what the pages contained and where to find what was needed, others could not hope to do so. To Birgitta, locating information in that great pile of parchments probably seemed akin to locating a needle in a large stack of hay.

I smiled at Birgitta's look of consternation. "I might be able to put these notes into some sort of order," I said.

"Yes," Birgitta said quickly. "That would be most helpful."

Hildegard took Birgitta's hand in hers. "Thank you for agreeing to do this," she said. "It will help me greatly to have one less responsibility."

Birgitta smiled and blushed a little. "It will be my honour and pleasure to serve you and the other women," she said.

Hildegard immediately seemed more relaxed, and I was relieved to see this. Her burden was still great, but this was, at least, a start.

Chapter 19

The new year began with a wintery blast, and remained cold until March. The monastery was always quiet at this time of year. Travellers were few, the days were short, and all outdoor activities were on hold. The indoor routines, of course, continued unabated, although it was especially difficult to leave one's bed when the bell rang in the middle of the night for Matins.

Once the worst of the weather was behind us, the outside world again encroached upon us. The visitors began to return in great numbers – word of Hildegard's healing abilities continued to spread, and she was able to devote more time to healing visitors and travellers, now that Sister Birgitta had taken over the physical care of the women's community.

The better weather also saw a resumption of enquiries from parents hoping for their daughters to join the women's community. One such enquiry was received with particular enthusiasm and excitement.

"Brothers," Abbott Cuno began at a Chapter meeting one fine spring morning. "I have excellent news concerning the women's community. We are to be blessed with the arrival of Richardis von Stade, daughter of a Marquess, no less! This is, indeed, a great honour for our monastery."

Excited murmurings erupted from all sides of the Chapter House. "The daughter of a marquess!" I heard someone say. "*Quite* an acquisition!"

As for me, I wondered if God really cared about the earthly status of those called to serve Him. Surely, we would all be judged on our merits, and not on the accident of our familial relations, on the Day of Judgment.

Richardis arrived about two weeks later. I met her in the afternoon following her evening arrival.

"You are very welcome here, Richardis," I said, smiling.

"I am very grateful to be here, Brother," she replied, smiling shyly at Hildegard. "It is my privilege to serve God in such a holy community."

Hildegard was also smiling. It was the happiest I had seen her for some time. Her bouts of ill health were growing longer and more frequent, and my concerns for her were continuing to grow.

Richardis joined our afternoon lessons, and I discovered quite quickly that she had already received an excellent education. Her knowledge of Scripture and Latin were well-advanced for a person of just 16 years, particularly for a girl. I also soon realised that she was very keen to learn, and was also eager to assist me, Hildegard, or any other member of the community who needed help. She fitted into the community quickly and well, and was liked by everyone.

Hildegard seemed particularly taken with her. I sometimes watched Hildegard watching Richardis, and wondered if Hildegard saw something of herself in the young oblate.

Richardis worked and studied harder than any of the other young women. She was an avid reader, as Hildegard had always been, and asked for texts on a wide range of subjects.

I was particularly impressed with her writing skills. While most of the nuns and oblates wrote neatly enough, Richardis' writing was exceptional. She took such care as she formed the letters into words and sentences, that it was as if she was creating a work of art each time she sat down to write. In a way, I suppose she was.

The women's community was flourishing. With the arrival of Richardis, there were now eighteen women, including Hildegard, and conditions were becoming quite cramped in the former anchorage. Although it had been quite generously extended when it was first opened up, over twenty years earlier, it was becoming clear that the building would soon be full to capacity. Would there be another extension? I wondered what was to become of this happy, vibrant community in future years.

Chapter 20

Despite my efforts to reduce Hildegard's burden and the resulting anxiety and fatigue, it came as no surprise when her ill health became too much for her to bear. Early in the summer of 1141, she took to her bed and did not speak or move for several days.

I sat with her as much as I could, talking gently to her, asking, even pleading with her to tell me what was causing her so much anxiety. Finally, about a week after her collapse, she began to speak.

"There is something I must reveal to you, dear Volmar, a matter that has weighed me down for some years," she began.

"I know you have been troubled," I said, "and I wanted to help you, but I also did not want to pressure you into speaking."

Hildegard smiled. "I am grateful for that," she said. "The pressure I was already receiving from God was as much as I could bear."

"Pressure from God?" I tried to sound surprised, even though I felt sure I knew what was coming.

"It is a long tale," she said. "If you are willing to listen, I will tell it to you."

"Of course, I will listen," I said. "I am always here for you."

She smiled again, closed her eyes, and remained silent for a moment. Then she began to speak.

"For as long as I can remember – from around the age of three, I think – I have sensed in myself the power and mystery of secret visions."

"Visions? Do you mean dreams?" I knew that she did not.

"No, not dreams. I do not perceive the visions in sleep, or delirium, or by the eyes of my body, or by the ears of the outer self. I receive them while awake and seeing with a pure mind and the eyes and ears of the inner self."

She paused. I wanted to hear more. "What do the visions look like?"

"It is hard to explain," she replied. "The things I see and hear are not like the words of human speech, but are like a blazing flame and a cloud that moves through the clear air. I can by no means grasp the form of this light, any more than I can stare fully into the sun."

We were both silent for a moment. Hildegard's description of her visions far exceeded my expectations, based as they were only on what Lady Jutta had been able to tell me. What did all this mean?

Hildegard continued. "Earlier this year, I had a particularly powerful vision in which I heard the voice of God giving me a clear command to record my visions in writing. I was very afraid to do this, and blushed at the thought of proclaiming what I had kept silent about for so long. This illness is God's punishment for my failure to obey him."

After another pause, she said, "When I was a child, before I came to the monastery, I used to see many things and talk about them quite openly, thinking that other people could also see them. After a while, I realised that other people could *not* see them, and I began to feel that I was different. I became worried about being so different, so I decided to keep quiet about what I was seeing and hearing."

"Are you willing now to make these things known to others?" I asked.

"I must obey God's command to write what I see and hear," she replied, "but I am uncertain how to proceed. As I said, the visions do not come to me in the form of human words."

"Perhaps I can help you to put your visions into words that people will understand," I suggested. "Messages from God should be made known to all of God's people."

"Yes," she said with a nod. "That would be helpful."

"Could you write down at least something of what you have seen and heard?" I asked. "I would like to think and pray about this."

"Bring me parchment and ink," she said, "and I will try."

A short time later, Hildegard handed me the parchment. I quickly read what she had written. It was hard to understand at first. The Latin was very rough, and the images that the words sought to convey seemed strange, but eventually, I made some sense of it.

"I saw a bright light," the writing began, "and in the light was the figure of a man the colour of sapphire, and it was all burning in a delightful red fire. And the bright light and the red fire mingled and shone together through the whole figure of the man, and formed one powerful light." This was truly stunning imagery!

Later that evening, after Compline, I stayed behind in the oratory to think and pray. I read Hildegard's writing again, and found it even more astounding than I had on first reading. What did it mean? I had my own ideas as to how it could be interpreted. Others, doubtless, would read it differently. *If Hildegard's visions are all like this,* I thought, *they cannot be made public without some form of explanation or guidance for ordinary ears and eyes.*

Putting that to one side, I had no doubt as to the authenticity and significance of these visions. I prayed to God for guidance that night, and felt sure that I was being called to assist Hildegard to make God's word known to many people.

Chapter 21

The next day, Hildegard was up and about as if she had not been ill at all.

"I feel as if a great weight has been lifted from me," she told me. "It is such a relief to have finally told you of my visions. I have wanted to for many years, but have been unable to speak of this matter since my childhood."

"I am honoured that you feel that you can confide in me," I said. "My only regret is that you have borne this burden in silence for so long."

"I was afraid of what people would think and say of me, but now that God has told me to be open about the things I see and hear, my fear has finally vanished."

That afternoon, Hildegard and I met to discuss our approach to the task of recording the visions.

"I will need Abbott Cuno's permission to spend additional time here," I began. "I was thinking that I should probably tell him about your gift in any event, with your permission, of course."

"Yes, I think he needs to be told," Hildegard replied. "We will, at some point, need the approval of the Church leaders to make these things known to people outside these walls."

Later that day, I went to see the abbott. He listened without interruption as I told him of Hildegard's disclosure to me. When I had finished, he sat silent for some time, examining his folded hands as they lay on his desk.

"I think we should keep this to ourselves for the time being," he finally said. "I would like to see these writings, and consult with the senior brothers as to the validity of the visions. If they appear to be genuine, we can consider taking the matter further. You have my permission to assist Hildegard with this work, in whatever way you can."

I bowed slightly. "Thank you, Father," I said. "I will try not to neglect my other duties."

"You will en*sure* that you do not," the abbott said, without looking up from the parchment he had begun to read.

The next afternoon, I met with Hildegard again, and told her of my discussion with the abbott.

"In short, I am permitted to assist you with this important work," I concluded, smiling.

"That is fortunate," Hildegard replied, "because it is also *God's* will that you should do so."

"God's will?" I asked, genuinely surprised.

"Last night, in a vision, I heard a voice telling me that whenever something is shown to me from on high, I must not publish it in the Latin language by myself, for I am not sufficiently skilled in this language. Rather, I must 'let him who has this skill finish it off in a form pleasing to the human ear.' That can only be referring to you, dear Volmar," she said.

I was truly amazed to hear that I featured in God's messages, but agreed that Hildegard's interpretation must be correct.

"This confirms my own conclusion," I replied, "that it is my duty to assist you with this work of God. It will, of course, also be my pleasure to do so."

Chapter 22

I had not told Hildegard of the abbott's final admonition to me as I left his chamber yesterday, but it troubled me. My relationship with the abbott was complicated by the fact that, as *Brother* Cuno, he had been my confessor for many years. Now, as *Abbott* Cuno, I knew that he had knowledge of all my deepest fears and secrets, and this often made me feel anxious. While I felt certain that he would never break the sanctity of confession by revealing this information to anyone, I knew that it must colour his opinion of me, particularly where Hildegard was concerned.

As a young man, I had struggled frequently with temptations of the flesh. My dreams were often filled with lustful images, sent by Satan's minions to torment me by night. I confessed all this to Brother Cuno, expecting harsh penance, certainly, but also hoping to receive some sympathy for my sufferings. In this, I was misguided and disappointed.

When I had finished my confession, Brother Cuno had curled his lip in disgust. "Perhaps some time in prayer, prostrate on the cold stone floor of the oratory will cool your unseemly ardour," he had said. He did go through the motions of forgiveness and absolution, but his feelings of revulsion were apparent.

I was required to spend one hour, every night for a month, face down on the floor after the singing of Compline had concluded. This was made even more onerous by the fact that I had made the mistake of confessing during winter. The floor, although always cold, was truly freezing. This penance certainly did have the effect of cooling my ardour and, indeed, my entire body. I was so numb after each session that I could barely rise from the floor and stagger to my bed.

After yesterday's meeting, I realised that the abbott's disapproval had not diminished over time. This was exacerbated by the fact that I would be working closely with Hildegard, and he knew that it had been that lady for whom I had longed. While I could do nothing to change our past dealings, I was determined that, from that day forward, I would never give the abbott any reason to doubt my obedience to my holy vows, especially the one concerning chastity.

Chapter 23

It took Hildegard a little while to decide the form that her writings should take. Then, about a month after our first discussion on the subject, she told me that she knew how to begin.

"In a vision, I saw that this book of visions is to be called *Scito vias Domini*, for it will come forth by way of the Living Light, and not through any human instruction."

"Know the Ways of the Lord?"

"Yes," Hildegard replied. "These are the visions I need to record at this time, the messages God wants to be made known to His people."

"Perhaps we could call it *Scivias* for convenience", I suggested.

Hildegard raised an eyebrow, then nodded. "Very well," she replied. "That is a well-known contraction of the phrase, I believe."

"What are the messages to be included in *Scivias*?" I asked.

"The visions that I have had, over many years and in no particular order, really cover the entire story of Christianity," Hildegard began, "beginning with Creation and the Fall, then moving on to our salvation through the Incarnation, leading to the Day of Judgment and the coming of God's Kingdom. All Christians know this story, but many have become very lax in their observance of the Christian way of life. God wants, through me, to remind, to warn, and to reinvigorate His people."

"That is no small task," I said, with a short laugh, "but I will do whatever I can to help you."

"Perhaps I could help, too?" said a voice behind me. It was Richardis. I did not know how long she had been there, or how much she had heard, but I had no doubt that her desire to help was genuine and well-intentioned.

Hildegard smiled. "I am sure you can, Richardis," she said. "Between the three of us, I am certain that, with God's help, we can complete this task to God's glory."

I was excited at the prospect of this work, but also apprehensive. What if I were not equal to the task? Then I looked at Hildegard and Richardis. They showed no such trepidation – they were happy, excited, and eager to begin. I suddenly felt such a strong bond of camaraderie with these two remarkable women, that all my doubts vanished. Thus, the 'team' was born.

"So, how shall we begin?" I asked.

Hildegard thought for a moment. "Each of these visions comes to me, in the first place, as an image, that I 'see' as clearly as I see you now," she began. "At the same time or shortly after the arrival of the image, come words of explanation." She frowned. "I do not think that the words, without the image, will convey the message clearly or even adequately."

"Can you reproduce the image?" I asked. "Perhaps, draw it?"

Hildegard looked doubtful. "I am no artist, but I could try. Even if I can produce only a rough sketch, it will be a place to begin."

An idea struck me. "I will be back in a few minutes," I said, as I hurried out of the house. I made my way briskly to the scriptorium, hoping that Brother Jurgen, who had recently taken on the role of armarius, was not there. He was quite difficult to extract materials from, if he did not believe they were needed, or could not see the value of the proposed work.

I stopped just outside the scriptorium and checked the interior before I entered. Brother Jurgen was nowhere to be seen. There were, as usual, a few brothers at work, but they did not even look up from their scribing when I entered.

A few moments later, I was back at the house, bearing a wax tablet and a clean quill.

"Perhaps you could try sketching an image into this," I said to Hildegard as I handed the items to her.

The following day, Hildegard showed me the image she had created. It was rough, but I thought I could make out a figure at the top of the image, with faces and stars below.

Hildegard sighed. "This is *not* what it looked like in my vision. As I thought, I am no artist, and it needs *colours*!"

Another idea came to me. "Richardis, is this something you could help with?" I remembered her beautiful writing, and wondered if she might have other artistic abilities.

Richardis looked closely at the wax tablet, frowning slightly. "I could certainly try," she replied, turning to Hildegard. "Perhaps you can direct me as to how it should look," she said.

"Back soon," I said. I again hurried to the scriptorium, hoping for another clear run. Luck was not with me on this occasion.

"You want *what*?" Brother Jurgen was aghast. "Parchment, *coloured* ink, and a quill for each colour? What on earth are you up to, Brother?"

I adopted a formal demeanour. "I am assisting the women with work approved by the abbott," I replied. "I cannot say more than that."

Brother Jurgen stared at me for a moment, then shrugged.

"Very well," he said. "Take what you want. Everything here is intended for God's work, I suppose."

"Just so," I said and went to the storeroom to see what I could find.

Moments later, I was back at the house. I placed the items on the table, where Hildegard and Richardis were sitting.

Richardis was open-mouthed. "Such beautiful colours! I will need to take great care – I would hate to waste any of this ink."

Several days passed before I was permitted to see the final image. It was my turn to be open-mouthed - the difference between the first sketch and the final image was astounding, as was the image itself. I had been right about the figure at the top of the image, but I could now see that this figure shone with radiance and had wings. Beneath this figure, which I thought must be God, were many windows, each containing a human head. There were two complete figures at the bottom of the image, but I could not tell what they were intended to represent.

"What a beautiful image," I said. It was of outstanding beauty and quite unlike anything I had ever seen.

Hildegard and Richardis both smiled. "Yes," said Hildegard. "This is what I saw in my vision. Richardis has done an excellent job." Hildegard smiled warmly at Richardis.

"What comes next?" I asked, keen to continue.

"I need to describe the image, in the words I was given. I will write the words as best I can, but you will need to correct the Latin," Hildegard said.

It took Hildegard a couple of days to write these words to her satisfaction. It then took me twice as long to edit the text into a form suitable for general reading. Hildegard was, as God had told her quite bluntly, unskilled in formal Latin, although I could understand what she was trying to say.

When I had finished, I showed Hildegard the text.

"This is beautiful prose," she said, shaking her head, "way beyond my meagre abilities." I felt myself blushing, and hoped nobody would notice. "The final thing I must do is write the words that I heard that explain the *meaning* of the vision. I will ..."

The bell rang for Vespers. Unusually for me, I was annoyed at this summons. I was keen to continue the work with Hildegard, but knew I must go to the chapel immediately.

By the next day, Hildegard had taken ill, so the work was delayed for a few days. About a week later, when I went to the house, Hildegard was still lying on her bed, but seemed quite lucid.

"I do not feel strong enough to write the words of explanation, but I think I could speak them. Could you write them down as I speak?" she asked.

"I think that should be possible," I replied. This seemed like a good way to keep the work progressing during Hildegard's bouts of poor health.

This process proved to be quite laborious, but I still thought it better than doing no work on the visions.

Hildegard spoke the words that she had heard, but could only do so in her unpolished Latin. I decided to write exactly what she said, and then to edit the rough draft later – I did not think I could 'translate' her words directly into polished Latin.

After a week of these, usually short, sessions, I had Hildegard's spoken words written on parchment. It then took me a few days to edit the work and prepare the final version.

I read what I had written to Hildegard as she lay resting. She listened with her eyes closed and smiled when I had reached the end.

"That is perfect," she said, then fell into a deep sleep.

The process that Hildegard, Richardis and I had adopted for recording the first vision was the one that we followed for the remainder of the work on *Scivias*. We could not always find time to devote to this work – there were sometimes quite long gaps of time when we were too busy with other tasks. Also, some of Hildegard's visions were more complex and multi-layered than others, and those took much longer to record to Hildegard's satisfaction. In short, it was not a full-time project, and it was, at times, extremely challenging, but it was fascinating and rewarding, and I always enjoyed the collaboration and camaraderie that flourished between the three of us.

It was around this time that Hildegard mentioned the possibility of engaging a new maid to assist in the women's community.

"We all miss Jutta," she began, "but I think it is time to find a replacement for her. We all need some assistance with household tasks."

I thought this an excellent idea. I was always concerned that Hildegard was doing too much, but even the other sisters needed more time to spend on their devotions and studies.

"I will speak to Brother Stefan," I said. "He has dealings with many of the townspeople, and may be able to find us a girl or young woman."

Brother Stefan wasted no time in fulfilling our request. About a week after I spoke to him about the matter, the local butcher's daughter, Bertha, had moved into the women's house and was quickly making herself useful. Bertha was around 14 years of age, but seemed older. She was tall and strongly built, and was confident in her dealings with the older women.

One afternoon, when Bertha had been with us for only a few days, Hildegard and I watched her scrubbing the floor with great vigour.

Hildegard smiled. "I think Bertha is going to be a valuable addition to this community."

I nodded and smiled. The women had been without a maid since Jutta's death four years earlier, and I was greatly relieved that Hildegard's burden was being further reduced to more manageable dimensions.

Chapter 24

By the spring of 1142, I had known Hildegard for over 25 years. I thought I knew her well, and felt sure that I was aware of the full extent of her God-given gifts and talents. I was mistaken.

One afternoon in mid-April, as I was walking to the women's house for lessons, I heard music coming from the house. This, in itself, was not unusual. Hildegard had taken great pains to teach the women the chants of the Divine Office, having learned them first from me, and I often heard them practising. This music, however, on this day, was unlike anything I had ever heard.

A single voice sang a phrase, followed by the rest of the women repeating the phrase. The melody flowed from low to high, then settled briefly in the middle range, before soaring higher still. It was captivating yet disturbing at the same time. It sounded – un*earthly*. Whatever else it was, it was beautiful.

I stopped outside the door, not wanting to interrupt the teaching of this beautiful music. I must have been heard, however, because the singing stopped in mid-air.

The door opened. "Volmar," Hildegard said, smiling. "Come in. I am just teaching the sisters a new antiphon."

"It is enchanting," I replied. "Who has created such beautiful sounds? Surely no human could have composed this."

Hildegard blushed and looked at the floor. "It is one of my humble efforts," she replied.

"You composed this? It is wonderful!" I said.

She looked up and smiled. "It is not really *my* doing," she explained. "I heard the Living Light sing to me, and I am trying to reproduce the song as closely as I am able."

I was amazed. I was well aware that Hildegard received words and images in her visions, but it seemed that music was another of these sensory, God-sent experiences.

"Do you see and hear the words and music together?" I asked.

"When the words come, they are merely empty shells without the music," Hildegard replied. "They live as they are sung, for the words are the body and the music the spirit."

Thereafter, I occasionally heard Hildegard teaching the women a new chant, each as glorious as that first one. Whenever I did hear these voices rising and falling together in perfect unison, I felt the music lift my soul and raise it closer to God in Heaven.

Chapter 25

In the year 1143, and after more than 30 years of construction, our new church was finally finished, and was dedicated by Henry, Archbishop of Mainz, on 29 September. On the same day, the relics of our holy patron, Saint Disibod, were freshly sealed and blessed in a stone tomb-shrine behind the high altar of the new church.

This was, indeed, a grand occasion, attended by all members of the men's community. I was greatly disappointed that the women's community could not attend. Ever since the Second Lateran Council of 1139, men and women were not permitted to co-celebrate the liturgy, and could only share church space if walls, grills and separate entrances were installed to separate the two sexes. This was, apparently, required to ensure 'the purity' of both. I considered these requirements to be heavy-handed and un-Christian. Had Jesus ever insisted on such segregation? I, of course, kept my opinions to myself, but Hildegard showed less self-control.

"This is outrageous!" she had declared, when news of the Council's ruling first reached us. "What a low opinion the authorities must have of we monastics if they think that such separation is required, and in church, of all places! What *do* they think we will get up to?"

I had noticed, since the papal dispute that began in 1130, that Hildegard was becoming more openly critical of certain aspects of the Church's leadership, albeit within the relative privacy of the women's house. While I generally agreed with what she said, I worried that by being too open about her feelings, she was running the risk of attracting unfavourable attention from the authorities. After all, we would eventually need the approval of these same authorities if we wished to make Hildegard's visions and writings widely known.

I need not have worried. While Hildegard had strong views on religious matters, she was also sufficiently worldly-wise to know when to speak and when to remain silent. As events would soon prove, she was also sufficiently skilled to secure the required approval from the highest possible earthly authority.

Chapter 26

One morning, early in the year 1146, I received a summons from Abbott Cuno.

"How is the work with Sister Hildegard progressing?" he asked without preamble. "It seems to be taking quite some time."

"The work *is* progressing, Father," I replied, "but not rapidly or even regularly. We are somewhat constrained by Hildegard's other duties and her spells of poor health, and also by the difficulty of the work. Some of the visions are complex, and it can be challenging to 'translate' the images she sees and the words she hears into language that other people might understand."

The abbott grunted. "That is all well and good," he said, "but I am eager to make these miraculous messages from God known beyond the monastery's walls. Can you estimate a completion date?"

"I will ask Hildegard, but I know that she is uncertain about the number of visions that are to be included in this work, and how long each will take to put into writing," I replied.

"I am not happy about the delay," the abbott said, frowning at me. "I would like to bring this matter to the attention of the archbishop. We will, at least, need his approval to make these visions public."

I conveyed this request to Hildegard later that day.

She thought for a moment, then said, "Yes, that is probably a good starting point. I have also been thinking of making my own approaches to secure such approval."

"From the archbishop?" I asked.

Hildegard smiled. "No. I will leave that to the abbott. I have another in mind."

I raised my eyebrows in enquiry. "Who might you approach?" I asked.

"I have been thinking for some time that it would be very helpful to seek the support of Bernard, Abbott of Clairvaux. I recall the great influence he brought to bear in resolving the papal dispute, and I am certain that he would be a powerful ally."

My eyebrows raised even further at this. Bernard of Clairvaux? That would be a bold move indeed. "Yes, I am sure you are right," I said. "He would, indeed, be a powerful ally, especially now that Eugenius is pope."

Pope Eugenius III had been elected the previous year, and was well-known to Bernard. As Bernardo da Pisa, Eugenius had been one of Bernard's disciples at Clairvaux before his elevation to the papacy. If Hildegard could secure the support and approval of these two leaders of the Church, there could be no earthly impediment to her work.

"My letter to Bernard must be carefully worded," Hildegard continued. "I must not appear to be self-promoting – from a woman, that would not be tolerated. I will tell him about my visions, and ask his *advice* as to whether I should make them known to others or keep silent about them."

"That sounds like a good approach," I replied. "If we allow him to take the initiative, we cannot be accused of over-reaching. I will help you with the Latin."

"Yes," Hildegard said. "The Latin must be flawless for *this* recipient. I will write a draft for you to edit."

A few days later, Hildegard gave me the draft letter. It was deferential and quite self-effacing. It began with, "O venerable father Bernard, I lay my claim before you, for, highly honoured by God, you bring fear to the immoral foolishness of this world."

Hildegard went on to say, "Wretched in my womanly condition, I have from earliest childhood seen great marvels which my tongue has no power to express, but which the Spirit of God has taught me that I may believe. Steadfast and gentle father, in your kindness respond to me, your unworthy servant, who has never, from her earliest childhood, lived one hour free from anxiety."

This last sentence caused my heart to grieve for her. *What a burden this has been!* I thought. *I had no idea that she suffered so.*

The letter then went on to describe the nature and content of the visions, and the great insights that had been given to her by this inward 'seeing'. Later, Hildegard asked Bernard to reveal to her "whether I should speak these things openly or keep my silence, because I have great anxiety with respect to how much I should speak about what I have seen and heard." This was the crux of the letter. If Bernard advised Hildegard to reveal her visions, then this was the authority and permission we required.

While my heart grieved, it was also gladdened by part of the letter. At one point she wrote, "With the exception of a certain monk in whose exemplary life I have the utmost confidence, I have not dared to tell these things to anyone. I have, in fact, told all my secrets to this man, and he has given me consolation." I knew that the 'certain monk' must be me, and I knew that Hildegard had known that I would read this. My heart (and face) glowed with pleasure when I read this passage.

I needed a few days to edit this draft and put it into the best Latin of which I was capable. I had never written to such a highly esteemed person before, and I was very anxious about the final result, and its reception and response.

As expected, several weeks passed before a reply came. Hildegard handed it to me, her hands shaking.

"Would you read it to me?" she asked.

I unrolled the parchment and scanned it quickly. The response was quite brief, but this was to be expected from such an important person with many demands on his time.

"What does he say?" Hildegard could wait no longer.

"It is a positive, albeit brief, response," I said. "He acknowledges that your gift is, indeed, from God, and 'urges and beseeches you to respond eagerly to it with all humility and devotion'. That seems to me to be encouragement to make your visions known to others," I concluded.

Hildegard thought for a moment, then smiled. "Yes," she said. "That is sufficient. Progress is being made."

I assumed that this 'progress' referred to a plan Hildegard had to gain full Church acceptance and authority. I did not know of any such plan and perhaps, at this stage, the details were not clear even to Hildegard. I did know that patience and tact would be required in this matter, and I also knew that Hildegard was fully possessed of these attributes.

Chapter 27

Towards the end of 1146, Abbott Cuno returned from a visit to Mainz with encouraging news. He made the announcement at a Chapter meeting in early December.

"Brothers," he began, beaming with uncharacteristic excitement, "I have spoken to the archbishop at length about Sister Hildegard and told him of her miraculous visions. After some thought and prayer, he advised me that he is certain that Hildegard is, indeed, receiving messages directly from God."

The normally quiet meeting erupted into a cacophony of astonishment and joy.

"What is more," the abbott continued, raising his hand to subdue the chatter, "he is proposing to bring this matter to the attention of Pope Eugenius at next year's Synod at Trier."

More excitement ensued. I was as pleased as anyone, but less surprised than most of those present. I, at least, had known of Hildegard's visions for some time, while for the rest of the brothers, it was an astonishing revelation.

"These are very exciting developments," the abbott continued, "for Hildegard, of course, but also for our community. Hildegard and the women of her community have already attracted many visitors and prospective members to Disibodenberg, but gaining the pope's attention will do even more to enhance our standing and reputation."

Everybody agreed that this was, indeed, very good news. The matter was, however, in abeyance until next year, so all we could do was wait and see how things developed.

Hildegard was also very pleased when I conveyed the news to the women's community later that day.

"Excellent!" she said. "Bernard will also be at Trier, with the pope, so I will have two eminent supporters in attendance." The 'plan', it seemed, was even closer to fruition.

Chapter 28

The year 1147 began unremarkably, but it would prove to be quite momentous.

We had a long wait for the Synod at Trier, which was not due to begin until late November. I tried to put it out of my mind by keeping busy. With my regular tasks and duties, and the work with Hildegard and Richardis, I succeeded in this aim.

Shortly before the Synod was due to begin, a 'sign' appeared in the sky. On October 26, the sun was transformed into the shape of a sickle, and cast darkness across the land.

"This *must* be a bad omen," Richardis said, frowning.

"Yes and no," Hildegard replied thoughtfully. "It is a warning to those who have not been living in accordance with God's ways, so, for those who do not heed the warning, it *is* a bad omen. On the other hand, I see it as a *good* omen for my mission."

Richardis looked as puzzled as I felt at this conclusion. Hildegard continued.

"Surely, it must mean that I will be allowed to spread God's word far and wide, to reinforce this call to repentance," she said.

I nodded at this reasoning, but said nothing. Hildegard seemed to be gaining confidence that the news from Trier, when it eventually reached us, would be in her favour. I certainly prayed that it would be so.

The Council of Trier began on 30 November 1147, although we did not know that until later. Early in the new year, everyone at the monastery was greatly surprised, and more than a little excited, when a delegation from Pope Eugenius arrived to enquire after Hildegard and her visions. It seemed that Archbishop Heinrich had, as promised, spoken to the pope about Hildegard, and the pope was keen to learn more.

The delegation was led by the venerable Bishop of Verdun, Albero. With him were his secretary, Adalbert, and several other senior clerics. They were an austere and imposing assemblage, all in black, with large gold crucifixes adorning their chests.

"We must speak to the lady privately," the bishop said to Abbott Cuno. Hildegard and I had been summoned to the abbott's chamber to meet the delegation, and we were now standing as near to the fireplace as rank allowed.

I looked with alarm at Abbott Cuno. I dared not speak in this company, but hoped that my look would convey my concern at the bishop's demand.

"Perhaps another nun ..." the abbott began, but was cut off.

"*Privately,*" the bishop repeated.

Hildegard gave me a warm smile. She did not appear concerned at the prospect of a private 'interview' with the delegation. Reassured, I bowed and left the room, followed closely by Abbott Cuno.

I returned to the women's house to wait. I paced up and down and I could see that Richardis was also not giving her full attention to her studies. After what seemed like hours, Hildegard returned to the house, clearly exhausted by the ordeal. She went straight to her bed to lie down.

All of the women stopped what they were doing and watched as Richardis and I went and sat on either side of Hildegard.

"Are you well?" I asked. "What happened?"

Hildegard smiled. "All is well," she replied. "I am quite tired from their rigorous questioning, but they appear to be satisfied that my visions are genuine, and are truly sent by God."

The women all burst into excited chatter at this news. Richardis' shoulders relaxed as she smiled broadly.

"That is wonderful," Richardis said, taking Hildegard's hand in hers.

I felt a surge of both excitement and relief. This was, indeed, a major step forward. If the pope were to be satisfied that Hildegard's visions were authentic, and said so publicly, there would be nothing to prevent Hildegard from making the messages from God known to all.

"They have asked for a sample of my writings to take back to His Holiness," Hildegard continued. "Perhaps they could take the first three of the visions from *Scivias*? I believe they are completed to the requisite standard."

"Yes," I replied. "Those would be a very good example of your work."

"I would also like to write a letter to the pope, pleading my cause. Would you help me to prepare it?" she asked, looking at me.

"Of course," I replied. "We must be swift, however. I understand the delegation is returning to Trier tomorrow morning."

Hildegard and I worked for most of that evening and into the night on this most important of letters. We finished just as the bell rang for Lauds.

A few hours later, the Papal delegation began its journey back to Trier, carrying a copy of Hildegard's first three visions and her letter to Pope Eugenius. I said a prayer as I watched them ride out through the monastery's main gate.

The letter to the pope was extraordinary and could not fail to convince. Hildegard adopted the same humble, self-effacing tone that she had used when she wrote to Bernard of Clairvaux, but it was also a more confident letter in many ways. Hildegard even included a short visionary passage, in which she described a 'mighty king' in his palace, surrounded by great, golden columns adorned with pearls and precious stones. This king touched a small feather, which flew miraculously and remained aloft due to a powerful and sustaining wind. Although no explanation was provided, it seemed clear to me that this king represented God, empowering Hildegard (the feather) by the Holy Spirit (the wind) to carry God's word to the people. The letter concluded with a direct request (instruction, even?) that the pope 'prepare this writing for the hearing of those who receive' God.

I knew we would have to wait some time for a response, but I hardly knew how I was going to stand the anticipation.

Chapter 29

The Council of Trier concluded in early February 1148. Shortly afterwards, Abbott Cuno was summoned to Mainz by Archbishop Heinrich. I was hoping that this summons concerned Hildegard and the reception of her writings, but, as usual, I was forced to wait to learn more.

Abbott Cuno returned a week later, and again delivered exciting news at a Chapter meeting.

"Brothers, I have the most marvellous news," he began, barely able to contain his excitement. "His Holiness the Pope not only received and read Sister Hildegard's writings, he also read part of them aloud to the entire gathering!"

Exclamations of surprise and delight erupted and filled the Chapter House.

The abbott continued. "His Holiness was so inspired by what he had read that he called on those present to praise and give thanks to God."

This was greeted by gasps, and several of the brothers fell to their knees in reverence.

"Then," the abbott continued, "no less a person than Bernard of Clairvaux stood and, before the assembly, urged the pope to confirm Hildegard's gift of grace by his authority. The pope agreed to do so, and has sent this letter to Sister Hildegard. I have, of course, not read this, as it is not addressed to me. Brother Volmar, will you pass this on to Sister Hildegard?"

"Yes, of course, Father," I replied, as I took the parchment. Had it been opened? I could not tell.

"There was also another letter from His Holiness given to me by the archbishop," the abbott continued. The room was now quite silent, in anticipation of further news. "I have read this letter, as it *was* addressed to me." He glanced at me, but looked away quickly. "This letter is also truly astounding, and I am most humbled to receive it." He paused and swallowed before continuing. "The pope has sent his congratulations to all of us here at Disibodenberg Monastery for the role we have played in nurturing and supporting Sister Hildegard, whom God has chosen to be the recipient of this most precious gift." Another burst of astonishment erupted. "Now, brothers, we must not allow the sin of pride to fill our hearts, but we can, I think, be humbly grateful for this recognition, from God's highest representative on earth, that we have well and truly served God to the best of our abilities."

I suspected that there was, in fact, a great *deal* of sinful pride in the room that morning, but perhaps God will not judge us too harshly for it. It was, after all, a truly momentous occasion for our community. To have come to the attention of the pope in such positive circumstances was rare enough, but to be congratulated by him was beyond all expectations.

After the meeting, I took the letter straight to the women's house. Everyone gathered around Hildegard, as she broke the seal and unrolled the parchment. She read the letter to herself, smiled, then handed it to me to read. It was good news, indeed. The pope, 'under Christ and in the name of blessed Peter', granted Hildegard permission to make known whatever she learnt through the Holy Spirit, and encouraged her to put what she learnt into writing. She had received the ultimate earthly approval. From now on, nobody could legitimately criticise Hildegard for making her visions known to all.

"This is wonderful," I said, passing the parchment to Richardis. We can re-double our efforts now, and complete *Scivias* in the knowledge that we have the pope's blessing."

"Yes," Hildegard said. "The way is now clear."

All the sisters read the letter, one after another, and there was much excitement. Hurrying away from the house in response to the bell for Prime, I could hear their happy chattering and laughing. Things were, indeed, in a happy state at Disibodenberg Monastery.

Chapter 30

It did not take long for news of the pope's approval of Hildegard's visions to travel far and wide.

Within weeks, Abbott Cuno was inundated with requests from noblemen to offer their daughters as oblates within Hildegard's community. While the abbott would happily have accepted all such offers, the women's house was quite full. The arrival of any new residents would have resulted in the accommodation becoming cramped and uncomfortable. It became apparent that further expansion of the house was required.

Abbott Cuno was more than happy to arrange for the building works to commence without delay. It was late spring, and the weather was ideal for such work. There was also no shortage of willing workers in the men's community and in the local villages.

Hildegard's increasing fame also brought many more visitors to Disibodenberg. People of both sexes, both local and from every part of France and Germany, came to see Hildegard for healing, advice or insight into God's intended purpose for their lives.

Letters also arrived in large numbers. These also sought information and advice from Hildegard on matters both physical and spiritual. Hildegard's workload became overwhelming.

After one particularly busy day, she sat down heavily on her bed and sighed deeply. "This is becoming too much," she said to me and Richardis as we came to sit with her. "I have no time for my own devotions, and we have not worked on *Scivias* for weeks."

"Perhaps we can share the burden with you," I said. "I am certain that Sister Birgitta can help with some of the physical ailments – she has become a skilled infirmarian these past few years. Richardis can certainly assist in the giving of spiritual counsel, and I can deal with most of the correspondence."

Hildegard smiled and looked much brighter. "That sounds like an excellent arrangement," she said, "but will people be happy to see or hear from someone other than the person for whom they have asked?"

As things turned out, most people did not seem to mind or feel that they had been 'cheated'. Hildegard made sure that she spoke to everyone who came to the monastery to see her and listened carefully to the reason for their visit. Only then did she decide to either deal with the matter herself, or, in very kindly tones, suggest that the visitor see either Birgitta or Richardis. Similarly, she read all of the letters addressed to her, and wrote all of the replies to people of high social or ecclesiastical standing. I prepared all other replies on her behalf, so that all she needed to do was simply sign them.

In this way, Hildegard was able to treat everyone with care and concern, while also reducing her burden. As her closest supporters, Richardis, Birgitta and I were more than happy to help, even though our own workloads became heavier. All four of us were busy but content, and I felt confident that this new arrangement would continue well into the future. As usual, I was mistaken.

Chapter 31

Towards the end of summer in 1148, I observed that, despite a more manageable workload, Hildegard was becoming anxious and short-tempered. I wondered at the reason for this, but was soon distracted by my own concerns and responsibilities.

In mid-September, I received word that my father was seriously ill and unlikely to live much longer. I obtained Abbott Cuno's permission to leave the monastery to go and see my father before he died, so I set off for Koblenz, my hometown.

I had not seen my father or any other family members since I first entered the monastery nearly 40 years earlier. Unsurprisingly, everyone had changed, almost beyond recognition. Apparently, I also seemed altered.

"Volmar!" my sister greeted me. "You look so ... *old*!"

I laughed. Hilda had always been blunt in her speech. "As do we all, sister," I replied.

"Come," she said, suddenly serious. "Father is asking for you."

My father was in bed, sitting propped up by pillows. He was, indeed, close to death, and looked skeletally thin. I sat with him, on and off, for hours that day, telling him about my life at the monastery, and prayed with him as he grew weaker. I have never been ordained as a priest, so I could not give him Extreme Unction, but I gave him my blessing and love as he died peacefully the next day, surrounded by the rest of our family.

I stayed to arrange and attend his funeral and to help my mother and sisters with various matters. After a week or so, I was glad to be leaving. This place had never felt like home, and seemed even more foreign after all these years. I set off for Disibodenberg without a backward glance.

When I arrived home, I was greeted by Richardis in a distressed state.

"Brother Volmar! I am so pleased you have returned," she said as I entered the main gate.

"What has happened?" I asked, dismounting. A lay brother took my horse to the stables.

"Hildegard is very ill," she replied. "She took to her bed shortly after you left, and has barely moved since."

We hurried to the women's house. There were building materials lying nearby, but work did not appear to have commenced.

As I entered the house, I was greeted by a group of anxious and tearful women.

"Brother, it is good to see you," said Birgitta. "I have done all I can for her, but she is not responding to any of the usual treatments. She seems quite delirious."

I went to where Hildegard lay, and sat on a stool beside the bed. I took her hand in mine, which seemed to settle her slightly.

"Hildegard? It is I, Volmar. What ails you?" I asked gently. *Has she had another vision?* I wondered. The last time I had seen her like this was when she was resisting God's command to make her visions known to others. *What is she attempting to conceal this time?*

As Hildegard's body relaxed, her breathing became slower and deeper. Then she opened her eyes. She was *look*ing at me, but did not seem to be *see*ing me.

"Oh, Volmar," she began. "There is a clouding over of my eyes, and I am so pressed down by the weight of my body that I cannot raise myself."

This illness seemed more serious than the last. I moved closer and lowered my voice. "Have you had another command from God?" I asked.

She nodded slightly. "Yes," she replied, "but this command is too much. It is beyond my abilities."

I frowned. "Surely God would not ask you to do something that you are unable to do," I said. "He knows your abilities. He *gave* you your abilities, as he did for us all."

"I have always believed the same," she said, "but the task He commands this time is of immense difficulty and will cause much distress."

"Tell me what it is," I said, squeezing her hand gently, "and we can deal with it together, all three of us." Richardis, who was sitting on the other side of Hildegard's bed, nodded her vigorous agreement.

Hildegard closed her eyes and lay silently for a moment. Then, tentatively, she began to speak.

"It was shown to me that I must move with my nuns from Disibodenberg to another place," she told us.

"Move?" Richardis and I exclaimed together. "Where have you been told to go?"

"To Rupertsberg," Hildegard replied. "I do not know the place, but I have been told that it is not far from here."

Rupertsberg! I *did* know the place. It was a cold, barren hilltop, named for St Rupert, whose story I also knew. Born in Mainz in the early 8th Century, he was only 15 years old when he made a pilgrimage to Rome with his mother, St Bertha. When they returned, they lived on a hill near Bingen, which came to be called the 'Rupertsberg'. Rupert used his inherited wealth to found churches and establish hospices for the poor and needy. Sadly, he died when he was just 20 years old, and his mother had a monastery built at the site of his grave. The monastery was now in ruins, but parts of the church dedicated to St Rupert were still standing.

A ruined monastery on a barren hill? Could God really be telling Hildegard to take her nuns there? I knew it was not my place to question Hildegard's visions, and even less appropriate that I should doubt the wisdom of God's commands, but my heart sank at the thought of living in the midst of another major construction project, such works being undoubtedly necessary to establish any decent place for the women's community.

I did not voice any of my doubts and misgivings. Instead, I said, "We must speak to the abbott as soon as possible. I do not think he will be very pleased about this development." Even as I spoke, I knew that I was understating the extent of the abbott's reaction.

"Impossible!" the abbott said, banging both palms on the table he was sitting at. "It is absolute insanity! Why would Hildegard want to take her nuns away from this safe, supportive environment, and move to that patch of wilderness? I know conditions are cramped in the women's house at the moment, but that situation is soon to be improved – we have already purchased the building materials."

I could think of no reasonable reply so thought it best to remain silent.

"Well," he continued, "she will receive no help from me or *anyone else* here." I had been examining the floor at my feet, but raised my head to see that he was looking at me with narrowed eyes. I swallowed, but still said nothing. "She is most ungrateful," the abbott concluded, "after everything we have done for her and her community."

I felt conflicted. The abbott's position seemed to have much merit, but my desire to help Hildegard to achieve her plans, especially those that came to her from God, outweighed any reason or logic. In any battle between my duty to the abbott and my devotion to Hildegard, I had no doubt that the latter would always prevail.

Hildegard had seemed much recovered after she had told Richardis and me of this new vision. As before, speaking of the vision had removed the burden of keeping it concealed. When I told Hildegard of my conversation with the abbott, however, she immediately relapsed.

Now her illness was even more severe. She was completely bed-ridden, and could not sit up even to eat or drink. Richardis wept, and I genuinely feared for Hildegard's life.

At the Chapter meeting the next morning, the abbott told the brothers of Hildegard's plan. This was met with a torrent of shock and disapproval. Some brothers even expressed opinions on the matter.

"Ridiculous!" said Brother Jurgen.

"Such ingratitude, when the abbott has so generously agreed to expand their facilities!" said Brother Arnold. This monk, a solidly built man about my own age, was the sacristan, and was responsible for, among other things, the maintenance of the monastery's buildings. He had also been closely involved in the building works around the monastery, and had recently been put in charge of the plan to expand the women's house.

Although it remained unspoken, I knew that the brothers were also concerned about the prospect of losing a major source of the monastery's income. The women's community, and Hildegard in particular, attracted many visitors who often brought generous gifts and donations with them. If the women were to leave, there would be few, if any, reasons to visit Disibodenberg.

"Surely Brother Volmar can talk some sense into Sister Hildegard," said Prior Adelbert. This silenced everyone. Now, they were all looking at me expectantly.

"Sister Hildegard genuinely believes, as do I, that it is God's will that she and the sisters should move to Rupertsberg," I began. "She would not have made this decision otherwise. She knows how much the men's community has done to help her over the years and she is very conflicted over this command from God, but cannot refuse to obey. For this reason," I paused and looked at Abbott Cuno, "I will do everything I can to assist her with this move." I then lowered my eyes, expecting a verbal assault.

To my surprise, nothing more was said on the subject. The brothers could hardly disagree with God, I suppose. I looked up at the abbott. His jaw was clenched tightly, and I knew that this matter was far from settled.

Hildegard remained rigid in bed for several days. We were able, with difficulty, to give her food and drink, but I knew that this situation could not be allowed to continue.

On several occasions, I went to Abbott Cuno to plead with him to change his mind and give his blessing to the women's move. He refused to do so. *They are as stubborn as each other*, I thought after one particularly heated exchange.

After two weeks had passed and Hildegard had still not moved from her bed, the abbott's patience was exhausted.

"I tire of this game," he said as I stood before him. "She cannot move, you say, Brother? *I* will get her to move."

I had to almost run to keep up with the abbott as he strode towards the women's house. When he entered, the sisters all stopped what they were doing. Some gasped. Everyone watched, wide-eyed with alarm, as the abbott advanced towards Hildegard.

"Come now, Sister," the abbott said mildly. "It is time to stop this pretence. Sit up now."

"I...I cannot," Hildegard replied.

"Let me help you," the abbott said, carefully sliding his hands under Hildegard's back. Several of the sisters gasped again. The abbott tried to lift Hildegard gently, then with increasing effort, but he was unable to move her.

The abbott removed his hands from Hildegard and stood up, red-faced from his exertions. "This matter requires further consideration," he said, before leaving the house quickly.

At the Chapter meeting the next morning, the abbott announced a change of heart.

"Brothers, I have considered Sister Hildegard's request to relocate her community, and have prayed most of the night for God's guidance. I am now certain that it *is* God's will that the women should go to Rupertsberg, and it is not right that any of us should stand in their way. On the contrary, I believe we should strive to help them as much as we can."

The response this time was muted. While clearly surprised by the announcement, most agreed with the abbott that no man should oppose a person seeking to obey a command from God. How could they do otherwise?

Brother Arnold remained unconvinced. He dared not voice his objection in the face of such unanimity, but I could see from his frown and the clenching of his jaw that he was not going to be co-operative.

After the meeting, Abbott Cuno came with me to the women's house to tell Hildegard of his decision. He told her, in the Lord's name, to 'rise up and go forth to the dwelling place prepared for her by heaven'. When Hildegard heard this, she rose quite briskly, as if she had not been incapacitated at all. Everyone in the house was amazed at this instant transformation.

"God has sent us a clear message," Richardis said, her hands clasped as if in prayer. "Now we must do all we can to obey His command to move."

By the time we received the abbott's consent to move to Rupertsberg, the cold weather had arrived. We decided to wait until spring to go and inspect the site of the women's new home.

Meanwhile, Brother Arnold continued to resist the women's move most obstinately, and seemed to be stirring up the other brothers to join in his opposition. I kept this information to myself, as I knew that it would cause Hildegard great distress and, possibly, more illness.

In late February 1149, I was relieved when Brother Arnold had to visit a property of the monastery near Bingen. *A few days of peace, God be praised,* I thought. About a week later, Brother Arnold returned to the monastery a changed man. He came straight to the women's house and told us all what had happened.

"While I was inspecting the property, checking for leaks in the roof, I was suddenly struck by a strange ailment. My tongue swelled up so grossly that I could not close my mouth over it." Some sisters gasped in horror. "As best I could, by using signs and gestures, I asked to be carried to the church of St Rupert. As soon as I vowed there that I would not stand in the way any longer but would strive to help Hildegard all I could, I immediately recovered my health."

There were more gasps and exclamations from Brother Arnold's listeners. Hildegard had been listening impassively, and smiled at Brother Arnold when his tale was finished.

"I am glad that you are now well, Brother," she said.

"Because of you, lady," Brother Arnold replied. He knelt in front of Hildegard. "I am at your service, for the rest of my days."

I was amazed and relieved at the same time. Having Brother Arnold as an ally could only help our cause, and at least now he might stop turning the other brothers against us.

Sadly, it was not only the brothers that were having doubts about the move. Several of the sisters had also voiced their objections. They had not spoken to Hildegard, however, but had taken their complaints directly to Abbott Cuno.

"They do not wish to leave Disibodenberg," the abbott told me, one afternoon in April. "They are comfortable here, and do not like the idea of starting over in a barren wasteland. In truth, I cannot blame them for feeling as they do."

They were quite right, of course. Brother Arnold and I had just returned from a brief inspection of the land at Rupertsberg, and it was, indeed, mostly barren, but I firmly believed that this was the place God had chosen for the women's new community. Surely God would not ask the sisters to move there without very good reason. What this reason might be, however, was beyond my humble capacity to perceive.

Chapter 32

In the mid-summer of that year, Hildegard had another vision. This time, fortunately, it was not accompanied by any illness, probably because she had no reason nor desire to suppress it.

"I have seen in a true vision," she began, "that God wants me to write about nature – stones, plants, creatures and so on." That seemed like a modest enough command. Hildegard was certainly very knowledgeable about such matters. She continued. "He also wants me to compose a musical work, to be called 'Symphony of the Harmony of Heavenly Revelations." This sounded more challenging, but also well within Hildegard's capabilities.

"That all seems quite reasonable," I said. "I hope I can help you with these tasks."

Hildegard smiled. "I am sure you will be a great help, as always, dear friend."

I felt my face grow warm at this, so hurried on. "Perhaps you can use the notes you have already made on medicinal plants as a starting point for the work on nature …"

"That is sound advice," Hildegard said.

"… and as for music, you have already composed many liturgical pieces. Could they be used for the 'Symphony'"?

"Yes," she replied. "I have composed around 40 pieces so far, and will continue to write more. The 'Symphony' might be an ongoing work."

She thought for a moment. "Both of these tasks will require thought and time, but I can begin now, while we are waiting to move."

I nodded and rose to leave, but she said, "Wait. There was another aspect to this vision."

More? I thought, but returned to my seat and waited for her to continue.

"In my vision, God also showed me an unknown language – letters and words that I had never seen before, but which made perfect sense to me."

I raised my eyebrows at this. This was something quite different.

"How many words did you see?" I asked.

Hildegard shrugged slightly. "There seemed to be hundreds of them, but I am not certain how many. I must write them down soon, before I forget them."

I nodded. "A good idea. I can certainly help with that."

So, our first task resulting from this latest vision was the recording of this unknown language. It took quite some time. There were approximately 1,000 of these strange words, formed from the letters of our own alphabet, yet quite unlike any words I had seen before. Around 250 of these words referred to the natural world, and nearly 150 others referred to the human body. Given these practical, everyday meanings, the words could have many uses. To what end I did not know, but we exhausted much parchment, ink and ourselves in their recording.

I surveyed the pile of parchments. "What shall we now do with these strange words?" I asked.

Hildegard thought for a moment, then smiled. "I think we must *use* them, else God would not have shown them to me. Perhaps this is meant to be a private language, spoken only in the women's community."

"There are certainly enough words for that purpose," I agreed.

"Perhaps, like music, the words are intended to transcend the ordinary," she mused, "and cross the boundary between Earth and Heaven, giving us an insight into the wonderful world to come."

This was another intriguing thought. We both smiled as we considered the possibilities. Before the community could do anything with these words, however, they would need to *learn* them. "I will arrange for copies to be made and distributed, so that we can all learn and use these strange and wonderful words."

This, of course, took some time, but as the copies began to circulate through the community, I became aware of a variety of reactions to the new language. Most of the younger sisters seemed excited at the prospect of a private language, known only to our community. One of the youngest, Sister Gertrude, was particularly taken with the idea.

"This makes us..." she paused, searching for the right word, "*special*," she concluded, raising her chin. Then she looked at me quickly. "Is that wrong?" she asked me, wide-eyed. "Is it sinful to feel such pride?"

I laughed. "Probably," I replied, "but it is a reaction common amongst humans."

Some of the older nuns were less than enthusiastic when presented with the words to learn.

"What is this nonsense?" Sister Ilse muttered when I handed her the parchments. She was one of the oldest sisters, and had always been somewhat resistant to new ideas and practices.

I explained how the words had come to Hildegard in a vision from God, and Ilse's face grew red. "Forgive my rudeness, Brother," she said quickly. "I will, of course, learn these words by heart."

The strange words even appeared in one of Hildegard's chants, an antiphon titled *O Orzchis Ecclesia* ('O Measureless Church'). As the sisters chanted this short antiphon, standing in two rows facing each other, I saw knowing smiles pass between some of them when they sang the words from their private language. Sinful pride? Perhaps, but the language had a powerful bonding effect on the small community and helped to remind them of their special vocation to serve God. Given the hardships they would soon be required to endure, this reminder was most opportune.

Chapter 33

Towards the end of summer, we began discussions to acquire the land at Rupertsberg. 'Barren wasteland' it may well be, but there were, presumably, owners of this land to consider.

At my request, Abbott Cuno made enquiries to identify the owner or owners of the land. He received the information quite promptly.

"The land on the hill belongs partly to the Canons of the Church of Mainz, and the estate with the oratory of St Rupert belongs to Count Bernard of Hildesheim," he told me.

"How am I going to acquire this land?" Hildegard asked me, when I reported the news. "I have no money of my own."

This was, indeed, a major obstacle. I also had no money, nor any wealthy relatives to approach. "We must pray to God for guidance in this matter," Hildegard said.

Several months passed without any progress. Then, early in spring 1150, the abbott made an unexpected visit to the women's house. He was bearing very good news concerning the Rupertsberg land.

"It appears that the transactions have been completed," he said.

"Completed?" Hildegard was puzzled, as was I. "How can that be?" she asked.

The abbott turned to Hildegard and explained. "It seems that a certain noble margravine that we know approached the archbishop and put the whole story before him. With his, and the margravine's generous assistance, the land has been acquired from its former owners, partly by purchase and partly by an exchange of property, using the offerings of the faithful which the fame of your reputation has attracted." The abbott then smiled at Richardis, who was also smiling at him.

Noble margravine? Whom did he mean? Suddenly I realised why Richardis was smiling. The abbott must be referring to Richardis' mother!

After the abbott had left the house, I asked Richardis if she knew anything of this matter.

"I *may* have mentioned to my mother in a recent letter that financial assistance and a bit of political persuasion might be required to advance Hildegard's plans," she said, still smiling.

Hildegard embraced Richardis and held her for a long moment. "I cannot thank you enough," she said, through tears. "God will reward you for your loyalty to me."

About a week later, Hildegard and I met with Abbott Cuno to discuss final arrangements for the move. Brother Arnold, who was to be the new community's sacristan, had gone ahead to clear the overgrown vineyards around the site where the nun's dormitory was to be built. We were expecting to follow him shortly, within the next month. It was mid-March, and the weather was improving, and a move in April would give us several months to get settled before winter arrived.

"What are your final numbers, then?" the abbott asked Hildegard.

"There will be 20 women, including me," she replied. The abbott nodded. "Five of the sisters are refusing to come," Hildegard continued. "I cannot force them to come with us, but I do not know what is to become of them if they do not."

"They will always have a home here," the abbott said, "although it will, once again, be a rather small community of women." He sighed and lowered his eyes.

Hildegard smiled. "Thank you, Father. That is a great relief." She paused for a moment, glancing at me. "Of course, Brother Volmar will also be coming, as my secretary and as provost of the new convent."

The abbott had been examining his hands, folded on the table in front of him, but he looked up sharply at this last statement.

"Brother Volmar? I do not recall agreeing to his departure. I accept that he will need to *visit*, to help with your writings, but I cannot allow him to move permanently."

"He *must* come with us!" Hildegard said, her voice rising. "I cannot possibly function without him. He is an essential part of our community."

"He is not a priest," the abbott replied, "so cannot give sacraments or say Mass. Surely his other tasks can be performed by the sisters or Brother Arnold."

"Brother Volmar is a gifted teacher and scribe. He has been an integral part of our community for many years now. He will continue to teach our novices, he will help with my correspondence and the recording of my visions, and he can give spiritual guidance and counsel to all. If you refuse to allow him to come, you are thwarting the fulfilment of God's command!"

Hildegard had become highly agitated. I decided I should also speak.

"Father," I began, "I must go with the women. I feel certain that it is part of God's plan for *my* life of service to Him. I have prayed to Him about this, and He has made my path clear – I am meant to go to Rupertsberg and serve God by serving Mother Hildegard."

The abbott opened his mouth to speak, but closed it abruptly. He again sighed deeply.

"I am not pleased about this," he said, "but I would never knowingly stand in the way of God's plans. Very well," he said, looking at me. "You may go with the women, but your services here will be hard to replace."

I was startled by this rare compliment, but greatly relieved that the matter was settled. Indeed, everything now seemed to be settled. After many obstacles and frustrations, Hildegard's vision that she must move her nuns to Rupertsberg was about to become a reality.

PART TWO

*Rupertsberg Abbey, near
Bingen, Germany*

Chapter 1

April 1150

On a crisp, clear morning in mid-April 1150, 21 people set out from Disibodenberg Monastery, bound for a new life at Rupertsberg. Some tears were shed, but mostly, there was an air of excitement about this adventure.

The women comprised Hildegard, Richardis, Birgitta, Bertha the maid, and 16 younger nuns. I was the only male on the journey, although Brother Arnold would also be a permanent member of the community.

Most of us travelled on foot, but Hildegard was on horseback. I led the other horse, which was pulling the cart carrying our provisions.

We stopped for a rest about halfway through the 15-mile journey. The countryside was already changing – the lush verdure we were accustomed to at Disibodenberg was gradually being consumed by a much rockier terrain.

In the middle of the afternoon, as we passed by the town of Bingen, we were surprised to see that many of the townspeople had come out to greet us. Hildegard's fame had travelled this short distance quite quickly, once she had received the public approval of the pope, and there appeared to be great excitement at the prospect of such a celebrated person establishing a community nearby. This greeting greatly lifted the spirits of the whole party, but especially the younger nuns, who were showing signs of fatigue from the journey. Their spirits did not, sadly, remain raised for long.

We reached Rupertsberg as the sun was setting. It had been a pleasantly warm day, but an evening chill was beginning to settle around our shoulders, and our feet throbbed from the long walk. In the fading light, the site of our new home looked barren and desolate. For most of the party, this was their first glimpse of the place, and I heard a few gasps and groans. I had seen it already, and knew that there was much to do.

Hildegard, by contrast, was ecstatic. "Praise God – our new home!" she cried out. "Let us give thanks to the Creator of all things for this wonderful place!"

Everyone followed her lead and knelt on the rough ground to pray. When Hildegard had finished leading us in prayer, she turned to more practical matters. "Now we must eat, drink and rest."

Brother Arnold, who had greeted us all most cheerfully, began to unpack food and ale, of which we were all greatly desirous after such a long, hard day.

After we had eaten and had a short rest, we sang Vespers. Then it was time to unpack the cart and set up the sleeping quarters.

The church dedicated to St Rupert by his mother so long ago was, miraculously, still mostly intact, although it was in great need of repair and restoration. This was to be our accommodation until other buildings were ready. I felt some discomfort at the thought of using a church as a dormitory, but I did not think that St Rupert would mind, given our circumstances.

After Compline, most of the women went to find their beds in the church and settled themselves to sleep. Hildegard and Birgitta stayed up a while longer, keen to begin plans for the following day. I noticed that Richardis did not join them.

Although it was a cool night, Brother Arnold had decided to sleep under the stars, wrapped in a blanket. "I will be fine, as long as there is no rain," he said with a grin. "I can keep watch better from out here." That was true, although I did not think there would be many people passing by this remote place, especially at night.

The next morning, we began our first full day in our new home by singing Prime. Hildegard and I had decided not to wake the sisters for Matins or Lauds, as they were all exhausted from the journey.

After Prime, we all met to discuss what needed to be done.

"We need gardens," Hildegard began. "Sister Birgitta will supervise this work. The building work will be directed by Brother Arnold, who has already done most of the necessary clearing. Thank you, Brother." Hildegard smiled at Brother Arnold, who bowed his head in acknowledgment. "Restoration of the church is of the utmost importance, but we must attend to our basic requirements first," Hildegard said.

After a few questions and some further discussion, everyone seemed clear as to what they were meant to do. The group dispersed to various parts of the site, and began their allotted tasks.

Over the next few weeks, the garden beds were cleared and prepared for planting. There were to be three gardens – one each for herbs, vegetables and flowers. The building work began slowly, but was greatly assisted by the arrival of men from the nearby villages. These men came and went as they were able, depending on their other responsibilities. There were usually five to ten such men assisting with the building work on most days, apart from Sundays, of course.

One of the builders, a cooper named Jakob, regularly brought his son, Roric, with him. Roric was about 12 years of age, so could not assist with the heavy work, but was most helpful with lighter tasks and the running of errands. He seemed particularly drawn to Brother Arnold, and I often saw them sitting together, talking, during periods of rest.

"He is a bright lad," Brother Arnold told me one evening as we were preparing for sleep. "Too bright to be a cooper, I fear. He is uncertain about his future, and I am doing my best to counsel and advise him."

I nodded. "He is fortunate to have your guidance," I replied.

The priority for the builders was to construct enough accommodation for the community, and storage facilities for food, drink, equipment and other provisions, before winter arrived. We also needed a kitchen quite soon. Cooking over an open fire was fine in the warmer months, but could not be continued into winter. Later, once the essentials had been built, we would also need an infirmary, a Chapter House, and probably also a bakery and alehouse. There was much work to be done.

Brother Arnold thrived in his role as supervisor. He seemed to enjoy barking instructions at the workers and checking the work to ensure that it was up to his high standards. He also contributed to the heavy manual labour, and did everything so cheerfully that he did wonders for the men's morale.

The women's morale, however, was another matter. While the gardening and building works were progressing, Hildegard, Richardis and I returned to our work on *Scivias*, which was finally nearing completion. I could see that Hildegard was distracted, and seemed not to be enjoying the work as much as she had previously. I was quite sure I knew the reason for this.

I had overheard some of the sisters complaining about the harsh conditions, and I knew that Hildegard was also aware of these discontented murmurings. When I asked her how she was coping with this dissent, she sighed and looked at me with tired, sad eyes.

"These trials that have come upon me are after the pattern of Moses," she said.

"Moses?" I raised my eyebrows.

"Yes. When he led the children of Israel out of Egypt across the Red Sea into the desert, they murmured against him, even though God had lit up their way with so many wonderful signs," she explained.

"Oh yes, of course," I replied, remembering the passages from Scripture.

"Likewise," she continued, "God has allowed me to be afflicted by some of my sisters because they lack 'necessities'. I have heard them, as I know you also have, say 'Why have noble and wealthy young women like us left a place where we lacked nothing, to come to such a place as this?' Yet it was God who showed me this place and brought us here, so we must be patient and wait for the grace of God to come to our aid."

I nodded. "As He surely will," I said. We were doing the best we could, under difficult circumstances, but I knew that God would not have brought us here without also providing for us.

Money, or rather the lack of it, was our most pressing problem, and it was this that occupied a great deal of my attention. While we had been truly blessed to have been given these lands through the generosity of others, there were still many expenses that we were unable to cover. The building labour was all being given freely, and we could salvage some building materials from the site and its surroundings, but most of the materials had been acquired from local tradesmen and had not yet been paid for. Then there were all the other items needed to maintain a community, including food, drink, blankets, clothes, shoes and writing supplies. How were these to be paid for?

I sometimes wondered if Hildegard could read my mind. When my attention returned to the present, I realised that she had been watching me, a concerned expression on her face.

"I have been thinking about the sisters' dowries," she said, seemingly from nowhere. "Why should they remain the property of the Disibodenberg Monastery? Any unused portions should be transferred to our control for our use, given that the sisters' needs have accompanied them here."

This was an excellent point and a very good idea. It would certainly solve many of our current financial problems.

"Brilliant!" I exclaimed. "I will write to Abbott Cuno at once. I am sure there will be no quarrel with this request — it is completely reasonable."

Now it was Hildegard's turn to raise her eyebrows, but she said nothing.

By late August, the building works were sufficiently advanced to allow us to address the issue of the church's restoration and repair. One mild evening, as I sat with Brother Arnold under the stars, I asked for his opinion on how to tackle this task.

He thought for a moment, scratching his chin. "The whole roof needs to be replaced," he began. "We should remove that first, repair the walls — they are in better condition - then build a new roof." He was silent for another moment. "I think we can make the whole thing *bigger*," he said. "It is quite small, already a bit small for the size of the community. If we want more nuns, we should have a bigger church."

This seemed sensible. "I will speak to Hildegard and ascertain her wishes," I said.

Hildegard was very enthusiastic about this proposal. "Yes," she said. "The church dedicated to St Rupert must be grand enough to honour our patron saint, and large enough to accommodate our growing community. This must be the builders' main priority, now that our basic needs have been met."

I told Brother Arnold of Hildegard's response, and he smiled broadly. "We will begin immediately," he said, rubbing his hands together. I could see that this was a challenge he would relish.

Chapter 2

In September of that year, Hildegard surprised Richardis and me by telling us that our work on *Scivias* was at an end. The three of us had collaborated on twelve of the thirteen visions, but Hildegard now wished to proceed unassisted. "I must complete this last vision alone," she told us.

I was curious to see this last vision and wondered how it differed from the others, but I left Hildegard to work on it in her own time and way. I certainly had plenty of other tasks with which to occupy myself.

Richardis, on the other hand, seemed to be at a loose end. She helped with gardening and food preparation but did not seem content. I mentioned this to Hildegard, but she appeared to be unconcerned. "It has been a difficult time for us all," she said. "I am sure that Richardis will be fine. She just needs to find work that satisfies her and makes good use of her talents. There are many tasks she could involve herself in. Perhaps you could help to guide her in this?"

I agreed to do so, and said no more on the matter. I was uncertain what I could suggest for Richardis to do, but I resolved to keep my eyes open for suitable opportunities.

Winter soon came to our home on the hill, but it was unusually mild that year. We had much less rain than expected, which was a blessing for our builders but proved to be a major problem for the region.

Lack of rain led to failed crops, which resulted in a famine that claimed many lives. We were still not self-sufficient at Rupertsberg – our gardens were only producing a fraction of what we needed – and we were forced to rely on the generosity of the people from local towns, especially Bingen. We also received some support from Disibodenberg, as they had not been as badly affected by the famine as some other areas. I say 'some' support, as I had not yet received a reply from Abbott Cuno concerning the matter of the sisters' dowries.

The year 1151 did begin with one positive event – Hildegard announced to the community that she had finished work on *Scivias*.

"I particularly want to thank Sister Richardis and Brother Volmar for their assistance," she said at a Chapter meeting in early February. "I could not have completed this work without them."

Although I would never have said so, Hildegard did, in fact, complete *Scivias* without us. I had still not seen the final section, which Hildegard had insisted on finishing alone, although Richardis did complete the artwork. When I finally did see this last vision, I was intrigued. The title of the final section was 'Symphony of the Blessed' and began with the description of a vision in which Hildegard 'heard different kinds of music, marvellously embodying all the meanings I had heard before'. After the vision came the words that accompanied the music, although the music itself was not recorded.

The first section contained songs of praise to the Virgin Mary, the choirs of angels, prophets, apostles, martyrs, confessors and virgins. Following these were laments and a prayer of intercession for sinners. Finally, there was a section headed 'The exhortation of the virtues and the fight against the Devil', which was written in the form of a play. It was both beautiful and fascinating.

"You are going to write down the music, too, I hope?" I asked Hildegard after I had read the final vision.

"Yes," she replied, "but this book is not the appropriate place to do so. The people who will read this book might not understand musical notation."

That was a good point. Reading music was a specialised and demanding skill, one that many people did not possess.

So, after ten years of very hard work, I was finally holding the completed *Scivias*. It was a magnificent work, and needed to be read by as many people as possible. This, of course, raised a problem – who was going to make the copies needed to make the work available to the public?

I raised this matter with Hildegard. "Perhaps the monks at Disibodenberg might help," I suggested half-heartedly. I doubted that they would. Hildegard shared these doubts. She shook her head.

"Many of the brothers are still furious that we left," she said. "No, we need to make other arrangements."

We thought for a moment, and then looked at each other.

"We can make our *own* copies!" Hildegard said, just before I said something similar. "We need our own scriptorium and our own scribes. I want the Rupertsberg community to be as independent and self-sufficient as possible, in *all* things."

This was, of course, the solution. "I can certainly teach some of the sisters how to produce books," I said. Then a thought struck me. "Perhaps this is something that Sister Richardis would like to be involved with. She is highly skilled in both writing and illustration."

"That is an excellent idea," Hildegard replied, beaming. "This is just the task she needs to find the fulfilment that she seems to have been lacking of late."

I raised this possibility with Sister Richardis later that day.

"That sounds like a good idea," she said without much enthusiasm. "You really do need your own scriptorium and scribes."

I frowned. "'*You*'? Surely you mean '*we*'!" I said.

She looked away quickly. "Yes, of course. *We*. That is what I meant to say."

I was not convinced that this was said in error. Sister Richardis might not have intended to *say* it, but I had a feeling that she *meant* it. Again, I felt uneasy about Sister Richardis, and what her, and our, future might hold.

Chapter 3

Early in the spring of 1151, my fears concerning Sister Richardis proved to be well-founded. I had hoped that I would be wrong to doubt her commitment to the Rupertsberg community, but, on this occasion, my instincts had been accurate. They have not always been so.

One sunny afternoon, I returned from a pleasant stroll to the nearby river and observed Sister Richardis rushing out of Hildegard's chambers, clearly in some distress. I went straight to Hildegard to seek an explanation for this odd behaviour.

When I entered the room, Hildegard was standing behind her table, facing the door, her face as white as snow.

"What has happened?" I asked.

"It is Richardis," Hildegard gasped. "She is leaving me, us."

My heart sank. "Leaving? Where is she going?"

Hildegard slumped into a chair. "She has been named 'mother' of a very eminent community in Bassum. She wishes to leave within a week."

I was stunned. This was completely unexpected. It was certainly a prestigious appointment for one so young, but I knew Sister Richardis came from a wealthy and noble family with much influence in both church and society. My heart ached for Hildegard. I knew very well how much she cared for the young nun, and I worried that she would become ill as a result of this emotional wrench.

"This is, indeed, surprising news," was all I could think to say.

"It is that brother of hers," Hildegard said. "I am certain that this is *his* doing."

The brother of which Hildegard spoke was Hartwig, Archbishop of Bremen. The Bassum community was in Hartwig's diocese.

"Did she say how this has come about?" I asked. I wondered if, perhaps, the move had been initiated by Sister Richardis herself, and not by her well-placed brother. She had certainly not seemed happy for some time. I decided not to voice this possibility to Hildegard.

"Oh, yes," Hildegard replied, sounding bitter. I had never before heard this tone in her voice. "She told me that God is 'calling' her to higher service. I am convinced that this is certainly *not* God's will. Hartwig is interested only in worldly matters such as social status and ecclesiastical power – God has *no* role to play in Hartwig's machinations."

"Is Sister Richardis willing to go?" I asked. I feared that she was.

"She says that she wants this new role, but she would have little say in the face of pressure from her family." Hildegard banged the table with her fist. "Well, I will not allow it. I will put a stop to this at once."

"How might you do that?" I wondered aloud. I feared that a conflict with this powerful family would be both futile and detrimental to Hildegard's health.

Hildegard thought for a moment, tapping the tabletop with her fingers. "I will write to Richardis' mother," she said decisively. "She was a great supporter of our move to Rupertsberg. I cannot imagine she would be pleased that her daughter would leave so soon, after such a generous endowment to this place."

"Do you need my help with this letter?" I asked.

Hildegard smiled grimly. "No, thank you, dear Volmar – I do not thank God enough for you, loyal friend. No, this letter will be informal, directly from my heart to the margravine's, mother to mother."

I did not see Hildegard's letter to Sister Richardis' mother, or the reply that came about three weeks later, but I certainly heard all about it from Hildegard.

She was pacing around her chamber, red-faced with fury, as she waved the letter in the air.

"It is the same pretence – Richardis feels 'called by God' to accept this post," she said. "I cannot accept that the margravine genuinely believes this. She, also, is being bullied by the archbishop."

From what I knew of the margravine, I doubted that she would allow herself to be bullied by anyone – archbishop, son, or Satan himself. Although I did not say it, and did not want to believe it, I now felt certain that the move was either instigated by Sister Richardis or, at least, agreed to by her. It is, after all, a rare human who is not tempted by the prospect of worldly advancement.

Some things, however, *were* going well at Rupertsberg. The builders had made remarkable progress on the restoration and extension of the Church of St Rupert, helped in large measure by the abnormally dry winter we had experienced. By late April, the church was finished and ready to be used.

On 1 May 1151, our new church was consecrated by Archbishop Heinrich of Mainz. On the same day, the archbishop gave the holy veil to several young women who had joined the new community at Rupertsberg. Two of these new nuns were particularly noteworthy – Sister Hiltrud, who was the niece of Lady Jutta of blessed memory, and Sister Clementia, who was Hildegard's niece. It seemed most fitting that these two young women, both related to the founders of this community of women, should become full members of the community on this special day.

It was a splendid occasion, made even more so by the inclusion of a major musical work written by Hildegard. This piece, entitled *Ordo Virtutum* (the Order of the Virtues), is a drama, sung in Latin, depicting the struggle between the Devil and the Virtues for the control of a wayward soul. Hildegard had told me when rehearsals began that the play was an extended and notated version of the drama with which she had concluded *Scivias*.

There are numerous singing roles in the play, including a chorus of patriarchs and prophets, a chorus of souls imprisoned in bodies, and sixteen virtues, led by Humility, their Queen. There was, however, only one speaking part, that of the Devil. That made sense – Hildegard always considered liturgical singing to be a sacred act and, consequently, beyond the purview of Satan.

The role of the Devil would, of course, need to be played by a male.

"I was hoping you would play the Devil, Volmar, although you are the least devil-like person I know," Hildegard had said to me with a smile.

"I was thinking that Brother Arnold would be ideal for the role," I had replied, smiling in return. "He has such a deep, raspy voice, after all, and is a much more imposing figure than am I."

When I suggested this to Brother Arnold, his face turned white. "I...I could not," he stammered. "I would be terrified of getting it wrong!"

I was surprised and amused by this response. Brother Arnold had always seemed, to me at least, to be utterly fearless, and yet here he was, terrified at the prospect of taking part in a play! As the only other possible candidate, the part of the Devil was assigned to me.

Everything went well on the day of the consecration. The play was particularly well-received. Hildegard led the way, in her lead role as Humility, and I think I did a reasonable job as the Devil – my first, growling utterance caused the archbishop to jump in his seat, so I must have been reasonably effective. The tension between Hildegard and Sister Richardis was forgotten, at least temporarily, and the whole occasion was both joyous and reverent.

Once the festivities were concluded and routines were resumed, the impending departure of Sister Richardis became a matter requiring Hildegard's urgent attention.

About a week after Hildegard received the margravine's reply, a delegation from Bremen arrived to escort Sister Richardis to her new community at Bassum. As I had feared, Hildegard was not prepared to concede defeat. She refused to let the delegation enter, and prevented Sister Richardis from departing. Thus thwarted, the delegation returned to Bremen.

Shortly after that confrontation, a very blunt letter was received from our archbishop, Heinrich of Mainz. Hildegard read the letter, turned a bright shade of red, then handed the letter to me.

It seemed that the delegation, having been refused entry into Rupertsberg, then made their way to Mainz, to petition Archbishop Heinrich for the release of Sister Richardis. In his letter to Hildegard, the archbishop wrote the following.

"By the authority of our position as prelate and father, we command you to release this sister immediately to those who seek and desire her. If you do not comply, we will command you in even stronger terms, and we will not stop until you fulfil our commands in this matter."

I rolled up the parchment and handed it back to Hildegard, who tossed it into the corner of her room.

"I do not think you can refuse any longer," I said sadly. "It would not be wise to make an enemy of the Church authorities, even if you do have God on your side." I was not convinced that she did have such divine support, but did not wish to contradict her on this point.

The Bremen delegation returned to Rupertsberg within a few days. This time, Hildegard did not refuse their entry. When Sister Richardis was leaving with them, every member of the Rupertsberg community, with one notable exception, gathered to bid her farewell. Hildegard stayed in her chambers and did not emerge until the party had departed.

I had hoped that this would be the end of this very sad affair, and that Hildegard would accept defeat and allow healing to begin. Not for the first time, I had greatly underestimated Hildegard's determination to succeed, made even greater on this occasion by the strength of her feelings for the young nun.

"They think they have won," she muttered later that evening, "but I have not yet exhausted all avenues open to me."

"What do you intend to do?" I asked, greatly alarmed.

"First, I will reply to the archbishop, letting him know in the strongest possible terms what I think of his 'command'," she began, pacing around her room. "It bears no weight at all, when compared to the will of God. Then, I will appeal to Pope Eugenius for his personal intervention. He knows that I speak with God's authority, on this as with other matters." She stopped pacing and sat in a chair, exhausted. "Will you help with these letters, dear friend?" she asked me, suddenly looking frail and vulnerable. "I am not equal to the task of writing in appropriate Latin to such people."

While it was true that the pope had been a great and highly influential supporter of Hildegard's visionary writings, I was doubtful that he would choose to intervene in what was, after all, a personal matter, even if it did involve ecclesiastical positions and movements.

"Of course, I will help," I replied. How could I refuse? *Should* I have refused? Was I being a good friend by assisting Hildegard to pursue this futile campaign? I have sometimes wondered whether I should have tried to reason with her, to persuade her to let go of Richardis, but I doubt she would have backed down, and I ran the risk of damaging our friendship. That was something I could not bear to do.

As expected, her efforts were in vain. The archbishop did not even reply to Hildegard's letter, which was, admittedly, somewhat vitriolic in tone. The pope did reply, but merely referred the matter back to the archbishop. Hildegard told me later that she had also written to Richardis' brother, the other archbishop involved in this matter. I never saw this letter, but assumed that it was a less formal, personal appeal to Hartwig to change his mind about his sister's appointment. This, of course, did not happen.

Winter was settling in, and Hildegard said no more about the matter, but I could see that she was greatly affected by the loss of her beloved friend and protégé. I did what I could to console and support Hildegard, but I feared that this was a wound that might never fully heal.

Chapter 4

While the winter of 1151 had been unusually dry, the following winter sought to redress the imbalance. In January 1152, the whole Rhine region experienced major flooding, which severely restricted the movement of people, goods and, most importantly, food. Once again, without the generosity of local townspeople, the Rupertsberg community would have experienced severe hardship.

Sitting high up on our hill, we could see the floods in low-lying areas below us. While we were cold and wet for most of that winter, our lands and buildings were spared any water damage.

Hildegard had not said a word about Richardis since her departure, but I could see that she missed her. At meals, I sometimes saw Hildegard gazing at the place where Richardis had regularly sat. Occasionally, during conversations, she would stop abruptly in mid-sentence when she had been about to refer to Richardis, before remembering that she was no longer with us. My heart ached for Hildegard, but I could do little to ease the pain of this loss.

Perhaps as a means of distraction from unwelcome musings, Hildegard threw herself into her work with alarming intensity. She spent a lot of time each day teaching the novices and less experienced sisters in both Scripture and more practical matters. She was a wonderful teacher, and was both strict and loving with these young women, as she was with all members of the community.

Having completed *Scivias*, Hildegard was also keen to spend more time on other writing. She began work on her nature book, which now had a title: *The Book of Subtleties of Diverse Natural Creatures.* Sister Birgitta had managed to organise the vast number of loose notes that Hildegard had made on herbs and flowers, and I reminded Hildegard of my earlier suggestion that this would be a good foundation on which to base the book.

"Yes, indeed." Hildegard agreed, "A good start, but this book will be, as God has directed me, about much more than plants. It will, of course, be a manual of herbal treatments, but I also want to write about other aspects of the natural world, including birds, fish and other animals, as well as stones and metals."

My eyebrows raised. "That sounds like an immense undertaking," I said.

"Yes," Hildegard replied, "but an important one. I must delay no longer on this task."

"Is there anything I can help you with?" I asked.

Hildegard smiled at me. "As always, dear friend, I will need your help with my Latin, particularly with some of the Latin plant names."

I smiled and nodded. "Yes, they can be quite complex."

"I also need to work on the Symphonia. I have sorted my compositions into a logical order, but there is much more work to be done." She sighed, then smiled again. "Still, it is good to be busy. The Devil finds work for idle hands," she said with a laugh.

I laughed, too. "I do not think Satan will find many idle hands around here," I said, thinking of all the things I and others in the community were required to do.

In early March, a new German king was crowned. Conrad III had died in February, and on 4 March 1152, the kingdom's electors designated Frederick, known as Barbarossa, as the next king of Germany.

"I must write to him," Hildegard said when the news reached us later in March. "I think it would be wise to establish a cordial relationship with our new ruler."

It was a cordial, respectful letter, congratulating Frederick on his election, and urging him to uphold justice in God's domain. About a month later, a reply came. Frederick thanked Hildegard for her good wishes, and expressed the hope that, at some future time, the two would meet.

"Well," I said, rolling up the parchment. "That seems promising. Hopefully, Frederick will be a wise and just ruler."

Hildegard looked thoughtful. "God knows, and time will tell," was all that she said.

The year then progressed as most do, with our routines providing comfort and order. Once the floods had subsided, the spring and summer were warm and fruitful.

By the time autumn came, Hildegard seemed to be back to her normal, happy, loving self. While it had taken some time for her to adjust to Richardis' absence, she now seemed to have done so, and I was relieved that her heartache had eased. Then, in November of that year, news arrived that restored her pain in full measure.

When Hildegard did not appear for the meal on that bleak autumn evening, I went to look for her. I found her sitting at her table, holding a parchment, sobbing. I was shocked. I had never seen her cry before, in spite of all her ill-health and frustrations.

"What has happened?" I asked.

Hildegard tried to speak, but could not manage to do so through her sobs. She handed me the parchment.

It was from Hartwig, Archbishop of Bremen, Richardis' brother. Suddenly, without warning or illness, Richardis had died on 29 October. Now, I was doubly shocked. Richardis was only 28 years old and had always been healthy and active. How could this have happened?

The letter did not reveal the cause of Richardis' death, but it was a great comfort to know that she had been able to make her last confession and was anointed with consecrated oil before she died. Of even more comfort to Hildegard, I felt sure, was the fact that Richardis had expressed a longing for Rupertsberg, and an intention to visit, had death not intervened so prematurely and cruelly.

I read the letter to the end, then rolled up the parchment and held it to my lips. Hildegard's sobs had subsided, and she was staring into her lap. Then she looked up at me.

"I did not even say goodbye to her," she said quietly.

"I know that she understood your reasons," I said. "She told me so at the time. You were angry and upset, and it may be better that you chose to stay away, rather than saying something you would regret now."

She smiled sadly. "You always know just what to say, dear, wise friend. If I have learned anything from this sorry tale it is that I must cherish those whom I love while I can, before it is too late."

My heart ached for her anew. "It may be too late in *this* life," I said, "but you *will* see Richardis again, and you know how much she loved you."

"As I loved her," Hildegard said, slowly rising from her chair. She suddenly seemed elderly, well beyond her 54 years. The death of Richardis was, indeed, a bitter blow, and I knew that Hildegard would need all the support that I could provide to get her through this time of grief.

Chapter 5

The year 1153 began with another unsettling celestial event. On 26 January, the sun was blocked by the moon, leaving only the edge of the sun visible as a bright, fiery ring in the sky.

The sisters working outside in the gardens shrieked, dropped their tools, and ran to the church. Hildegard and I were inside at the time, but could not have failed to notice the sudden shift from day to night.

"I wonder what this one is trying to tell us," I said with a laugh as we both hurried to the church.

Hildegard looked grim. "I feel that trouble is brewing," she murmured.

I wondered what this 'trouble' might be, but did not question her. Once we had calmed the frightened women, the day had reappeared as if nothing had happened, and everyone slowly returned to their work.

For a short while, I felt concerned by Hildegard's words of foreboding, but when nothing extraordinary occurred, I forgot the eclipse and any warnings it might have wished to convey.

Spring that year began with an unexpected visitor. I was working in the scriptorium one sunny, April morning, when Brother Arnold appeared in the doorway, looking slightly agitated. He indicated with his head that I should join him outside.

"What has happened?" I asked.

"It is Roric, the cooper's son," he replied. "He is here. He wishes to join our community!"

I tried not to laugh. "He cannot join *this* community," I said. "This is a convent!"

Brother Arnold smiled. "Yes, I told him that. He feels he is being called to God's service, and this was the first place he thought to come to."

"Well, the obvious place for a boy would be the monastery at Disibodenberg, of course. I will speak to Hildegard and see what can be arranged."

Hildegard was surprised and pleased to hear of Roric's wish to enter God's service. "I remember him from the building works," she said. "He seemed a nice lad. I will write a letter for him to take to Abbott Cuno. I am sure the abbott will be pleased to receive a keen novice."

Hildegard wrote the letter and gave it to Roric with her blessing. His face shone as he rose after having knelt to receive the blessing. "We will pray that your calling is pleasing to God, and that you have a long and blessed vocation," Hildegard said.

Sometime later, we heard that Roric had been accepted at Disibodenberg. "That is good news, indeed," Hildegard said. We were all pleased, but none more so than Brother Arnold.

Towards the end of June, the 'trouble' that Hildegard had predicted came to pass. The eclipse, it seemed, had been right in its foreboding.

At the Council of Worms, held on 7 June, two papal legates - Bernard of St. Clement and Gregory of St. Angeli - had deposed Archbishop Heinrich of Mainz, our archbishop, even though Bernard of Clairvaux spoke in Heinrich's defence. He was to be replaced by one Arnold of Selenhofen, a close associate of our recently elected king.

I was shocked by this news. "Why would Pope Eugenius have authorised this?" I asked Hildegard. It was a warm evening, and we were walking in the garden, waiting for the summons to Vespers. Recent unseasonal rain, together with the summer warmth, had made everything grow, including the weeds.

Hildegard sighed deeply, frowned at a particularly large weed, then bent down to remove it. "I have heard that Heinrich was opposed to Frederick's election last year. This seems to be nothing more than petty retribution," she told me as she straightened herself, tossing the weed to one side.

I frowned, too. "I had hoped that our new king would be more just than this," I said. "Hopefully, the king's man will, at least, be a good archbishop."

Hildegard grimaced slightly as she tugged at another, even larger weed. "That might be too much to hope for," she said. This weed proved to be more stubborn than the first, but, after a brief tussle, Hildegard prevailed.

Chapter 6

Towards the end of 1153, stories began to reach us concerning a nun in our region who was claiming to be receiving 'visions' from God. This young woman named Elisabeth, was, apparently, a nun at the double monastery at Schoenau, and it was the leader of the monastery, Abbott Hildelin, who was speaking of these visions at various churches near to Schoenau.

Hildegard was most intrigued. "I wonder what she claims to see?" she said to me one afternoon in November of that year.

"I have only heard of one such vision," I replied. "Brother Arnold heard it discussed when he was in Bingen on business last week. The vision sounded quite fantastical."

"Tell me what you remember of it," Hildegard said, leaning forward with keen interest.

I thought for a moment, calling to mind the details. "This is what was told to Brother Arnold, of course, so it may have altered after several retellings," I said by way of caution.

Hildegard nodded. "I will make allowance for that," she said.

"Well, it is said that Elisabeth had a vision in which she saw the Virgin emerging with the sun surrounding her on all sides, and the Virgin's great brilliance seemed to illuminate the entire earth," I began. "Along with this great brilliance, a dark cloud appeared, which Elisabeth described as 'extremely dark and horrible to see'. She asked the holy Angel of God, who appeared to her during the vision, what it all meant. The Angel told her that the Virgin represents the humanity of the Lord Jesus. The Angel went on to explain that the darkness represents God's anger with the world, but that the brightness signifies that he has not altogether stopped watching over the earth." I had been watching Hildegard while I was telling the story, to observe her reaction. Apart from a slight raising of eyebrows, her face remained unreadable.

"Interesting," she said. "I think I will write to Abbott Hildelin to find out more about this young nun and her visions."

Although Hildegard did not need my help to write this letter, she showed it to me before it was dispatched. It was a courteous and respectful letter, in which she enquired about the young nun and her visions. She also offered her assistance to the abbott and his community, should it be required at any time.

We were, of course, expecting a written reply from Abbott Hildelin, so were very surprised when, about a month later, in early December, the abbott presented himself at the Rupertsberg gatehouse. I was summoned to greet him.

"Abbott Hildelin!" I said, smiling. "What an agreeable surprise. How may we serve you?"

"I was delighted to receive Hildegard's letter," he said, "and do, indeed, require her assistance."

The abbott was not a young man, and the journey from Schoenau seemed to have greatly tired him. It was late in the afternoon, so I escorted him to the guest house to rest before the evening meal.

After the meal, Abbott Hildelin and I met with Hildegard in her audience chamber to discuss the purpose of his visit.

Bertha served us all wine, which we sipped for a few moments before anyone spoke.

"I am pleased you have made contact, Father," Hildegard began. "Brother Volmar tells me that you have come to seek my help. I will do whatever I can for you."

"Thank you, Mother," the abbott said, then took another sip of wine. "It is... well... it is Sister Elisabeth, really. I do not know what to do about these visions she claims she is having. I know you are also blessed by God in this way, so I have come for your advice as to how I should manage the situation."

Hildegard nodded. "Has Sister Elisabeth been having the visions for long?" she asked.

The abbott thought for a moment, then shook his head. "As far as I know, they only started after she was unwell for an extended period of time - nearly three years it was."

Hildegard and I exchanged a look. This sounded quite familiar.

"What was the nature of this illness?" I asked.

"Nobody could say with any certainty," the abbott replied, "but I do worry about her ascetic practices. She is very hard on herself. She fasts excessively, and I suspect she also performs rituals of self-mortification, although, of course, I have never been witness to this." His face reddened slightly.

Hildegard raised her eyebrows. "That must be stopped," she said, shaking her head. "I have seen the results of such practices before. They are most injurious to health, and I do *not* believe that God requires them or even welcomes them. How can we do His work here on Earth if we damage the vessel through which we do such work? I have never understood this."

"You make a good point, Mother," said the abbott. "It is not, however, something that *I* feel comfortable discussing with the young woman ..."

"No, of course not, Father," Hildegard replied, lowering her gaze. "Perhaps your prioress could speak to Elisabeth about such personal matters."

The abbott frowned. "That is a good suggestion," he said, "but I fear my prioress and Sister Elisabeth do not have a good relationship. The prioress is, how to say, very *proper*, and does not approve of Elisabeth's conduct."

"What do you mean by 'conduct'?" I asked. "What has the sister done to offend the prioress?"

"Although I have not seen it happen, I am told that Elisabeth has her 'visions' during the women's liturgies. She goes into a fit of...of *ecstasy,* I suppose is the best way to describe it. She loses all awareness of her surroundings and seems to be interacting with someone that nobody else can see. The prioress does not believe that these experiences are genuine. She believes, I think, that Sister Elisabeth is merely seeking attention for herself."

Hildegard nodded. She seemed to be deep in thought, looking beyond the abbott into an unseen distance. After a few moments, her focus returned to the abbott. "Please ask Sister Elisabeth to write to me about her experiences, if she feels comfortable doing so," she said. "I would be more than happy to guide and console her through this. I have, as you probably know, had a good deal of experience in this area, and know very well how troubling it can be."

We were all silent for a few moments, lost in our own thoughts. I was thinking about the story that Brother Arnold had brought back from Bingen about Elisabeth's vision. I told the abbott what we had heard and asked him if it was an accurate account.

He nodded sadly and looked at the floor. "Yes, that is a fair description of the vision, as told to me by Elisabeth. I do not think I should have told people about this or any of her visions. I thought it a wondrous gift, to be shared with all God's people," he said, looking at Hildegard. She smiled and nodded her understanding. "Some people were filled with joy to hear such things, but I fear others have been harshly critical in their judgment of the young nun. Again, I seek your advice on how to proceed."

"I will need to devote both thought and prayer to this matter," Hildegard said. "I may need some time to do this. It is a serious matter that requires careful consideration."

"Yes, of course, Mother," the abbott said. "I will take no more of your time. Thank you for seeing me with no warning of my coming."

Abbott Hildelin returned to Schoenau the following day, promising to convey Hildegard's offer to correspond with Elisabeth.

Within a week, a long, somewhat rambling letter arrived from Elisabeth for Hildegard. It was clear from the speed and content of her response that she was sorely troubled by the hostile reaction that her visions had provoked in some quarters.

After reading the letter slowly, Hildegard handed it to me. As I read, my heart began to ache for the young woman.

"May the grace and consolation of the Most High fill you with joy," the letter began, "because you have been kindly sympathetic to my distress, as I have understood from the words of my confessor. For just as was revealed to you about me, I have been disturbed by a cloud of trouble lately because of the unseemly talk of the people who are saying many things about me that are simply not true. Still, I could easily endure the talk of the common people, if it were not for the fact that those who are clothed in the garment of religion cause my spirit even greater sorrow. For stirred by I do not know what spirit, they ridicule the grace of the Lord in me, and they have no fear of making hasty judgments about things that they have no understanding of. They have slandered me by claiming that I have prophesied about the day of judgment – which, certainly, I have never presumed to do, since such knowledge is beyond the ken of any human being." I paused at this point and looked up at Hildegard.

"It is disturbing that Elisabeth is being criticised unfairly by people *within* the Church," I said. "Surely they should reserve judgment until they have seen and heard the young nun for themselves."

Hildegard nodded and sighed. "I fear the matter has not been well handled," she replied. "As you know, I did not make *any*thing public until I was certain that senior members of the Church had been given the opportunity to pass proper judgment."

That was true. Hildegard had been very careful to inform the appropriate people and obtain the necessary approval. Neither of these steps appeared to have been taken in relation to Elisabeth's visions.

I nodded. "Yes," I agreed. "They do seem to have been a bit premature with their disclosure."

"I also think that the *nature* of Elisabeth's visions may have led to the scepticism and criticism she has received," Hildegard continued.

"The nature of the visions?" I asked.

Hildegard smiled. "Keep reading," she said.

I returned to the letter. "As you have heard from others, God has, through His angel, frequently disclosed to me the things that are about to befall his people unless they do penance for their sins. Seeking to avoid arrogance and not wishing to spread novelties, I sought, to the best of my ability, to keep all this hidden. Yet on a Sunday when I was, as usual, in a state of ecstasy, the angel of the Lord stood before me and said, 'Why are you hiding gold in the mud? The word of God should not be hidden but made manifest to the praise and glory of our Lord and to the salvation of His people.' And after he had said this, he lifted a scourge up over me, and as if in great wrath he struck me harshly five times, so that for three days thereafter, I suffered from that beating in my whole body. It was after this that my abbott began to tell people about my visions, lest we incur the angel's wrath a second time."

My eyebrows were well and truly raised by the time I had finished reading this passage. "This is most ... un*usual*," I said. "I have never heard that someone could be beaten by an angel. This is nothing like the visions that you have experienced."

"No, it certainly is not," Hildegard agreed. "I have no doubt that different people see and hear God's word in different ways, but this is quite extreme."

I nodded. "I am certain that Elisabeth would benefit from your wisdom and guidance," I said, rolling up the parchment. There was more to read, but I felt that I had gleaned the gist of the letter.

"I will write to her at once," Hildegard replied, looking out the narrow window. "I think I will also invite her to come and stay with me for a short while. It would be good to discuss these matters in person."

Hildegard did not show me the letter that she wrote to Elisabeth, but she told me what she had written to the young nun.

"I tried to console her about her present difficulties," she told me, "and I assured her that those of us inspired by God to directly see and hear His word were often afflicted by the devil. I did try to warn her, however, that those of us who long to complete God's works must always bear in mind that we are fragile vessels, for we are only human. We can only sing the mysteries of God like a trumpet, which only makes a sound but does not function unassisted, for it is Another who breathes into it that it might give forth a sound."

I nodded. Hildegard had always been adamant that it was God speaking *through* her, and not *her*, who spoke the things she saw and heard. Elisabeth also needed to adopt this attitude of humility, which would probably help to lessen some of the criticism she had received.

I hoped that Elisabeth would come and visit us one day soon. I was intrigued to meet this new 'visionary' and hoped that Hildegard would be able to provide the guidance and support that she so obviously required.

Chapter 7

By 1155, the community at Rupertsberg was well-established. The number of sisters had increased to 40, with enquiries from interested parents arriving regularly. Fortunately, when we had first built the sisters' dormitories, we had allowed sufficient room to accommodate such expansion. "I do not wish to repeat the mistakes made at Disibodenberg," Hildegard had said when the building works began.

Rupertsberg was, mostly, a very happy community. Hildegard embraced her 'daughters' with great affection, and the 'daughters' submitted themselves to their 'mother' with such reverence that it was hard to decide whether the mother surpassed the daughters in virtue, or *vice versa*.

Hildegard was a model of virtue, admired by everyone. She was firm but fair when it came to matters of discipline in the community, and generous to all who sought her advice or counsel. Her health, as ever, was up and down – at times it was quite good; at other times it was very poor, but she rarely allowed even poor health to keep her from her work. She was a fine example for us all to follow.

On ordinary days, the sisters worked hard in the well-fitted workshops, making and weaving material into robes and altar cloths, which were used by us or sold to other communities. Other sisters worked in the various gardens - we now grew all our own fruit, vegetables and herbs. In our scriptorium, a few of the more gifted sisters copied, illustrated and bound books under my tutelage and direction. Our library was beginning to grow, and some of our books were sent as gifts to other monasteries and convents. Everyone in the community worked hard, often performing the work of their choice, and all were pleased to seek their beds after the singing of Compline.

Feast days, however, were another matter entirely. On these days, the sisters stood in the church with unbound hair, wearing white silk veils that touched the floor, while singing psalms set to Hildegard's heavenly music and wearing gold rings on their fingers. They also wore crowns of gold filigree, into which were inserted crosses on both sides and the back, with a figure of the Lamb on the front.

Perhaps unsurprisingly, there were people in the broader church who did not approve of these 'unusual' practices. One such person, one Tengswich, *magistra* of a foundation of canonesses in Andernach, wrote Hildegard a letter that, although overtly polite, showed clear disapproval of the way in which the nuns 'adorned' themselves on these festive days.

Hildegard's reply was equally polite, but she made no apology for these liturgical practices.

"These practices celebrate the virginity of the Brides of Christ and are in no way caused by worldly vanity or excess," she wrote. "Virgins are married with holiness in the Holy Spirit, and so it is proper that they come before the great High Priest as an oblation presented to God."

Tengswich did not reply to Hildegard's letter, but other mutterings reached us concerning the Rupertsberg community's unusual practices. Hildegard acknowledged the mutterings, but was not at all troubled by them.

For me, these feast day liturgies were a sensual feast for the eyes and ears, and I always felt particularly close to the Heavenly realm on these days, even as a mere (male) spectator.

Financially, matters were greatly improved in the five years since our arrival at Rupertsberg. We received gifts from wealthy donors who wished to bury their relatives in the

Rupertsberg cemetery. One wealthy nobleman, a certain Count Embricho, even paid a substantial sum in advance of his own death, such was his desire to secure his final resting place at Rupertsberg.

This measure of prosperity was tempered by the fact that its source was unpredictable and finite – there were only so many people we could appropriately lay to rest in our grounds. The matter of the sisters' dowries had still not been resolved, and the community did not own the freehold of the Rupertsberg lands. Both of these important assets were still under the control of Abbott Cuno of Disibodenberg Monastery.

Early in the summer of that year, Hildegard suddenly became very unwell. She took to her bed, and tossed and turned feverishly for several days. By then I had learned to recognise the signs – we were about to take delivery of an important vision from God.

A few days after the onset of this illness, Sister Birgitta was holding a cold compress against Hildegard's forehead, and I was sitting on the other side of the bed, praying quietly, when Hildegard suddenly sat up and said, "I must go to Disibodenberg."

Sister Birgitta and I both jumped, startled, but I was more surprised at Hildegard's utterance than the sudden movement.

"Why Disibodenberg?" I asked.

"I must speak directly to Abbott Cuno about our land and dowries, before it is too late," Hildegard replied, staring straight ahead.

"What do you mean, 'too late'?" asked Sister Birgitta.

"The abbott is very ill," Hildegard replied. "I must go immediately."

I had not heard that Abbott Cuno was unwell, but this did not mean that it was untrue. Hildegard often 'knew' things before she could have actually heard of them. I was concerned for the abbott, but more concerned about Hildegard's health.

"I do not think you are well enough to travel, Mother," I said. "Perhaps I could go instead."

"No," she said, turning to look at me. "I must go, alone."

"You will *not* go alone," I said, with more adamance than was usual for me. "It is not safe for you to travel alone. I will come with you."

"Very well, but we must go now," Hildegard said, rising unsteadily from her bed.

Within an hour, Hildegard and I rode out through the main gate and headed south towards Disibodenberg. It was a warm day, and wildflowers bobbed and swayed in the fields and woods. Hildegard would usually have been delighted by the sights and smells, but she was preoccupied with the task at hand. We barely spoke during the entire journey.

By the time we arrived at Disibodenberg, it was nearly dark, and I could hear the brothers chanting Vespers. When they emerged a few minutes later, I noted that Abbott Cuno was walking very unsteadily, until Prior Adalbert came and took his arm.

Hildegard and I had been waiting just outside the chapel. The abbott and prior both looked up and saw us.

Abbott Cuno's face broke into a smile, while the prior's expression travelled in the opposite direction.

"What are *you* doing here, and at this late hour?" the prior asked, looking first at Hildegard and then at me.

"Prior, that is no way to greet guests," said the abbott, still smiling at us.

"Forgive me, Father," said the prior, with a slight bow. He turned to us. "How can we be of assistance to you, Brother Volmar, Mother Hildegard?" he asked with feigned courtesy.

"I must speak with Father Abbott," said Hildegard. "It is a matter of the utmost importance."

"Out of the question," the prior snapped. "The abbott is quite unwell and needs to rest. Perhaps you could let us know when you intend to visit in future?"

"I think it is for me to decide if they may speak with me," said the abbott, raising his eyebrows at the prior.

"Yes, Father, of course," said the prior, bowing again. "I will leave you with your ... *guests*." He gave us a sour look and stalked towards the cloister, doubtless to ensure that the brothers were all diligently engaged in their sacred reading.

The prior's abrupt departure had left the abbott unsupported. He swayed unsteadily, so I took hold of his arm and helped him to his chambers, followed closely by Hildegard. Once there, I settled him into a comfortable chair.

"It is lovely to see you both," he said, smiling warmly. "Please, be seated," he said, indicating a bench along the wall.

It had, admittedly, been five years since I had last seen the abbott, but this was not the man that I remembered. Aside from the inevitable physical deterioration, he had mellowed considerably. I was sorry for his infirmity, but hoped that his changed demeanour might make this visit a bit easier than I had anticipated.

"How can I help you?" he asked, leaning forward. He then started coughing so violently that his whole body convulsed. There was a pitcher and cup on his desk, so I poured him some wine, and passed the cup to him. He sipped the wine slowly and seemed to recover slightly.

"I am so sorry to trouble you when you are unwell, Father," Hildegard began, "but I have been compelled by God to speak to you." The abbott sat up straight. "I have seen in a vision that I must make it known to you that our lands at Rupertsberg, with all that belongs to it, should be separated from this place, and that we will owe deference and obedience to the servants of God here, only as long as we find good faith in you towards us."

The abbott had turned quite pale as Hildegard spoke. He glanced at me quickly. "I have, of course, received your letters concerning the sisters' dowries, Brother Volmar, but there is considerable opposition amongst the brothers to your request that these dowries should be relinquished." He took another sip of wine. "As for the lands at Rupertsberg, I expect I would receive a similar response. However, a directive from God is always to be obeyed. I shall, of course, take immediate steps to see that this is accomplished."

Hildegard smiled warmly at the abbott. "Thank you, Father. I knew we could rely on you to do the right thing."

Hildegard and I ate a good meal and spent the night at the monastery's guest house. Early the next day, we headed back to Rupertsberg. I felt happy, optimistic that all would soon be settled, but Hildegard was not so certain.

"I will not relax until matters are completed and formalised in writing," she said as we rode.

About a week later, we received word that Abbott Cuno had died on 2 July. We were all greatly saddened by this news. Although he and I had had our differences over the years, he had been a highly competent and caring abbott to both the men and women of Disibodenberg for 19 years, making him the longest to serve in that role to date. He would be sorely missed and difficult to replace.

Hildegard decided not to attend Abbott Cuno's funeral. "I think my presence would be a distraction," she said, "given the circumstances of my departure." I agreed that it would be better if I went alone.

The funeral was a suitably sombre and grand occasion, as befitted a respected leader of this highly regarded community. It was well attended by local townspeople and clergy from near and far.

After the funeral, I stayed at Disibodenberg for a few days to spend time with members of my former community with whom I had been close. While there, I tried to ascertain what steps were being taken to transfer the land and dowries, but was unable to learn anything about the matter.

When I returned to Rupertsberg, I broached this subject that I knew was on Hildegard's mind.

"I am not sure whether Abbott Cuno was able to take any action before he died," I said. "I heard no mention of these matters in my discussions with the brothers. I feel certain that I would have, if it had been discussed in Chapter, as it would have been unpopular with some members of the community."

Hildegard said nothing for a moment. "I suppose we will just have to wait and see if anything happens," she said. "Do you know who the next abbott might be? Will it be Adalbert?"

I shuddered. "No, I do not think so," I replied. "I think he enjoys being prior — he has power with*out* responsibility." Hildegard laughed.

"From what I heard from the brothers, it is likely to be Brother Helenger," I said. Hildegard stopped laughing and looked at me, wide-eyed.

"Helenger?" she gasped. "He is no great supporter of the women's community, as I recall."

I nodded. "No, I do not think he is," I said. "It might not be him, of course. Gossip is not always accurate."

My optimism proved to be misguided. Helenger became the next abbot of Disibodenberg Monastery on 17 July 1155, the fifth person to perform this role.

Hildegard and I both thought it best to give the new abbott some time to settle into his new role before we approached him with the proposal agreed to by his predecessor. By the beginning of Advent, we had heard nothing at all from Disibodenberg, and Hildegard was becoming agitated.

"Should I visit him? Write to him? I think he has had enough time to consider the matter," she said to me, one chilly morning in November.

I remembered our last, unscheduled visit, and decided that a letter might be a safer strategy.

"Perhaps we could start with a letter, and see what comes of that," I said.

A few days later, a letter to Abbott Helenger, written by Hildegard and edited by me, was dispatched by way of messenger on horseback. Would we receive a prompt reply? Would we receive *any* reply? Would it be favourable to us? Only time would tell, and we were required, yet again, to sit and wait.

Hildegard's letter was very polite and deferential in tone. She described the circumstances of our last meeting with Abbott Cuno, and gently enquired whether any steps had been taken as a consequence of that meeting.

A week before Christmas, Abbott Helenger's reply was delivered to us. "Read it aloud," Hildegard said anxiously, handing the parchment to me.

This letter was polite in neither tone nor content, and was certainly *not* favourable to the Rupertsberg community. Not only did the abbott refuse to honour his predecessor's undertakings regarding the Rupertsberg land and the sisters' dowries, he denied that any such undertakings had ever been given. Alternatively, if Abbott Cuno *had* given such undertakings on the occasion of our last visit, the new abbott could not be obliged to honour these, as Abbott Cuno was so close to death as to be not of sound mind.

Hildegard was angrier than I had ever seen her. Her face was red as she paced rapidly around her chamber, and her attempts at speech were incoherent splutterings.

I tried to remain calm, for both our sakes. "Abbott Cuno was obviously unwell," I said, "but he seemed perfectly lucid while we were with him."

"Of course, he was!" Hildegard managed to say. "I would never have *sought* such an undertaking from a person who did not fully understand what he was agreeing to!" She continued to pace around the room. I scanned the rest of the letter, as it clearly had more to say. I hesitated to read the next paragraph aloud, but knew that I must.

"There is ...more," I said, looking nervously at Hildegard. She stopped pacing and stared at me wide-eyed.

"More?" she said, then sighed. "Go on."

"It seems that the new abbott is demanding that I return to Disibodenberg immediately. According to his 'understanding', my move to Rupertsberg was intended to be temporary, solely for the purpose of assisting you to complete the work on *Scivias*. Now that that work is finished, I must return to Disibodenberg, which continues to be the place at which I vowed my service to God." I felt sick.

Hildegard's face went from brightest red to palest white in an instant. She swayed slightly, then sat down in the nearest chair. I feared that she would faint from the shock.

She closed her eyes and took several deep breaths. Then she spoke quietly as she placed her head in her hands, elbows on knees. "This is too much. Why does God allow these devils to torment me so?"

That was a question I could not hope to answer, but it seemed a reasonable one to ask. Just when we thought we were nearing a resolution of these financial arrangements, a change of abbott had sent us back to the beginning of the negotiations. I sighed deeply. I feared that this would not be a very happy Christmas for Hildegard or any of us in the Rupertsberg community.

Chapter 8

In the summer of 1156, Sister Elisabeth finally came from Schoenau to Rupertsberg for the visit suggested by Hildegard two years earlier.

It was a hot day in mid-June when Elisabeth arrived, and I was called to the gatehouse to greet her. As I approached, I saw a small, fragile young woman looking around anxiously.

"Sister Elisabeth!" I called. "Welcome!"

She turned to me as if startled and stared at me with dark brown eyes that seemed too large for her otherwise delicate facial features.

I took her directly to meet Hildegard, and they greeted each other like old friends. Elisabeth visibly relaxed in the company of the older woman.

Although Elisabeth slept with the other nuns and attended the Offices with them, she spent a considerable amount of her visit in private time with Hildegard. They talked and prayed together for hours, and this seemed to have a positive impact on the younger woman.

After several weeks at Rupertsberg, Elisabeth had gained some weight and seemed less anxious than when she arrived.

"I think I have persuaded her to be less self-punishing," Hildegard told me one evening. "There really is nothing to be gained from starving oneself to death." I readily agreed with that assertion.

When Elisabeth departed to return to Schoenau in late August, Hildegard seemed quite sad but optimistic.

"I have enjoyed her visit," she told me, "and believe that we have both benefitted from our time together. Elisabeth has promised to maintain a regular correspondence with me, and I am very interested to see how her visionary gift develops. She certainly seems to have unique abilities."

I smiled and nodded. 'Unique' was certainly one way of describing the young nun, yet I had found that I liked her very much. She had a naivety appropriate to her years, but a wisdom that was way beyond them. In this respect, she reminded me of the young Hildegard I had known many years before.

It seemed to me that they had enough in common to form the basis of a solid friendship. This was something that I felt Hildegard had lacked since Richardis' departure and subsequent death. Although she loved and got on well with all the women under her care, there had never been a special friend to take the place of Richardis, and I fervently hoped that a friendship with Elisabeth could, at least in part, help to fill that void.

Chapter 9

Towards the end of 1157, Hildegard received a letter from Elisabeth, with an accompanying document titled *Liber revelationum Elisabeth de sacro exercitu virginum Coloniensium* (Book of the Revelations of Elisabeth about the Holy Army of the Virgins of Cologne).

"This sounds *very* intriguing," I said, as I passed the documents to Hildegard.

She read the letter quite quickly, but lingered over the *Liber*, her face becoming quite animated as she read and then re-read the neat lines of script.

"This is quite remarkable!" she said, handing the documents to me. "I knew of St Ursula and her virgins, of course, but I did not know the full story, and it is wonderful that the relics have been verified."

I knew that a large number of bones had been discovered in Cologne earlier in the century, and there was conjecture as to whether or not these belonged to the saint and her companions. *How could this have been verified?* I wondered, but all became clear as I read Sister Elisabeth's words.

"At the Mass on the Feast Day of St Ursula of Cologne, the blessed lady herself appeared to me in a vision and told me many things. She told me that she was the daughter of a British king. While still very young, a pagan king of Anglia had wanted her as a wife for his son, Aetherius. She agreed, on condition that she be allowed three years to go on a pilgrimage to Rome. On the way home, they stopped in Cologne, which was under siege by the Huns. The wild hordes murdered Ursula's companions (said to have been 11,000 virgins) and, when Ursula refused the advances of the Hun prince, she was also killed. Then, a company of 11,000 angels appeared and put the Huns to flight. In gratitude for their deliverance, the people of Cologne made St Ursula their patron saint.

"The blessed lady also confirmed that the remains uncovered near Cologne nearly sixty years ago are hers and those of her companions. She wishes this to be made widely known, so that the relics of these holy martyrs may be given due reverence and be used in furtherance of God's work."

I, also, knew of St Ursula, but the version of events described by Sister Elisabeth was, as Hildegard had said, remarkable.

About a month later, shortly before Christmas, I heard Hildegard teaching the sisters a beautiful new chant. I stopped, transfixed by the glorious sound.

Later that day, I asked Hildegard about the new chant.

"It is one of the chants I have composed that is dedicated to St Ursula," she told me as she went to a shelf to retrieve several parchments. "I was so inspired by Sister Elisabeth's vision of St Ursula and her brave companions that I just had to compose music and words in their honour."

She handed the parchments to me, and I examined them. There were six new pieces, some short, some much longer.

"You have written these so quickly!" I said, amazed at the quantity and the complexity of the work.

"They came to me in just a few days," Hildegard said. "Both words and music flowed from me with such ease that I had trouble writing it all down quickly enough."

I smiled and shook my head slightly. There were two antiphons, one short and the other much longer, two responsories, and a hymn. There was also a sequence, intended to be sung between the Alleluia and Gospel at Mass, and it was this work that most captured my attention.

"O Ecclesia," I read aloud.

"That was the chant you heard us practising," Hildegard said.

I continued to read aloud:

'In a vision of true faith, Ursula fell in love with the Son of God and renounced her man and all the world, and gazed into the sun and called to the most beautiful youth, saying: In great yearning I have yearned to come to you and sit with you at the heavenly wedding feast, running to you by a strange path like a cloud that runs like sapphire in the purest air.'

"These words are beautiful!" I said. "They evoke such vivid images in my mind."

Hildegard smiled. "I take no credit for them," she said, as she always did. "The words are given to me by God, as is the music."

The beautiful words, of course, became even more beautiful when sung. I was clearly not alone in thinking that this chant was special, as I soon heard the sisters humming fragments of it as they went about their daily tasks. We prepared for the Christmas of 1157 in good spirits, which I mostly shared. There was, however, still a dark cloud that continued to hover over me, a cloud that could be described in one word: Disibodenberg.

Chapter 10

By 1158, copious quantities of parchment and ink had been expended in the ongoing battle between Hildegard and Abbott Helenger regarding the transfer of the Rupertsberg lands and the sisters' dowries. There were still 15 sisters at Rupertsberg who had begun their service to God at Disibodenberg, and had paid substantial sums on their arrival at the latter place. These sums would have been of great benefit to the community at Rupertsberg, and it seemed right and proper that the funds should be at the place where the sisters were *currently* performing their service to God. Abbott Helenger disagreed.

The dispute concerning *my* place of service to God was also not yet resolved, although I had remained at Rupertsberg while the matter was being settled. Regrettably, nothing had been committed to writing regarding my role and tenure at Rupertsberg, and the abbott who had given me permission to move to Rupertsberg as its provost had now been dead for over two years.

In mid-January 1158, Hildegard became seriously ill – worse than I had ever known her to be. She seemed to be burning alive, from the inside out, and no remedy that Sister Birgitta tried was of any help. Sisters Birgitta, Clementia and Hiltrud took turns to sit with Hildegard so that she was never alone. I also came and sat and prayed by Hildegard's bed whenever I could.

We were so certain that Hildegard was about to depart this world that we laid her inert body out over a haircloth on the ground, as we had done for the Lady Jutta. Members of the community and neighbours came in great mourning to farewell Hildegard on her final journey, which seemed imminent. She remained in this state for 30 days, hovering between life and death. As Hildegard told me later, she did not pass out of this life, but was not fully in it either.

After 30 days had passed, Hildegard opened her eyes and sat up slowly. Amazed and full of joy, Sister Birgitta and I helped Hildegard onto her bed, where she lay back down again while remaining awake.

"Are you feeling better, Mother?" asked Sister Birgitta.

Hildegard nodded slightly.

"What has been happening to you?" I asked, scarcely believing our good fortune.

"It was the most evil spirits of the air, those who commit all the punishing tortures of human beings, who have been attacking me relentlessly," Hildegard began. "They rushed at me, crying out, 'Let us seduce this woman so that she has doubts about God, and criticises Him for allowing such suffering to be inflicted upon her.'" She paused and gasped for air. Sister Birgitta lifted Hildegard's head and gave her water to drink. Hildegard then continued.

"To be truthful, I was terrified of these spirits, but God strengthened me to bear my suffering with patience. The worst of it is now passed, and there is much I must do."

Both Sister Birgitta and I protested at this. "You are much too weak to do anything for the time being," I said.

Hildegard nodded slightly. "I will rest and recuperate for a short while," she said, "but there is something you must do for me, Volmar, dear friend."

"Of course! Anything!" I replied a little too eagerly, but I was still overcome with joy and relief that Hildegard had come back to us.

"I need you to send a message to Abbott Helenger," Hildegard said. I frowned at this. I did not think this was the time to continue the argument with the abbott, but I fetched parchment, ink and quill, and waited for further instructions.

After a few moments, Hildegard began. "Tell him this: 'I am commanded by God to go to Disibodenberg to announce the words He will show me. I must speak these words to the whole community, gathered together in one place. I will come to you on the 1st day of March. You must obey this command from God, as must I.' That is all." Hildegard closed her eyes and slept peacefully for the next 12 hours.

On 1 March, at first light, Hildegard and I set out on horseback, once again headed to Disibodenberg. It was a cool, crisp morning, and the horses' hooves made crunching sounds as they trod on the frosty grass.

We arrived at Disibodenberg around dusk. We were greeted at the main gate by Prior Adalbert. A young novice led our horses to the stables, while the prior escorted us to the Chapter House.

As we entered, the brothers fell silent. The room was full. The benches around the walls were packed, and younger brothers sat cross-legged on the hard stone floor.

Hildegard went to stand behind the plain wooden lectern. She looked around the crowded room, then began to speak. Her voice did not sound like her own. It was loud, deep and resonant, and seemed to come from all around us.

"I have been commanded by God to speak these words to you," she began. Everyone stiffened, sitting bolt upright. "The Rupertsberg convent, as well as the alms accruing therefrom, must be free and clear from the control of Disibodenberg." Her eyes then fixed on Abbott Helenger, sitting in his chair at the back of the room. "To you, Father Abbott, I have this message from the Serene Light: 'You should be a father to this woman's community, for the salvation of the souls of My daughters abiding there. The alms given to them have nothing to do with you or your brothers, but your monastery should be a place of sanctuary for them. But if it is your will to persevere in gnashing your teeth at them with your verbal assaults then woe will be upon you. And if any among you …' she looked around the room, 'say to yourselves maliciously: We intend to diminish their holdings – then I Who Am say that you are the worst sort of despoilers.'" Hildegard's gaze returned to the abbott. "'If you attempt to take from them the shepherd who applies spiritual medicine …' I assumed this was a reference to me … 'then again I say to you that you are not considering the justice of God, and, for this reason, the justice of God will destroy you.'"

Hildegard stopped speaking. The brothers had been getting more and more agitated as she spoke. They all looked terrified – pale-faced and wide-eyed. Some of the younger brothers were crying. Once Hildegard had stopped speaking, pandemonium erupted.

The abbott got up and moved to the front of the room. He tried to regain order by raising his hands and crying, "Peace! Peace!"

When the crying and shouting had subsided, the abbott turned to Hildegard.

"Of course, Mother Hildegard," he said. "It will be done, just as you have decreed."

"It is not *I* who have decreed this," said Hildegard, her voice returned to its normally calm, clear tones. "It is God who has spoken to you, *through* me."

The next day, at first light, Hildegard and I rode out of the Disibodenberg gates and headed back to Rupertsberg. We rode side by side where the path allowed, and I glanced at Hildegard from time to time, trying to gauge her mood. She looked pale, her face drawn. She barely spoke a word all the way home. It seemed clear to me that the extraordinary events of the previous evening had taken a toll on her already weakened state.

When we got back to Rupertsberg, everyone was in the refectory eating, while Sister Hiltrud read aloud. We joined them for the meal, and Hildegard went straight to bed immediately afterwards. She did not emerge from her sleeping chamber for several days.

"How did it go?" Brother Arnold asked me, as we prepared for bed in the small room we shared.

I thought for a moment. Then laughed slightly, from amazement more than amusement. "It was astounding," I finally said. "If *that* does not settle the matter, nothing on God's Earth ever will."

I described the events to Brother Arnold, who was open-mouthed at the tale. "What will happen now?" he asked.

"Now we will wait, again," I said, pulling the blanket up to my chin. I laughed again, quietly, then slept through the night.

For once, we did not have to wait long for a response. Towards the end of May, Hildegard received two documents from Arnold, Archbishop of Mainz. Hildegard read them silently to herself, while I sat opposite, trying to read her facial expressions. She remained impassive until she had finished reading, and then she smiled before handing the documents to me.

I skimmed quickly over both documents, trying to determine whether their contents were favourable or not, then returned to the beginning and read both carefully. The contents were, indeed, very favourable to the Rupertsberg community.

The first document, signed under the archbishop's seal on 22 May 1158, was a document confirming as a freehold possession of Rupertsberg the gift of Count Herman and his wife Gertrude of their property in Bingen, and also confirmed other transfers and purchases of real property. It was a considerable parcel of land, comprising fields, vineyards and houses, and put the Rupertsberg community in a very comfortable financial position.

It was the second document, however, that directly addressed the matters that Rupertsberg and Disibodenberg had been disputing over the past eight years. This document, dated and sealed as was the first, confirmed that the sisters at Rupertsberg were to have freehold possession of both the Rupertsberg land and their estates in independence of the Disibodenberg brothers, and were to 'incur no hindrance from them on any pretext whatever'. I laughed out loud at this point, then continued reading.

The document went on to state that the Abbott of Disibodenberg, both present and future, was required to provide priests for the Rupertsberg community, that is, 'monks of worthy reputation, who shall care for them in all things according to their need and petition'. Importantly for me, the document also stated that the abbott was not permitted to 'remove' any such monk without the sisters' consent. I felt my shoulders relax. I was safe.

I was amazed by what I had read. It seemed that all our prayers had been answered. I looked up from the parchment and saw that Hildegard was watching me, smiling.

"Well," I said, rolling up the parchments, "that seems to have settled everything very well."

Hildegard sighed deeply. "Yes," she said. "Finally, I am free to begin my most important work."

I frowned slightly. "What do you mean? You have been working for God for as long as I have known you."

"That has all been important work, of course," she replied, "and I will continue to write down my visions and compose music for the liturgy, but there is much more to be done. You see, dear Volmar, I did not reveal *all* that God commanded during the 30 days when I hovered between life and death."

Hildegard paused. I waited, wondering what she was about to reveal.

"God also commanded me to go to communities in other places, and reveal to them the words that God has shown me. So, I must prepare for this task at once."

I could scarcely believe what I had just heard. Travel to other communities and preach God's word to them?

"But you are still far from well," I said. "How are you meant to travel when you are still so weak?"

"God and my faithful helpers will assist me," she said, smiling. "You know as well as I do, dear friend, that nothing is impossible for God."

I knew there was no use in trying to dissuade Hildegard from her intentions, so I resolved to assist her as much as I possibly could. I agreed that nothing was impossible for *God*, but I was starting to wonder how much more Hildegard could be expected to do in His service.

Chapter 11

After resting for only a few days, Hildegard threw herself into the planning of her proposed preaching tour.

We were seated at her table, on which was laid a large map of the Rhine region. Peering intently at the map, I followed her finger as she showed me where she intended to go, which was in an easterly direction and mostly along the river Main.

"It will be much quicker if we can sail, rather than ride," she said.

"That is true," I replied, "but we do not have a boat."

"Yes," she replied. "That *is* a problem."

I mentioned this to Brother Arnold that night as we were getting ready for bed, and was greatly surprised by his response.

"You need a boat?" he asked. "I can help you with that. I grew up around boats!"

The next day, Brother Arnold and I rode to Bingen to search for a boat builder. It did not take us long to find a large, busy boatyard on the banks of the Rhine, not far from the centre of the city.

We wandered around, looking at boats at various stages of construction or repair. I knew nothing at all about boats, so had no idea what we were looking for. After a few moments, Brother Arnold slapped the side of what looked like a finished boat and said, "Ah! This is it. This is what we need."

"What type of boat is this?" I asked. It was quite small compared to some of the others, but looked quite sturdy.

"This is a cog," Brother Arnold replied, walking around the boat and peering over the top to look inside. "It is perfect for river sailing. See the single mast and flat bottom?"

I saw these features, but did not recognise their utility. "Why is a flat bottom a good thing?" I asked.

"The boat can be landed more easily, anywhere there is a riverbank. Also, it can sail in much shallower water than a boat with a pointed keel."

I nodded. That sounded reasonable.

"These are quite easy to sail, too," Brother Arnold continued. "The single sail is controlled by a central rudder – see that handle?"

I nodded again. I hoped it would be easy to sail, as I was the person most likely to be given that task.

While we were talking, a middle-aged man came up to us. "You are looking for a cog, brothers?" We nodded. "You will not find a better one than this," he said proudly. "Made from local oak, caulked with tarred moss – unsinkable."

That sounds perfect, I thought, but said nothing. I did not wish to betray my complete ignorance on the subject, so I left the negotiations to Brother Arnold and wandered along the riverbank.

As we rode back to Rupertsberg, Brother Arnold described the deal that had been struck. "I will return tomorrow with the purchase money," he said. "The boat is ready to go – it just needs the sail to be fitted, so you can start the journey in a few days."

That sounded straightforward, although I was still concerned about controlling the boat and said so.

"Yes, well, it will be a bit difficult heading east," Brother Arnold mused.

"Why is that?" I asked.

He looked at me, amused. "Because the Main flows west." I did not know how to respond to this. How could one sail *against* the flow?

Brother Arnold and I went to discuss the arrangements with Hildegard as soon as we arrived home. He explained the challenging nature of the outward journey.

"It is easy once you know how," he said, "but I gather Brother Volmar is quite - inex*perienced.*" That was an understatement.

Hildegard thought for a moment, then sighed. "I was hoping you would be our male companion, Volmar, but perhaps it would be better if Brother Arnold sailed the boat, and you stayed behind to take care of things here."

I sighed, too, then nodded. "You are right, of course," I said.

"I will teach you everything you need to know when we return," Brother Arnold said to me, slapping my shoulder to console me. "Then you will be ready for the next journey."

Next journey? I thought. *Surely there will only be one!* I did not trust myself to speak, so I merely nodded and forced my face to smile.

I did not *feel* like smiling. Hildegard would be gone for – how long? Months, at least. The thought of not seeing her for so long made me want to weep. I should be going with her!

By mid-June, all the necessary plans had been made. The whole community gathered in the forecourt to bid the travellers farewell. Hildegard had chosen Sister Hiltrud, the niece of Lady Jutta of blessed memory, to be her female companion – she could not travel with a man alone – so these three, Hildegard, Sister Hiltrud and Brother Arnold, headed out of the main gate and headed to Bingen, where their boat was waiting for them.

I stood at the gate and watched them go, until I could no longer see them. I then turned back into the forecourt, and walked slowly into my time of desolation.

Chapter 12

They were gone for nearly five months. It felt like an age. I had no difficulty in keeping busy – there was always so much to do – but my mind was rarely fixed on what *I* was doing. Instead, I tried to picture what *they* were doing and where they were, but I could not picture what I did not know. Although I knew their itinerary, I had no idea how long it would take them to reach each destination or how long they would remain in each place. My mind was a blur of uncertainty and anxiety. This was not a happy time for me.

Then, one afternoon early in November, a young novice came running up the hill. "They are back! Mother Hildegard is back!"

We all dropped what we were doing and hurried out of the main gate to greet them as they climbed the hill from the river. I saw Brother Arnold and Sister Hiltrud first, then breathed a sigh of relief when I saw Hildegard just behind them. They were all tired – this was to be expected – but they all seemed well, and very happy to be home.

After a brief rest, the travellers joined us in the refectory for the evening meal. Tonight, it would be a celebratory feast. We usually took our daily meal in silence, listening as one member of the community read to us from the Scriptures. On this evening, however, we all listened to Hildegard, as she told us of her travels.

"Our first stop was at Klause," she began, "where we visited a small foundation of the monks of St George. We stayed there for a few days only. Next, we visited the convent of Wechterswinkel at Winkel, where we stayed for one week." She paused briefly to eat and drink a little.

"We were greeted with great enthusiasm by both brothers and sisters," Sister Hiltrud said, then clapped a hand over her mouth, wide-eyed, horrified that she had spoken during the meal.

Hildegard laughed. "You may speak, dear Sister," she said. "This is your story, too." Hiltrud removed her hand from her mouth, but her cheeks remained red. Hildegard continued.

"I spoke to both communities about the Rule, and how they can best live in compliance with its requirements. These communities were not in any great error regarding their behaviour, but a gentle reminder does no harm."

In the silence that followed, all that could be heard was the clicking of cutlery on crockery. Everyone was listening intently.

"Our next stop was at the Cistercian Abbey at Eberbach." She looked at me. "You will remember how Abbott Eberhard of that place offered us assistance while we were establishing Rupertsberg?" I nodded and smiled. I did remember this abbott – a very kind and pious man. I also recalled that Hildegard had sent him a copy of *Scivias* as a token of her gratitude. This was, indeed, a rare and precious gift.

"Next we went to the ancient Benedictine convent at Kitzingen founded by Saint Adeloga sometime in the 730s," Hildegard continued, frowning slightly. "I had received a letter from the abbess, Sophia, just before we departed on this journey. She was very disturbed about the many conflicts in her community, and about her inability to regain order and stability under the Rule. I knew that this community would need a stern lesson.

"The community gathered in their Chapter Hall when it came time for me to speak to them. I could hear some murmuring among the sisters, but they did me the courtesy of falling silent when I began to speak. I began by warning them that I would need to speak harsh words to them, which caused many of the sisters to glance nervously at each other. I told the older women that they were far too harsh on some of the younger sisters, but were also far too lenient on other, less deserving sisters, all according to their own whims. I then told the young women that some of them were vain, for which reason there was great strife among them, with the vain attacking the harsh, and the harsh attacking the vain. I told them all that this behaviour must stop, but that none had strayed so completely from their sacred calling that they could not return to the path of righteousness. All that was required was that they should live according to the discipline of the Rule, and obey their abbess, who is a good and holy woman. 'Turn back!' I told them, 'as God has so instructed me to say, before it is too late.'"

Many of the Rupertsberg listeners were open-mouthed at this tale, including me. How could a community behave in this way? I felt compelled to ask Hildegard how the Kitzingen sisters had reacted to these stern warnings.

"Nobody moved or said a word as Sister Hiltrud, Brother Arnold, and I left the Hall," she said. "The silence was thick with fear, guilt and recrimination. Afterward, Abbess Sophia, moved nearly to tears, thanked me. 'I have no doubt that God's words, delivered by you, will have a positive impact on everyone,' she told me."

"'Sweet lady,' I said to her, 'I trust in God that the darkness that has surrounded your cloister will be banished by God's words and your actions.' I then told her that I felt that most of the sisters were good, faithful women, but that she would do well to dismiss the sub-prioress, who seemed to be causing the unrest by her own lax morals. 'This will also send a clear message,' I told the abbess, 'so as to put fear into those other sisters who might disobey you in future.'"

Some of our people gasped at this part of the story. Dismissal was, indeed, an extreme measure, but was occasionally necessary, particularly where the welfare of a whole community was threatened.

Hildegard finished her meal and smiled at the gaping faces, all fixed on her.

"While I intended this tour to be largely concerned with monastic communities and how they should live according to the Rule, I also wanted to preach publicly, to spread God's word far and wide. I did this in two major cities, Wurzburg and Bamberg. In these places, I addressed both clergy and laity, urging them all to repentance, conversion and penance. I was particularly keen to convey this message to the clergy. As many of you know, since the papal schism some years ago, there has been much corruption and sin in the Church, and I was very clear in my criticism of this conduct." I heard some appreciative murmurings from some of the listeners.

"Surprisingly perhaps," she continued, "and in spite of my sometimes-stern admonitions, my message was well received everywhere I preached."

"That is true," said Brother Arnold. "Many people spoke to Sister Hiltrud and me after they had heard Mother Hildegard preach, and many were moved to tears by her powerful words and presence. Nobody was in any doubt that God was, indeed, speaking to them through this holy woman, and they praised God greatly for sending this messenger to them."

Hildegard smiled warmly at him. "Thank you, Brother, and thank you for all your help. My journey would not have been possible without you."

I should have been happy that Hildegard had had the support of such a loyal follower as Brother Arnold on her long journey. I *should* have been happy, but mostly what I felt was envy. I felt my stomach tighten and my fists clench. It should have been *me* on that journey with Hildegard.

I immediately regretted these sinful thoughts, and resolved to confess and do whatever penance was required of me. I knew that a man of my position and experience should be better than this, but Hildegard had always been my Achilles' heel, and I doubted that this would ever cease to be so.

Chapter 13

Once the excitement of Hildegard's return had subsided, routines were resumed, and I finally managed to spend some time alone with her.

"The preaching seems to have gone well," I said.

"Yes," she replied. "I am pleased with how things went. I have completed *this* part of God's plan for me, but there is still much for me to do."

"Surely you can rest for a while?" I asked, hopefully.

"Maybe briefly," she replied, "but not for long. I had a vision while we were in Bamberg, and I must get to work."

"What was God's message to you this time?" I asked.

Hildegard took a deep breath and then spoke. "I heard a voice from heaven saying to me, 'From infancy you have been taught, not bodily but spiritually, by true vision through the Spirit of the Lord. Speak and write now, therefore, according to me and not according to yourself.'" She paused and closed her eyes.

"What is it that God is telling you to write?" I asked.

Hildegard opened her eyes. "I see a man who is so tall that he extends from the depths of the oceans up into the heavens," she began. "The man turns his eye to look in six different directions, one at a time, I mean, and he speaks of what he sees and hears, and interprets their meaning."

After another brief pause, Hildegard continued. "He speaks of the challenges of daily Christian life, the temptations that humanity comes across and can resist with the help of God. I am to tell God's message that it is to humans' advantage to live a virtuous life, one that will glorify God, by offering suggestions about how to atone for sins by penitence."

I thought about this for a moment. It sounded like another ambitious work, just as *Scivias* had been.

"I will help you with the Latin, of course," I said. "Will this work have illustrations, like *Scivias*?" I asked. Hildegard winced. I remembered Richardis, too late. I could have torn my tongue from my mouth.

Hildegard looked away from me and gazed out of the narrow window. She sighed. "There can be *no* pictures like those in *Scivias*, ever again," she said softly. She looked back at me and smiled sadly. "No. I do not think this volume will require images."

"I am sorry," I said. "I was thoughtless."

She smiled again. "We must carry on," she said, "and be grateful for those who *are* here."

I smiled in return. She was quite right, of course, and I thanked God that He had guided Hildegard safely home.

Chapter 14

Hildegard began work on her second volume of visions, to be called 'The Book of Life's Merits', towards the end of 1158, but not until she had finished the two works begun nearly ten years earlier – 'The Subtleties of Diverse Natural Creatures' and 'The Symphonia of the Harmony of Celestial Revelations'. So much had happened since our move to Rupertsberg that it was hardly surprising that Hildegard had taken so long over these writings. She had worked on them whenever she could spare some time, but her many spiritual and administrative duties often kept her from her writing.

Shortly after her return to Rupertsberg, Hildegard handed both of these works to me for copying and binding. I could see that the scribes would be kept busy for some time to come. Both volumes were substantial, to say the least.

Like everything Hildegard ever produced, the 'Natural Creatures' work was astounding. What had begun as loose parchments containing information about our local plants – herbs, flowers and trees – had become a comprehensive encyclopedia of what seemed to be the entire natural world.

It was divided into nine sections, each treating a different aspect of the natural world. The first was on plants (213 varieties), the second on the four elements (hot, cold, wet, and dry), the third on trees (55 kinds), the fourth on precious stones and gems (26 types), the fifth on fish (37 kinds), the sixth on birds (68 types), the seventh on animals (43 varieties), the eighth on reptiles (18 types), and, finally, the ninth on metals (only 8 of these)! Each of these 'creatures' was described with reference to its wholesome or toxic properties, and its medicinal uses, if any.

In addition to my usual task of 'polishing' Hildegard's Latin, I had assisted with this work by furnishing Latin equivalents to the German names of local things and creatures, thereby ensuring that this wonderful book could be read by people beyond the German borders. Apart from that, the work was based partly on earlier works I had found for Hildegard in the Disibodenberg library, but mostly on her keen observations of, and conclusions about the natural world around her.

The other newly completed work, the 'Symphonia', was as different from the 'Natural Creatures' work as it could possibly be. The 'Symphonia' was a collection of Hildegard's liturgical pieces, including both text and music. It comprised the 14 liturgical pieces first published in *Scivias*, and those that Hildegard had composed since the completion of *Scivias* seven years earlier. These new pieces had often been sung at Rupertsberg, and included 'Symphonies' of Virgins and Widows, an antiphon for the dedication of our new church, three pieces for the feast of St Rupert, and antiphons and responsories for the Virgin.

"This is really a work in progress," Hildegard told me as I scanned the pages. "I will keep composing for as long as I am able, but I wanted to collect what I have written so far. I can add new pieces to the collection later."

I never ceased to be amazed by Hildegard's compositions - the beautiful words paired with the strange and unheard-of music. We were so blessed to have a spiritual leader with this musical gift from God. It helped us all to transcend the ordinary, the here and now, and to catch a glimpse of the beauty that waited for us in Heaven.

Chapter 15

The year 1159 began with a wintery blast. We shivered and huddled together as we scurried from building to building as quickly as we could and as infrequently as we could. Apart from the keen gardeners amongst us, who missed their outdoor activities, everyone was happy to be busy inside.

Hildegard was writing her second book of visions, 'The Book of Life's Merits'. The scribes, under my guidance, were making copies of the 'Natural Creatures' and 'Symphonia' books. The music notation in the latter book required special care and skill. I had chosen Sister Clementia, Hildegard's niece, for this task, as she had previously demonstrated skill with quill and ink that was up to the challenge. Other members of the community prayed and read, and we all, of course, sang the Office eight times each day.

The Rupertsberg convent was, finally, fully established and self-sufficient. Our buildings were completed, our gardens were mature enough to provide many of our needs, and we had achieved financial and administrative independence from the monastery at Disibodenberg. For the first time in years, I felt that life was safe, secure and stable.

Winter finally gave way to spring, a lovely time of year when our gardens burst forth into new life. The weather improved rapidly. Cold, wind and snow were replaced by warm, sunny days and light breezes, and, although I dreaded the prospect, I decided it was time to remind Brother Arnold of the offer he had made to me nearly nine months previously.

"Sailing lessons?" he said, frowning slightly. "Oh yes. I did offer to teach you, did I not!"

"You did," I replied.

The next day, we descended the steep hill to the riverbank below, where our cob was secured to a tree. Brother Arnold untied the rope, and together we dragged the boat to the water. He leapt gracefully into the boat, and helped to haul me over the steep side.

"Now," he began. "If the wind is behind you and you are sailing *down*stream, there are no problems. Any fool can sail in those conditions. Just point the rudder in the direction you wish to go and keep away from the riverbanks. The two main difficulties are where the wind is *not* blowing behind you, or you are attempting to sail *up*stream, against the flow of the river. And if you are *really* unlucky, you might have both wind and river flow working against you. That can get very tricky."

I groaned. How would I ever be able to master this? I might have conceded defeat even before I began, but I was determined that, if Hildegard ever again went on a journey that involved travel by river, *I* would be the boatman.

Brother Arnold was looking amused at my dismay. "Fear not," he said. "We will begin simply, and work from there. Today, there is very little breeze, so we will sail downstream a short way, and then I will show you how to sail upstream as we return home."

Using a long pole, Brother Arnold pushed the boat away from the bank, into the flowing water. He was correct about sailing *down*stream – that *was* easy. I even quite enjoyed it, until it was time to turn around.

Again using the pole, Brother Arnold turned the boat back towards Rupertsberg, and showed me a technique he referred to as 'poling'. As the name suggests, this involved pushing the boat along in the desired direction pushing the pole into the riverbed.

"Obviously," he said with a laugh, "this can only be done in water that is shallower than the length of the pole. Here, Brother. You give it a try."

I took the pole and did as Brother Arnold had been doing. It was quite simple, but I imagined it would become rather tiring quite quickly. I said as much to my instructor.

"Yes, that is true," he nodded, "but the more you do it, the more you *can* do it, if you see what I mean."

I nodded. I was certainly not as fit or strong as Brother Arnold, but could probably improve in both respects with a bit of work.

Another day, when the wind was behind us and we were sailing upstream, Brother Arnold showed me how to tack against the current. This involved sailing at an angle across the river, with each tack taking us further forward. He showed me how to adjust the sail so that it caught as much wind as possible, allowing the boat to move forward more quickly. Even so, it was a slow, laborious process.

On another occasion, we sailed downstream and against the wind. This also involved tacking, but seemed much easier than tacking against the current. I felt quite pleased with my efforts that day, but hoped that this would be the last lesson I would need.

"Very good, Brother," said Brother Arnold. "I think we have covered most situations. Now you just need to practise. I will come with you until you are ready to sail alone."

For the next few months, I practised as often as I could. Initially, I would only sail if Brother Arnold was available, but by the beginning of summer, I felt confident enough to sail alone. I even got to prefer the solitude, and looked forward to sailing on a pleasant summer's afternoon. I was amazed at what I could now do, and knew that I would be ready for any future journey Hildegard might wish to undertake.

Chapter 16

The summer of 1159 was hotter than any I remembered, but the heat was tempered by the breezes we felt on our hilltop. A curse in winter, our elevated exposure to the wind was a blessing this summer.

While life at Rupertsberg was happy and orderly, the same could not be said for the events unfolding beyond our walls.

The King of Germany, Frederick Barbarossa, had also been crowned Holy Roman Emperor by Pope Adrian IV in 1155. The relationship between emperor and pope had been shaky from the outset, but had deteriorated even further in the years since this second coronation.

I asked Hildegard if she knew why this had happened. She acquired information regarding events beyond our walls from her many visitors, some of whom were high-ranking clerics.

"The emperor and the pope have fallen out, it seems. The reasons are, of course, political rather than spiritual," she began.

I nodded. This was usually the way of things.

"Frederick had agreed to help the pope restore his authority in Rome and in the other territories controlled by William, King of Sicily, but he later reneged," Hildegard continued. "As a result, Pope Adrian broke the alliance that had been established with Frederick, and has made peace with William instead."

I nodded again. "That is disturbing," I replied. "Discord between pope and Holy Roman Empire cannot be a good thing." We were soon to discover the truth of these words.

Towards the end of October, I went to speak to Hildegard in her chamber, and was startled to see that she looked pale, as if in shock.

"What has happened?" I asked.

"Pope Adrian died on 1 September," she began. That *was* a shock. He was several years younger than I. "A mere three days later," Hildegard continued, "an election was organised, but the cardinals could not reach unanimity on any of the candidates. The result was – and I cannot believe that this is happening again – the election of *two* popes."

My jaw dropped. "Two? Again? Who are they?" I could not believe what I was hearing.

"Rolando of Siena, to be known as Alexander III, was chosen by the majority of the cardinals, while Ottaviano de Monticelli, to be known as Victor IV, was elected by the remaining cardinals." Hildegard was shaking her head. "Have these men learned nothing from recent history? Their loyalties obviously do not belong to God, or this would never have happened!"

"Why *has* this happened?" I asked, genuinely puzzled. "Why are the cardinals in such disagreement with each other?"

"It seems that two factions have arisen within the cardinals," Hildegard continued. "The majority remain in favour of the position adopted by Adrian towards Sicily, while a small but determined minority remain loyal to Frederick."

"Surely, if the majority voted for Alexander, he will be recognised as the true pope," I said.

"Much will depend on Frederick's response, I think," Hildegard replied.

We did not have to wait very long for this news to reach us. Towards the end of April 1160, Hildegard reported what she had been told by several visitors.

"In the week after Easter, Frederick convened a council in Pavia, and invited both Alexander and Victor to attend. Alexander refused to do so. As only Victor was present, he was declared by the council to be the rightful pope. Alexander, of course, continues to assert that *he* is the rightful pope, but without the support of the emperor, it is difficult to see how he can maintain his position."

I shook my head. Words rarely failed me, but I could say nothing to make sense of these events. Nor could I say anything to placate Hildegard, who was seething with rage.

"I must speak out against this intolerable intrusion of worldly politics into the affairs of the Church," she said, pacing up and down. She stopped pacing, thought for a moment, then looked at me. "I must embark upon another preaching tour," she said with determined finality.

My heart sank. "Are you certain this is what God desires?" I asked, already knowing the answer.

"Yes! This is, indeed, what God wants me to do," she said. She went and sat at the table. "We must get organised at once. Fetch the map and ask Brother Arnold and Sister Hiltrud to join us."

Within half an hour, we were all seated around the table in Hildegard's chamber, poring over the map. I wondered which direction she would choose to travel this time.

"I feel I must go to Trier," Hildegard began. "That is an important city in which to deliver God's message." We all nodded. "Then," she continued, "I will go to Metz, then to Krauftal, then home."

We had all been following Hildegard's finger as it moved south along the Mosel River, and then headed north/east overland to Krauftal. Brother Arnold was frowning.

"You can take the boat as far as Metz," he began, "but not to Krauftal, obviously," he said with a slight laugh. "How will you bring the boat home?"

Now I was frowning. I had prepared myself to sail the boat on any future journey Hildegard embarked upon, but Brother Arnold was making a very good point. How *would* we get the boat home overland?

Hildegard thought for a moment. "Perhaps it might be possible to use another's boat - for payment, of course — and then leave it in Metz for them to collect."

We all nodded again. That sounded feasible, if we could find such a boat.

"That should, indeed, be possible," Brother Arnold said. "I will go to Bingen tomorrow and ask the boatwright. He should know how to make such an arrangement."

We all met again two days later. Brother Arnold had made the necessary arrangements with the boatwright. We could collect a boat similar to ours from him in Bingen, and begin our journey from there. The boat was available immediately, so we prepared to depart.

The community gathered again in the forecourt to farewell Hildegard and her companions. Everyone, except Brother Arnold, was surprised to see that I would be going on this trip instead of him.

"Are you able to sail the boat?" Hildegard asked me, smiling broadly.

"I have taught him everything he needs to know," Brother Arnold said, slapping me on the back so hard that I staggered forward slightly.

"Wonderful!" said Hildegard. "Then let us be on our way." She turned to the gathered community. "Sister Clementia will be in charge while Brother Volmar and I are absent," she said. Sister Clementia looked both surprised and pleased at this sudden promotion.

I had not told Hildegard of my sailing lessons for two reasons. First, I was uncertain whether I would ever be called upon to use these new skills, and secondly, I thought it would be a nice surprise for her. It seemed that I was correct about the latter, if not the former.

"I am *so* pleased you are able to accompany us on this journey, Volmar," she said as we headed for Bingen. "Brother Arnold was an excellent companion last time, but I did miss your counsel and advice on theological matters."

I glowed at this compliment. *I missed you with my whole heart,* I thought. "I am always happy to be at your service," I said.

Brother Arnold and I had studied the map before our departure to discuss navigating the Mosel as far as Metz. "We are sailing south, so I expect this river flows north," I said wryly, hoping to be wrong. I was not.

Brother Arnold laughed. "Quite right, Brother, but do not be concerned. You know what to do." My heart sank, but then recovered. Brother Arnold was right – I *did* know what to do.

We arrived in Trier on the afternoon before Pentecost. Hildegard was expected at the Cathedral the next morning.

"Archbishop Hillenius was very pleased to invite me to preach when I sent word that I was coming," Hildegard told us that evening.

The next morning, the Cathedral was full to capacity. Word of Hildegard's visit had spread, and there were clergy from Trier and the surrounding villages in attendance.

At the appropriate point in the liturgy, Hildegard walked slowly to the pulpit, climbed the stairs, and looked around at the expectant faces. Sister Hiltrud and I were seated at the back of the Cathedral. I thought that would be a good position to observe the listeners' reactions.

"I, a poor little figure without health or strength or courage or learning, have heard these words addressed to the prelates and clergy of Trier, from the mystical light of the true vision," she began. A few people gasped.

"You have been completely lax in your duties, failing to sound the trumpet of justice, and prey to all manner of evils as a result." More gasps.

"I pray that you can still be filled with the fiery love of the Holy Spirit, though I believe this to be doubtful. In truth this is a womanish time, with a tyrant at the head, exhorting all sorts of malice forth. I speak to you in a true vision, that many will be disciplined as the head of the household, who is God, must treat his children when they act with such reckless provocation."

My heart leapt in my chest when Hildegard referred to the 'tyrant at the head'. Everyone would know that she was referring to Frederick Barbarossa, and I feared that it was dangerous to be so openly critical of him. The mutterings in the congregation also made me uneasy.

Hildegard went on to tell the listeners that their laxity was a result of seeking favour from the secular authorities for reasons opposed to the spiritual goal of Christian people. Chasing after wealth and privilege instead of spiritual goods, placed the 'shepherds' and the people in danger of great distress.

"The law is neglected among the spiritual people, who scorn to do and teach what is good. And the masters and prelates sleep, while justice is abandoned."

The muttering had stopped. People were looking at each other, open-mouthed and wide-eyed.

"Hence, I heard this voice from heaven saying: 'O daughter of Sion, the crown will tumble from your head, your riches will vanish, and you will be banished from God's kingdom. Many cities and monasteries will be destroyed by the powerful, by the princes from whom you seek favour."

The mood seemed to be a mixture of fear and anger. I was hoping Hildegard would finish soon. Fortunately, she concluded on a more positive note.

"Heed these warnings, brothers, and repent. It is not too late to seek God's forgiveness, to realise and reform the errors of your ways. Then and only then can you know God's mercy."

Hildegard, Sister Hiltrud and I left the Cathedral immediately after the sermon. I do not know if they continued with the liturgy. I was keen to place some distance between the congregation and ourselves.

As we walked away from the Cathedral, Hildegard seemed exhausted. Her face was pale, and her gait was slow and unsteady. Sister Hiltrud was shaking, whether from fear or excitement I could not tell. She and I assisted Hildegard back to our lodgings, where we stayed until the following morning.

I had no particular desire to remain in Trier, but Hildegard wanted to visit the monastery of Saints Eucharius/Matthias. She had been on good terms with Abbott Ludwig and his monks for a number of years, and had exchanged many letters with the abbott. This community had been one of the first to commission Hildegard to compose music for them, including two songs written for St Eucharius, the monks' original patron, as well as a hymn to St Matthias when the community was rededicated to that saint in 1148.

We stayed at the monastery for several days. We ate and sang the Office with the brothers, but slept in the very comfortable guest house. Hildegard had several long conversations with Abbott Ludwig, and spoke to the brothers at a meeting of their Chapter. She was, however, keen to keep moving south, so we left a couple of days before I thought she was quite recovered from her exhaustion.

Our next stop was in Metz, which was a week's sailing from Trier. Sailing against the current is a slow, laborious business, indeed. We arrived in the second week of June. The weather was hot, and the town was bustling.

Our stay in Metz was quite brief. Hildegard preached in the cathedral, and called upon the clergy to 'sound the trumpet of justice', as she had done in Trier. The sermon in Metz was not, however, as fiery as that in Trier, and Hildegard was well received by her listeners.

Hildegard also wanted to visit one of her correspondents who lived in Metz, one Bertha, who happened to be the sister of Frederick Barbarossa. I hoped that news of Hildegard's oblique reference to the emperor during her sermon in Trier had not reached Bertha's ears but, of course, it had.

Bertha raised the matter herself, and laughed at my obvious consternation.

"Do not worry yourself, Brother," she said. "I quite agree with that description of my brother. He always *did* insist on getting his own way, even when he was a little boy."

I laughed then, relieved. Hildegard sat smiling throughout this exchange. She did not appear to be embarrassed that Bertha had heard of her 'tyrant' reference.

"I pray daily that he will mend his ways," Bertha said.

After a few days of rest in Metz, we headed northeast to Krauftal on horseback. This took us two weeks of steady riding, and was the most arduous part of the journey thus far.

We arrived in Krauftal late in June, and stayed at the Benedictine abbey where Hazzecha, another of Hildegard's correspondents, was abbess. Hazzecha had written to Hildegard for advice and assistance when she found her tasks as abbess too onerous to bear. She had, Hildegard told me, expressed a wish to flee from the abbey, and instead live in solitude in a hermitage. Hildegard had urged the abbess to remain at Krauftal, and to persevere in the work that God had called her to do there. During our visit, Hildegard also urged the sisters to assist their leader, by curbing their unruliness and showing appropriate obedience and respect.

We stayed a week at Krauftal, then began the last leg of our journey back to Rupertsberg. This took another two weeks, so that we arrived home towards the end of July, exhausted but happy with our efforts.

I was certain that Hildegard's message would be spread far and wide by those who had heard her speak on this tour. The Church would begin to mend its sinful ways, and would maintain appropriate boundaries between itself and earthly powers and rulers. All would be well.

As was often the case, I could not have been more mistaken.

Chapter 17

It had been late in the evening when Hildegard, Sister Hiltrud and I arrived home from our travels, so we all went straight to our beds with barely a word to anyone.

At the Chapter meeting the next morning, we heard the dreadful news from Mainz. Archbishop Arnold had been murdered.

Sister Hiltrud gasped. Hildegard's face paled. The archbishop's unpopularity was known to all, but we were shocked to learn of such a wicked crime.

Since Arnold's appointment as archbishop in 1155, Hildegard had been kept informed of his activities, and had, in turn, passed the news on to me. She had been right to have had misgivings about the emperor's choice. Arnold's incumbency had lurched from one disaster to another. Shortly after his appointment, he had attempted to regain the lands that previous archbishops of Mainz had alienated. Predictably, the current holders of the lands had objected to these attempts.

Arnold's strongest opponent was the Count Palatinate, Hermann of Stahlbeck. In addition to being of senior imperial rank, Hermann was also married to Frederick's aunt, thus making him 'family'.

While Frederick was absent on the first of his Italian campaigns, hostilities between the archbishop and the count's vassals had escalated into a regional war. Hermann's troops destroyed castles and manors, plundered churches and monasteries, and abducted monks and nuns.

Frederick returned from Italy towards the end of 1155. At the next meeting of the princes, in Worms around Christmas time, both Arnold and Hermann were convicted of having 'breached the peace'. Quite an understatement, I would have thought.

Later, in 1158, Arnold imposed a tax on the citizens of Mainz in order to raise funds for Frederick's military endeavours in Italy. When the citizens refused to pay, Arnold excommunicated the entire city of Mainz. Hildegard had been apoplectic with rage when she told me of this particular development.

Unbeknownst to us, matters in Mainz had continued to deteriorate while we were away from Rupertsberg. Once we arrived home, Brother Arnold filled in the gaps in our knowledge.

Earlier in 1160, Brother Arnold told us, while Archbishop Arnold was away in Italy working for the recognition of Frederick's anti-pope, Victor IV, the leading citizens of Mainz rebelled. When the archbishop returned, and negotiations with the citizens had failed, he was murdered on 24 June in the forecourt of the monastery of St Jakob. Hildegard, Sister Hiltrud and I were travelling from Metz to Krauftal at that time, and the news had not reached Krauftal while we were staying there.

We all sat silently when Brother Arnold had finished the tale. Sister Hiltrud cried. Hildegard looked utterly defeated.

"I try *so* hard to do God's work, to spread His message, but who is listening? This is an outrage!" she said.

A few months passed, and we received further news in bits and pieces. After the murder of the archbishop, the rebel citizens had, apparently, 'persuaded' the clergy to install Rudolf, son of the Duke of Zahringen, as the next archbishop. Frederick, however, appointed Christian I as archbishop, thereby creating yet *another* schism in the Church of God.

"There is nothing God-ly about this Church of evil men," Hildegard said, when this news reached us towards the end of the year. "They are appointed by secular powers, for secular reasons. I fear for the safety of all our souls, with such men as these as our spiritual leaders, so called."

The affairs of the Church had, once again, been intruded upon by worldly matters and people. I agreed with Hildegard. How *could* our souls be safe when the Church was so utterly corrupted and tainted? What would become of our community with such turmoil in the Church? We seemed safe enough for now, but nothing could be certain. As always, we could only wait, watch and pray.

Chapter 18

We began 1161 with two popes and two archbishops of Mainz. The world had, seemingly, gone mad!

At Rupertsberg, we kept to ourselves during the cold winter months. I continued to supervise the work in the scriptorium, which was plentiful. Hildegard was as busy as ever, teaching, writing, composing and running the affairs of the community. I often wondered how she managed to fit so much into each day. She was, truly, an inspiration to all of us, and although we tried to follow her example, we were not equal to the task.

Hildegard was progressing steadily with her second volume of visionary writings, 'The Book of Life's Merits', and I assisted her to the best of my ability. I remembered with both fondness and sadness how Hildegard, Richardis and I had worked together on *Scivias*, and wondered if Hildegard did the same. I did not repeat my mistake of reminding Hildegard of Richardis' absence in this process. She had suffered enough grief from that significant loss.

By spring, news had reached us from multiple sources of a new threat to the Church: the heresy of Catharism. The Cathars had, apparently, been moving north from Italy and were now establishing themselves in Germany, particularly in and around Cologne.

I had, of course, heard of the Cathars, but I did not know as much about their beliefs as did Hildegard.

"They believe in *two* Gods: one good and the other evil," Hildegard told me. "The good God, they say, is the God of the New Testament, creator of the spiritual realm, whereas the evil God, also called Satan, is the God of the Old Testament, creator of the physical world."

I was horrified. "How can they think that the beauty that is God's creation is evil, a work of the Devil?" I asked.

"What is more," Hildegard continued, "they do not believe that Christ was physically incarnate! They say that he was an angel in human *appearance* only. He had no substance, they say. He was merely illusory."

I shook my head on hearing these things, which were completely at odds with the orthodox teachings and beliefs of the Church. I could well understand why Hildegard was so alarmed at the spread of such falsehoods, but wondered who, among the faithful, could possibly believe such things.

"Surely, good and faithful Christians do not believe those teachings," I said.

"Good and faithful Christians have been so seriously neglected by the Church leaders that they are looking for an alternative, no matter how false or dangerous it might be," Hildegard replied. "They are not being taught true doctrine. They are not being led by the example of good, pious men. It is the fault of our lax, corrupt clergy that people are being led astray by these heretical teachings."

We sat in silence for a while. I was still shaking my head, still not understanding how anyone could believe these things. Hildegard was sitting opposite me, her jaw and fists clenched tight.

She looked at me with sudden resolve. I knew what was coming.

"I must speak out against this heresy!" she said. "I must travel to Cologne."

I sighed inwardly but smiled. "I will make the arrangements," I said.

Hildegard smiled. "Thank you, dear friend. I can always depend on you to do what is right."

199

Chapter 19

We spent the next two weeks planning our journey and contacting the people we hoped to visit. Hildegard decided that she wanted to go even further north than Cologne. There was a monastery that she wished to visit in Werden, which was at least 100 miles to the north of Cologne. It was becoming clear that we would be away from Rupertsberg for quite some time.

"This journey is going to take longer than the previous two," I said, looking up from the map, frowning slightly.

"Yes," Hildegard replied. "It will be challenging, but I must do it. Perhaps we can stay in some places a bit longer than planned, in order to rest and restore our energy."

Sister Hiltrud and I both nodded. That seemed a sensible idea.

On a cool morning in late April 1161, Hildegard, Sister Hiltrud and I were again farewelled from the forecourt of the Rupertsberg convent. Sister Clementia, who was again chosen to be the acting prioress in Hildegard's absence, led the community in praying for us on our journey. Some of the sisters struggled to hold back tears, and I knew that Hildegard would be sorely missed by them.

I was pleased that we were able to use our own boat on this journey. Although the borrowed vessel had been quite similar to ours, I still felt more comfortable with the boat on which I had received my training.

We sailed north along the Rhine River, heading for Andernach, which was our first official destination. For once, we were sailing *with* the flow of the river, although the winds were not always helpful.

Andernach was nearly sixty miles from Rupertsberg, and we made slow but steady progress. After a brief stop in Koblenz, where I paid a short visit to my mother and sisters, we arrived at Andernach towards the middle of May.

We were to visit and stay with the canonesses of St Mary, at the invitation of their superior, Tengswich. I was quite nervous about the meeting between Hildegard and Tengswich. Although nearly ten years had passed, the correspondence that had passed between them regarding some of the less common liturgical practices at Rupertsberg had been quite strained. I need not have worried. They embraced like old friends, and clearly felt deep affection and respect for one another.

We were made to feel very welcome at St Mary's, and I was interested to observe their daily practices and rituals. As a house of canonesses regular, they followed the Rule of St Augustine, rather than our Benedictine Rule. The former is somewhat less prescriptive than the latter, and is more flexible in its demands on individuals within the community. As a result, life at St Mary's was somewhat more relaxed than at Rupertsberg.

In early July, while we were at St Mary's, more news reached us regarding the situation in Mainz. Recognising the impracticality of having two archbishops, Frederick had convened the Synod of Lodi, and had persuaded his anti-pope, Victor IV, to depose both Christian and Rudolph. In their place, Frederick appointed Conrad I of Wittelsbach to be the new, and only, archbishop of Mainz, thereby eliminating at least one of the ecclesiastical schisms.

"Let us pray that this appointment by Frederick is more successful than his appointment of Arnold proved to be," I said to Hildegard when we had heard the news.

"Yes," Hildegard murmured. "Let us pray, indeed."

By September, Hildegard was ready to keep moving north.

"I want to reach Siegburg before the weather becomes too harsh," she said, so we bid our farewells and gave our thanks to Tengswich and her canonesses, and headed further north along the Rhine.

At the junction of the Rhine and the much smaller Sieg River, we followed the latter and arrived in Siegburg in mid-October. We were expected at the Benedictine monastery, Michaelsberg Abbey. The monastery was situated on the Michaelsberg (St Michael's Mount), about 130 feet above the town of Siegburg.

Hildegard was greeted at the abbey with great affection. She had been in correspondence with the brothers for some time, and many of them told me that they revered her as their spiritual mother.

Winter came early that year, and was in no hurry to depart. We stayed at Siegburg for six months, during which time we were included in daily life as if it were our home. Hildegard had many private discussions with individual brothers, always with Sister Hiltrud in attendance for the sake of propriety. Hildegard also led regular group discussions, in which Sister Hiltrud and I were also included. These covered a wide range of topics, reflecting Hildegard's broad knowledge and insight. We discussed Holy Scripture, theology, herbal medicine and music, among other things. We also discussed the worrying state of God's Church, and the brothers shared Hildegard's outrage concerning the heresies being promoted in our region.

When the spring of 1162 finally came, I was expecting to head to Cologne, which was only about 20 miles northeast of Siegburg. Hildegard, however, had other plans.

"I really want to be in Cologne on the feast day of St Ursula," she told me one chilly afternoon in mid-March. We were strolling in the monastery's orchard, the air nipping at our noses.

"October 21st?" I asked, knowing the date, and the saint, quite well.

"Yes," Hildegard replied. "I propose that we go to Werden next, and then go to Cologne as our last stop, on the way back to Rupertsberg."

That seemed as good a plan as any. I had no particular preferences as to how the journey should be organised, so I agreed to send messages to both Werden and Cologne, advising the church authorities of our travel plans.

We set off for Werden towards the end of March. The weather was still cold, but the snow had vanished, and new life was emerging in the forests and fields.

It took us a month to reach Werden. We sailed back along the Sieg River until it joined the Rhine, then headed north to where the Rhine met the Ruhr River. We then headed east (against the flow of the river, again!) along the Ruhr until we reached Werden. That was the most difficult sailing I had faced on this journey thus far.

Werden Abbey was an ancient place, founded by St Ludger at the end of the 8th Century. It was also wealthy, with possessions in Westphalia, Frisia, eastern Saxony and around the abbey itself, where it had territory of nearly 80 square miles. Despite this prosperity, daily life at the abbey was strict and austere, at least when we were there.

While we were treated with respect and courtesy by the abbott and brothers, I did not feel as welcome here as we had been made to feel in Andernach and Siegburg. There was a feeling of tension in the air, the source of which I could not identify, but it made me uneasy. I suspect Hildegard had the same feeling of dis-ease, as we departed after three months instead of the six we had originally intended.

The trip from Werden to Cologne was much more direct than the previous stage of the journey, but almost as challenging. Once we were back on the Rhine, we needed only to head south to reach our final destination but, as often seemed to be the case, the flow of the river was against us, and we did not reach Cologne until August.

Cologne was hot and crowded, and more than a little noisome, but this was to be expected in a large town during the summer months. We were to stay at the Monastery of St Mary's in the Capitol, which lies on the south side of the sprawling town. As we made our way there, I heard and then saw a crowd of people surrounding a single man, who was raised above the crowd, standing on a log. Initially, I feared for this man's safety, but quickly realised that the crowd was loudly indicating its agreement with what he was saying.

"You must renounce the evil God," the speaker said, "and devote your lives to the good God, the God who saves. Renounce also all pleasures of the flesh, which are the invention of the evil God." The cheers were a little less enthusiastic at this exhortation.

"You must renounce your material self if you are to break the cycle of reincarnation and achieve salvation through the *consolamentum*," the man continued. "Only then can you return to the good God as a perfect being." The cheers grew loud again on hearing this.

What? Reincarnation? Good and bad 'Gods'? It was then that I realised that this man must be a Cathar. Hildegard's face had been growing redder and redder as the man continued to speak, and her fists were clenched as if she intended to strike him. She opened her mouth to speak and began to move towards the crowd, but I seized hold of her arm and prevented her from doing so.

"Not here, Hildegard," I hissed. "Not now. We are hugely outnumbered and might well be set upon if the crowd becomes angry."

She relaxed her arms and hands, and stood still, limply. I released my grip on her arm.

"This *must* be stopped," she said softly, nearly in tears. "It is an abomination."

We hurried on to the monastery, where we were greeted with great enthusiasm by the abbess, Mother Gertrude. Her smile turned quickly into a frown.

"Mother Hildegard!" she said. "Are you unwell?" Hildegard was now pale and trembling as a result of our encounter with the preaching Cathar and the enthusiastic crowd.

I explained to Mother Gertrude what had just happened. She crossed herself rapidly three times.

"They are everywhere," she said. "One cannot go anywhere in town without hearing their lies. Please come in, everyone. You are safe here with us."

It was fortunate that we did not need to leave the confines of the monastery any time soon. Established around 100 years earlier, St Mary's was a well-equipped, self-sufficient community of devout sisters and brothers. Hildegard spent many hours in discussions and prayers with the sisters, while I was made to feel very welcome by Abbott Georg and the brothers.

By October, the weather was cool but pleasant. The Feast of St Ursula was fast approaching, and Hildegard and Sister Hiltrud were looking forward to the occasion eagerly.

On 21st October, we attended mass at the recently completed church of St Ursula, erected on the site where the saint's and her followers' remains had been discovered nearly 60 years earlier. It was a solemn and moving occasion, yet full of the joy felt by the truly faithful. Hildegard's face shone as she entered and worshipped in this beautiful church, remembering this holy woman and her brave companions.

After the mass, Hildegard remained in the church and prayed for hours, until it was nearly dark. I prayed for part of this time, but my knees became sore, so I sat and waited just outside the church. Sister Hiltrud joined me a bit later. She had prayed longer than I, but also could not continue kneeling any longer.

When Hildegard finally emerged, she smiled at us, her face a picture of both joy and serenity.

"What a great privilege it was to be here, in this holy place, on this day," she said, as the three of us walked back to St Mary's.

We remained at St Mary's during Advent, and celebrated Christmas there in much the same fashion as we would have done at Rupertsberg. I often thought about our community, and wondered how they were coping without Hildegard. We had been away for nearly two years by then, and had only received news from them occasionally.

Since we first arrived at St Mary's, Hildegard had been working, intermittently, on a sermon to preach to the clergy of Cologne. By January 1163, she was satisfied that the sermon was ready.

On a cold, clear Sunday morning in late January, Hildegard, Sister Hiltrud and I left St Mary's for the 20-minute walk to Cologne Cathedral. This is, indeed, an imposing structure. Built around 200 years earlier, it was by far the largest building I had ever seen.

Despite its enormity, the Cathedral was full that morning. At the invitation of Archbishop Rainald, we sat near the front of the congregation, on the same side as the pulpit. At the appropriate point in the liturgy, immediately after a reading from the Gospel according to St John, Hildegard rose from her seat and made her way to the pulpit. Memories of Trier came flooding back, and I hoped that this sermon would be less confronting. My hopes were soon to be dashed.

The silence was palpable. I realised I was gripping my seat so hard that my knuckles were white. I took a deep breath and tried to calm myself.

Hildegard collected her thoughts for a moment, and then began to speak.

"We must give thanks to God for all He has done for us, and for all of His created things, for these are the materials for the instruction of mankind. All that God creates is good."

This was not the opening I was expecting, but it was explained soon after.

"There is a terrible and dangerous heresy, abroad in our cities and towns, that seeks to refute the goodness of God's creation, and strikes at the very foundation of our faith: namely, the incarnation of our Lord Jesus Christ."

Some murmurings of agreement rippled through the congregation. I began to relax slightly. There was nothing controversial about this view.

"It is, of course, the Cathars of whom I speak," Hildegard continued. "Their beliefs are false and heretical, yet they are permitted to preach wherever it pleases them to do so. I have seen and heard them myself in this great city of Cologne."

There were disapproving murmurings at this, but I assumed these were directed at the Cathars.

"Yet you clergy do nothing to stop this outrage," she continued. My heart sank. "The Cathars are attracting followers, because they are passionate about their beliefs, and appear to lead simple, ascetic lives. But you are a bad example to others, since no rivulet of good reputation flows from you, so that, with respect to the soul, you have neither food to eat nor clothes to wear, but only unjust deeds without the good of knowledge. Therefore, your honour will perish, and the crown will fall from your head."

Now the murmurings sounded like disapproval of Hildegard, and I felt as anxious as I had in Trier. While everything that Hildegard was saying was true, it was not popular amongst those on the receiving end.

"Wake up!" Hildegard said, suddenly much louder. I jumped in my seat. "The misguided people of today have no idea what they are doing. They will fear these heretics, but serve them slavishly and imitate them as much as possible. And, when enough of the people have fallen into this error, they will persecute and exile the teachers and wise men who remain true to the Catholic faith."

Now the congregation seemed frightened, as well they might be. Hildegard sought to console them.

"Do not despair! They cannot drive away those of you who are mighty knights for God's justice. Moreover, they will not be able to influence and sway those who have a good grasp on their faith in doctrine and practice. So there can be hope for Cologne, but if the rest do not wake up to the situation and lend a hand to correct and drive out this heresy, then there *is* much to despair of."

Most of those present now sat quietly. They certainly had been given much to think about, but Hildegard had not quite finished. Her shoulders sagged slightly, and she sighed, before concluding.

"I have worn myself out for two whole years so that I might bring this message in person to the magistrates, teachers, and other wise men who hold the higher positions in the Church. Do not allow my efforts to have been made in vain."

Hildegard quietly stepped down from the pulpit and returned to her seat between Sister Hiltrud and me. After a brief pause, the liturgy resumed its normal course.

After the mass, we slipped away quickly and returned to St Mary's. Hildegard went to the room she was sharing with Sister Hiltrud, and did not emerge until the following day. It was clear that our journey had, indeed, worn her out, and it was now time to go home.

Chapter 20

It took us around three weeks to travel from Cologne to Rupertsberg, so we arrived home in late February 1163.

Our homecoming was a joyful occasion, for both the travellers and the waiting community. We had been gone for nearly two years, and I had never been more pleased to enter the large gates of the abbey and then hear them close with a satisfying thud behind me.

Dinner that evening was not a silent affair. Hildegard told of our journey, and answered the many questions that came from her listeners. Sister Clementia and Brother Arnold then reported the happenings at Rupertsberg in our absence. Fortunately, no major catastrophes had befallen the community while its leader was away.

The following day, Hildegard and I were walking in the flower garden, discussing our travels, when we were approached by Sister Birgitta. She looked downcast. Was there bad news that we had not yet been told?

"I am sorry to trouble you when you have only just returned, Mother," she began, "but I fear there may not be much time left, so I must speak to you now."

Hildegard and I exchanged looks of alarm. "What has happened?" Hildegard asked.

"It is Bertha," Sister Birgitta told us. "She is very ill and close to death. I have tried all that I can, but to no avail."

The three of us went to the infirmary where Bertha was in a bed, propped up by pillows. She was clearly having trouble breathing, and the reason was readily apparent. There was a huge tumour on her neck and chest.

"She has been unable to eat for many days and cannot even drink now," Sister Birgitta told us, choking back tears.

It was a shocking sight. Bertha had been such a faithful, devoted servant to the women, both at Disibodenberg and then at Rupertsberg. I closed my eyes and silently asked God to relieve her from her suffering.

Hildegard sat next to the bed and took Bertha's hand. Hildegard prayed for a few minutes, and then traced the sign of the Cross over the affected parts of Bertha's body.

Almost immediately, Bertha's breathing became less laboured. She began to breathe deeply, then fell into a deep sleep. I was amazed at the instant relief that Hildegard had been able to give the dying woman.

Hildegard laid Bertha's hand gently on the bed and stood up. "She needs to rest. Please keep me informed of her condition," she said to Sister Birgitta.

By the following day, Bertha was awake and asking for water. Within a week, the tumours had shrunk noticeably, and Bertha was able to eat again. Nobody could believe what they were seeing.

"This is a miracle, that *you* have performed," I said to Hildegard.

Hildegard smiled and shrugged slightly. "It is God's will. For God, anything is possible."

A few weeks later, Bertha's tumour had vanished, and she was back to her duties as if nothing had happened.

"Mother Hildegard saved my life," Bertha told me. "I thank God for her daily."

This was the first of Hildegard's miraculous healings that I bore witness to, but there have since been many other such instances, both within and beyond the Rupertsberg community.

On one occasion, one of the young nuns, also named Hildegard, was beset by a recurring fever, and could not be cured by any of Sister Birgitta's remedies. When Mother Hildegard heard of this, she went to the infirmary, placed her hand on the young nun, and by her blessing and prayers cast out the fever and healed her.

Another time, a certain Swabian from the village of Thalfingen had swollen up through his whole body and was in great pain. When he heard of Hildegard's miraculous powers of healing, he made the long and difficult journey to Rupertsberg to seek her help. Hildegard kept the man with her for several days. Finally, she traced over the weak man with her hands and blessed him, and he was almost instantly restored to full health.

Hildegard also cured many people who could not make the journey to Rupertsberg, even though she was also not able to travel to them. A certain Arnold of Wackerneim, whom Hildegard had known for some time, experienced such pain in his throat that he was having great difficulty drinking, eating, and even breathing. He wrote to Hildegard, begging for her prayers and intercessions on his behalf. Hildegard, of course, did as he asked, but decided to do even more. She blessed some water and sent it to the sick man. He later reported that, after he had sipped some of the blessed water, the pain left him completely and did not return.

Other people also gained immediate relief from sipping water blessed by Hildegard. In Bingen, the daughter of a woman named Hazecha fell ill, and was unable to speak for three days. When Hazecha came to Rupertsberg to seek Hildegard's help for her daughter, she was given some of this blessed water. She later told us that when her daughter sipped some of it, she immediately recovered her voice and strength.

In the same town and at the same time, a young man was beset by so severe an illness that he was thought to be close to death. Hazecha still had some of the water sent to her daughter, who was now well and no longer required the precious gift. Hazecha gave the young man some of the water to drink and then bathed his face with it. Hazecha told us that he quickly recovered his strength and was healed.

Many people also reported the restorative powers contained within small portions of Hildegard's hair or clothing. For example, the wife of the mayor of Bingen was experiencing a dangerously long labour, and fears were held that she would die. When a messenger ran swiftly to our convent, Sister Birgitta gave the messenger a plait of Hildegard's hair that she had kept for some time, and gave instructions that this should be girded around the woman's body. When this was done, the birth came to a swift and happy conclusion for both mother and child.

These are some of the more noteworthy instances of Hildegard's immense skill as a healer of the sick, but many more could be related. Hildegard refused to take credit for any of the healings.

"This is God's doing," she would say. "I am merely the conduit through which God's mercy is delivered. The true miracle is that God has chosen me, a poor little form of a woman, to be so honoured."

Whether the healing power should be attributed to God, Hildegard, or both, I could not say. I am not wise enough to speak with any authority on such matters. The only thing I knew for certain was that we were truly blessed to have Hildegard as the leader of our community, and, like Bertha, I thanked God for Hildegard every day.

Chapter 21

While we were on our travels, Hildegard and I had been able to make good progress with the writing and editing of her second book of visions. It was all but finished by the time we got home, so I was able to take it to our scriptorium for binding and copying shortly thereafter.

As I had done after the completion of *Scivias*, I assumed and hoped that Hildegard would not embark upon another major written work, at least not for the time being. I also hoped that she would be able to stay at home and rest. These major tours took quite a toll on her health, both physical and mental, and she was still exhausted after our most recent journey.

"Hopefully you will be able to rest now for a while," I said.

Hildegard smiled. "For a while, perhaps," she replied, "but it will only be a *short* while." As always, her prediction proved to be correct.

We had been home from our travels for around a month when a startling piece of correspondence arrived at Rupertsberg. It was an invitation (command?) from Emperor Frederick to Hildegard, asking her to visit him at the Imperial Palace at Ingelheim, where he was currently holding court. It seems that the emperor was very keen to meet the now-famous lady.

"This is excellent," Hildegard said when she had read the letter. "There is much I wish to discuss with our secular leader." My stomach tightened slightly on hearing this. I hoped Hildegard would not be too forthright in her discussions with this important and powerful man.

Ingelheim was less than a day's journey from Rupertsberg on horseback. Hildegard decided that a third person was not required for such a short journey, so only she and I would go.

On a cool but clear morning in mid-April, we set out early and headed east to Ingelheim. It was late afternoon by the time we reached Ockenheim, and Hildegard decided that we should stop there for the night. We could have reached Ingelheim by evening, but did not want to impose on our royal host. We had not, after all, been invited to *stay* at Ingelheim.

We found a small inn in Ockenheim. There was only one room available, so Hildegard slept in that, and I shared the stable with our horses. I would have been quite comfortable, if not for the snoring stablehand.

We left Ockenheim early the next day and covered the remaining five miles to Ingelheim by midday. When we arrived, our horses were led away by a groom, and we were escorted to a large, lavishly furnished antechamber. A young page invited us to be seated while we waited to be seen by the emperor.

We could hear voices coming from the adjoining room, one of which was decidedly raised. An angry man was making his displeasure abundantly clear to at least one other person. Hildegard and I exchanged anxious glances. I was not sure that I wanted to meet Frederick if he was in a bad mood.

The recipient of this tongue-lashing, a middle-aged man in military uniform, came out of the room after a few minutes and closed the door carefully. He looked at us and then hurried away, red-faced.

The young page then knocked quietly on the door. "Enter!" was bellowed in response. The page entered the room and closed the door. The voice was less heated now, but could still be heard. We waited a few more minutes until the page came out.

"Emperor Frederick will see you now," he said, holding the door open for us. Hildegard and I entered this even larger, more lavish room, and the page closed the door quickly behind us. We were now alone with this famous and powerful man, and I had to fight an urge to turn and run.

Frederick was seated on the other side of a large table, facing us but studying what appeared to be several maps spread out before him. His brow was furrowed, and his hirsute chin was resting in his large left hand. After a short time, he looked up, smiled when he saw Hildegard, and rose to greet her.

"My lady Hildegard," he said, coming round the table and toward us. "I am honoured that you were able to accept my invitation."

"I was honoured to receive it, Your Majesty," Hildegard replied, curtseying.

I bowed, then examined the approaching figure. Frederick known as Barbarossa was an impressive presence. He was not overly tall, perhaps half a head taller than I, but he was solidly built and carried himself with an air of unquestioned authority. The bushy red beard, for which he was well-known, was also most striking. He turned from Hildegard to me, and his smile vanished.

"This is Brother Volmar," Hildegard began, "my ..."

"Thank you, Brother," Frederick interrupted. "I wish to speak to the lady in private. You may wait outside."

I hesitated, looking from Frederick to Hildegard. Despite my earlier urge to flee, I did not think I should leave Hildegard alone, unattended, with such a man.

"*Thank* you, Brother," Frederick repeated through gritted teeth as he glared at me.

I looked at Hildegard again. She smiled and nodded at me, so I bowed again and retreated backwards out of the room.

I might have stood close to the door in an attempt to overhear the conversation between Frederick and Hildegard, but the young page was in the anteroom and motioned for me to sit in a chair that was well away from the door. I could hear voices, but could not discern the words being spoken.

After what seemed an age, but what was, in truth, about an hour, the door opened, and Hildegard emerged, her face impassive. I tried to read her expression. Was she happy? Sad? Angry? She did not seem to be any of these things. I could not tell whether she was pleased with her audience with the emperor or not. When she looked at me and smiled, I smiled back and felt more relaxed.

Frederick followed Hildegard into the anteroom and instructed the page to arrange a meal for us. I was quite hungry from our journey, and the food at the inn had been quite poor. I was pleased to hear that we were to be fed before we set out on the return journey.

Frederick returned to his room and closed the door without another word. Hildegard and I were escorted to the large dining room, where we were served an excellent meal. Feeling well satisfied, we left the palace in mid-afternoon.

I was not keen to spend another night at Ockenheim, so we stopped at Gau-Algesheim. It was, in truth, too early to stop for the evening, but there were no other suitable places before Ockenheim.

The food and accommodation were much better in Gau-Algesheim, although we did have a much longer journey the following day. We did not reach Rupertsberg until after Vespers, and went straight to our beds.

On our journey home, I had hoped that Hildegard would relate details of her discussion with Frederick. She did not seem keen to do so, and I have never liked to press her when she was unwilling to speak. Consequently, I resigned myself to the fact that I might never know what had passed between them.

Towards the end of April, a document arrived at Rupertsberg which seemed to give some indication of at least one matter that was discussed by Frederick and Hildegard. It was a formal charter, signed and sealed by Emperor Frederick, and dated 18 April 1163, the day following our visit to Ingelheim.

The Charter proclaimed that Emperor Frederick took 'the monastery of Rupertsberg located at Bingen and its nuns who serve God there, and their possessions both movable and immovable and their fields and all matters belonging to the aforesaid place' under his protection, so that 'it should always continue free and secure from all attacks and injustices.'

I frowned as I read the document. Imperial protection was all well and good, but why was such protection deemed necessary? Surprising as this was, I was even more astonished to note that the protection was acquired 'through the intervention and petition of the venerable abbess, lady Hildegard.'

I looked up from the document with raised eyebrows. '*You* requested this from Frederick?" I asked, breaking my usual rule of never questioning Hildegard's decisions and actions. "Why?"

Hildegard looked away. "I fear we live in troubled times," she replied. "I felt that such a Charter was necessary to protect the wellbeing of this community."

I rolled up the parchment and handed it back to Hildegard. She appeared to know more than she was willing to say, but I decided not to push the matter further. She was, after all, a very wise and intelligent leader of our community, so I knew that her reasons for taking this action would be sound.

Later that year, a letter arrived for Hildegard from Emperor Frederick. As Hildegard's secretary, I read all correspondence that arrived for her, to determine its importance. Letters concerning matters of significance were always referred to Hildegard, while more routine correspondence was often dealt with by me or another member of the community. This was obviously a letter of significance.

After the standard greeting, it read as follows.

'We inform you, holy lady that we now have in hand those things you predicted to us when we invited you to our presence while we were holding court in Ingelheim. We will continue to strive with all our efforts for the honour of our kingdom.'

It seemed that Hildegard had predicted future events during her discussion with Frederick at Ingelheim. This was not something that Hildegard often did, although she did occasionally predict the dire consequences likely to flow from the bad behaviour of sinful clergy. Whatever the predictions had been concerning Frederick, they had obviously been accurate! The letter went on.

'Please be assured that with regard to that matter you directed to our attention we will be swayed by neither the friendship nor the hatred of any person, but with respect to justice alone, we intend to be equitable.'

This was intriguing. Hildegard had obviously been giving advice to the emperor as to how he should deal with a particular situation, but I had no idea what that situation might be. Once again, I was disappointed that Hildegard had not seen fit to disclose the details of their discussions, but I accepted that this was her decision to make and not for me to question. I could only hope that Frederick did, as he

promised, act with justice and equity in this and all matters
that might impact upon the life of our community.

Chapter 22

The year 1164 began peacefully enough, but all good things must come to an end.

On 20 April, the antipope Victor IV died.

"What will happen now?" I asked Hildegard when the news reached us in early May.

"Let us hope that the schism is ended," Hildegard replied. "There is no need for an election, as Alexander continues on, so there cannot be another disputed election."

I nodded. That seemed perfectly reasonable, but the ways of men can often be quite *un*reasonable.

About a month later, news reached us that a small number of cardinals who had supported Victor had met in Lucca to elect Victor's successor. They chose one Guido of Crema, who took the name of Paschal III.

Hildegard was horrified. "This is madness!" she exclaimed. "Surely the emperor will put a stop to this. A *second* antipope is unthinkable."

"We can only hope that the emperor will do the right thing," I replied, shaking my head. "We will have to wait and see."

As if that were not enough, tragic news of a more personal nature reached us in late June.

Hildegard received a letter from Abbott Hildelin of Schoenau, advising that Sister Elisabeth had died on 18 June. She was only 34 years old.

I was with Hildegard when she opened and read the letter, and could tell at once that the news was dire. As she quickly read the letter, her face grew pale, she drew in a sharp breath, and then began to weep. I could see that she would be unable to tell me anything, so I gently removed the letter from her hand and read it for myself.

It seemed that Elisabeth had returned to her harshly ascetic and self-punishing practices which had, quite predictably, taken a mortal toll on her already fragile body. Hildegard was inconsolable, and my heart, again, ached for her. Another close friend, taken far too young. Had God not given this poor woman enough grief for one lifetime?

Chapter 23

Early in 1165, more news arrived about the ongoing papal schism. Frederick had, apparently, been lukewarm in his reception of Paschal. In order to gain support from Frederick, Paschal had canonised Charlemagne in a magnificent ceremony at Aachen. This proved to be a wise move by Paschal. Frederick was so pleased with this new German saint, that he crushed all German opposition to the new antipope, and embarked upon a fourth Italian campaign to prevent the formation of an alliance between Pope Alexander and the Byzantine Emperor, Manuel I.

Hildegard was furious. "So much for 'the honour of the kingdom'," she fumed. My stomach tightened. What would she do? "I cannot remain silent this time," she went on. "I will write to Frederick to express my disapproval of his actions." I closed my eyes and groaned inwardly.

As I did with all of Hildegard's formal correspondence, I helped with her letter to Frederick by ensuring that the Latin was as polished as possible. I did not dispute her choice of words, however, and I prayed that our Charter of Protection would prove to be effective. The letter read as follows.

'O King, there is great necessity that you be careful in your dealings. I see you, in mystical vision, like a child playing insanely before the Living Eyes. You have yet time to get earthly things in control. Be wary, lest the highest King strike you to earth for the blindness of your own eyes, which do not see rightly how you would hold that sceptre in your hand for right ruling. So look to it. Be such that the Mercy of God does not die out in you.'

When I had put these words into the best Latin I could, I stared at the parchment for a few moments, horrified. Then I looked at Hildegard.

"Do you think it is – er – *wise* to call the emperor an insane child?" I knew I was breaking my 'no questions' rule again, but I was quite reluctant to send this letter in its current form.

Hildegard raised her eyebrows, perhaps surprised at my query. "It is not *I* that name him thus," she replied. "I am merely the conduit that conveys God's words."

I nodded, and smiled weakly. I hoped Frederick would recognise that this was so.

The continuation of the papal schism also had consequences for our diocese of Mainz. Archbishop Conrad, with whom Hildegard had established a good relationship, continued to support the legitimate pope, Alexander and refused to accept a second antipope. Later that year, Conrad was forced from his position in Mainz, and fled to France and then Rome, where he supported Alexander in his efforts against Frederick.

To our amazement, Conrad was replaced by a previous incumbent, Christian von Buch, who had held the position briefly after the murder of Archbishop Arnold. Hildegard was not pleased when this news reached us.

"He is not even an ordained priest!" she said. "Can these men do nothing in the best interests of God and His Church?"

I was uncertain how to respond to this question. I had no doubt of their *ability* to do the right thing, but it seemed clear that they were un*willing* to act in the way they should. This, of course, made their behaviour all the worse.

Hildegard did not seem to be expecting an answer, so I murmured sympathetic agreement but remained otherwise silent. I, like she, despaired for the Church, which seemed to have lost all connection with a loving, Christian God. All we could do was serve God to the best of our abilities and nurture and guide the community at Rupertsberg to do likewise.

Chapter 24

By the spring of 1165, it had become apparent that our community had grown almost to bursting point. As expected, our numbers had increased considerably since we established Rupertsberg Abbey 15 years earlier, but we thought, when designing and constructing the buildings, that we had allowed ample room for such expansion. It seemed that we had underestimated the extent of the desire to join Hildegard's holy community.

Brother Arnold and I surveyed the Rupertsberg grounds one morning in April. He scratched his chin as he looked around with an expert eye. "We cannot expand at ground level," he said. "The slopes make that too difficult."

I could also see that that was not possible. "Perhaps we could build upwards," I suggested. "We could add upper levels to at least some of our existing buildings."

"My thoughts exactly," Brother Arnold replied, smiling.

We took our idea to Hildegard. She listened intently, nodding as we spoke.

"Hm, yes. That is a good suggestion, but I have another idea, one that struck me as we were returning from Cologne," she told us.

I raised my eyebrows. Cologne? That was two years ago. Hildegard had obviously foreseen the need for us to expand some time ago.

"On the other side of the Rhine, about four miles to the north, I noticed the ruins of a large stone building. It looked like an old monastery. The nearest town to the building is Rudesheim, so I wrote to the local priest, Father Robert, to ask what he knew of the place. He came to see me a short time later, and told me that the building had been an Augustinian canonry until quite recently."

"Recently?" I asked. "So why is it in ruins?"

Hildegard looked sombre, and paused before replying. "It was destroyed on the orders of the emperor in 1160 when the canons voiced their disapproval of Frederick's endorsement of Victor IV as pope."

The hair on my head, or what little of it remained, stood on end. That fate might have befallen Rupertsberg if we had voiced our objections at that time. Apart from her oblique criticism of Frederick during her sermon in Trier, Hildegard had said nothing public about the emperor, and nothing at all about the schism. I now saw the wisdom in this, and also the reason for obtaining the Charter of Imperial Protection.

"I have not been to the place," Hildegard continued, "so I do not know if we can use it for a second convent. Perhaps you can go and inspect the site for me," she said, smiling and looking at both of us.

About a week later, when some wet weather had passed, Brother Arnold and I set out in our little cog to see what, if anything, could be done with the ruins.

The canonry had been situated at a place called Eibingen. We were able to land the boat on the riverbank below the ruins, and make our way up the hill to the site.

When we reached the top of the hill, we stopped to survey the scene. Neither of us spoke for a moment. We looked at each other, open-mouthed. What appeared to have been an extensive and well-resourced community was now a scene of utter devastation.

"They did a thorough job on the place," Brother Arnold finally said.

"This was a wicked deed," I said quietly. I sighed deeply and waited for my anger to subside before speaking again. "Do you think we can make any use of these – remnants?" I asked.

"It will be a major undertaking," Brother Arnold said with a sigh, no doubt remembering the time and effort required to bring the Rupertsberg site to an acceptable standard.

"Still," he said, brightening. "I like a challenge and, if truth be told, I am a little bored at present. Everything is running so smoothly at Rupertsberg that there is often not much for me to do."

I laughed. "Well, *this* will keep you busy for quite some time, I would think."

We returned to Rupertsberg and reported our findings to Hildegard.

"I will seek the necessary permissions from the archbishop," she said. "I would like the work to begin by the end of spring, if possible."

Permission was obtained from Mainz, but not from Christian. The archbishop was on campaign in Italy with Emperor Frederick. Apparently, our archbishop very rarely even *went* to Mainz!

"That might be a blessing," Hildegard had said when we were told. "He can cause less trouble if he is absent."

Work began at Eibingen in late May. Brother Arnold was in his element, supervising and directing the building works, which provided much employment for the men of the nearby villages.

Hildegard and I visited the new site several times during summer. She seemed pleased with what she saw.

"This is going to work well as a sister convent," she said one day towards the end of July. "We will be able to accept many new novices."

"Are you going to run both houses?" I asked. "I think that would be an onerous undertaking." I had been wondering about this for some time, so seized this opportunity to raise the matter.

"I will retain ultimate authority and responsibility," she said, "but I will need to appoint a senior nun to live permanently on site as my deputy."

I nodded, relieved. That seemed like the best solution. "Who will you choose for this task?"

"I have been praying and thinking on this matter," she replied, "but have not yet decided. God will reveal the right person to me."

About a week later, Hildegard told me what she had decided. "The leader of the Eibingen convent must be a mature, experienced sister whom I can fully trust. I have, therefore, asked Sister Hiltrud to take on this responsibility. She does not believe that she is worthy for this honour, but I think I have persuaded her otherwise."

"She is an excellent choice," I said. Hildegard had spent a lot of time with Sister Hiltrud while they were together on Hildegard's preaching tours, and I also had the opportunity to get to know her well. There was no better candidate in the whole community for this post. She was pious, devoted to God and Hildegard, and had gained excellent administrative skills while assisting Hildegard in the running of the Rupertsberg community.

"The Eibingen convent will also need its own infirmary," Hildegard continued, "and I have asked Sister

Birgitta to be the new infirmarian there. We will miss her greatly, but she has trained many sisters to take on the infirmary duties here in her place. Sister Mathilde, in particular, has shown considerable skill and devotion in her work in our infirmary. She is ready to assume leadership, I believe."

I nodded in agreement. "Both are excellent choices," I said. I would miss Sister Birgitta, whom I had known since she arrived at Disibodenberg as a novice many years earlier. She had been a wonderful infirmarian and a much-loved member of our community. Sister Mathilde had rather large shoes to fill, but seemed capable of doing so.

By the end of October, enough of the building work had been completed to allow a small group of nuns to take up residence at the new convent. Sister Hiltrud, Sister Birgitta and ten other nuns, including three novices, made the journey. There was still building work to be done. The chapel, for instance, was only half-finished, but there were places to sleep, eat, and meet for worship.

Some work was possible during the winter months, but the majority of it was completed during the spring of 1166. In May of that year, the rebuilt chapel was completed, and was dedicated in honour of the Holy Virgin Mary by the Bishop of Bamburg.

Around this time, Hildegard started visiting the new convent twice a week, to ensure that everything was running smoothly. I accompanied her on these trips whenever I could, which was nearly always. This was a happy time for both of us, I believe. The establishment of this sister-convent was a source of great joy and accomplishment for Hildegard.

"I see the establishment of this new community as another aspect of the work I am doing to spread God's message," she said as we returned to Rupertsberg one evening in mid-summer, "but there is still much that I must do, while I am able."

I frowned at this. "You are *more* than able," I said.

Hildegard smiled, but the smile was wistful. "For now," she said, then looked away. She said nothing more for the rest of the short journey, and I wondered what she knew that I did not.

Chapter 25

In August that year, on a hot summer afternoon, I was summoned to the gatehouse to greet a visitor. As I approached the gatehouse, I could see a tall Benedictine monk standing outside the gate, looking at the view from the top of our hill. When he turned and saw me, his handsome young face broke into a beaming smile.

"Brother Volmar!" he said. "How wonderful to see you again!"

I returned his infectious smile, but wondered if I knew the man.

"Good day to you, Brother," I said. "You are very welcome, of course, but – have we met before?"

"I suppose I probably *have* changed since we last met," he said with a laugh. "It is I, Roric. Brother Roric now, as you can see."

I laughed with surprise and delight. "Roric! Yes, you *have* changed, but for the better. You look very well."

"Thank you," he replied. "As do you. How is Mother Hildegard? I hope she is also well."

"Yes, quite well," I replied. "How is it that we may serve you this day?"

"I would very much like to speak with Mother Hildegard and you on a personal matter, if I may," he replied.

I gestured toward the abbey's front door. "Of course. Come this way. We will see if she is available."

Hildegard was both available and intrigued by the young monk's visit. The three of us gathered in Hildegard's audience chamber, and sipped wine that Bertha served us.

"I will be brief," Roric began. "I know that your time is God's, and not to be wasted." Hildegard nodded and smiled. Roric took another sip of wine before continuing.

"Ever since I first came to Rupertsberg as a boy with my father – you might remember me at the building works – I have longed to be part of your holy community here." He laughed nervously. "You may also remember, as I do with embarrassment, that I came here when I was 14, seeking to join your community of nuns." Hildegard and I both smiled. That was not an event to be forgotten easily. "You very kindly assisted me to enter the monastery at Disibodenberg," Roric said to Hildegard, "where I have been for the past 13 years. I have been very happy there, and it has been a privilege to serve God as part of that community." He paused, sipping his drink.

I wondered where this conversation could possibly lead, and could see that Hildegard also looked puzzled. Roric finished his drink and placed his cup on the table. He looked at the floor for a moment, then looked up at Hildegard with a sudden look of great determination.

"I wish to become an anchorite, attached to this holy community, and live out my days in solitary service to God through prayer and fasting," he said rapidly, then bit his lower lip, waiting for Hildegard's response.

Hildegard's eyebrows arched in surprise. "I see," she said, sounding calmer than she looked. "This is, of course, a matter of which I have some personal knowledge and experience," she continued.

Roric nodded enthusiastically. "Yes," he said. "I have been told of your confinement with the Lady Jutta at Disibodenberg. It was this that has inspired me to follow this path."

Hildegard and I looked at each other. I felt lost for words. I remembered the day I had witnessed Lady Jutta and Hildegard being sealed into their 'tomb', and had never quite managed to quell my revulsion at the idea of this drastic form of service to God. Why would this healthy, apparently intelligent young man wish to live like this? I did not understand, but decided not to voice my opinions on that occasion.

"We will, of course, need to discuss this in Chapter," Hildegard said, looking back at Roric. "For myself, I would have no objection to accepting you as an anchorite, and would welcome such devoted service to God being associated with this community." She smiled warmly at Roric, and he beamed at her, his face glowing as it had when she blessed him at age 14.

I felt a moment of irrational, sinful jealousy when I saw how he looked at Hildegard, but quickly dismissed this and chastised myself. I probably looked at her in exactly the same way when I was young. Indeed, I well understood how easy it was to be overcome by her presence.

Hildegard rose from her seat. "Please feel welcome to stay at our guest house this night, before returning to Disibodenberg in the morning. I will take this matter to Chapter, and advise you of the community's decision as soon as is possible."

Roric bowed and thanked Hildegard. I escorted the young monk to the guest house and arranged a room for him. "You are welcome, of course, to join us for prayer and our evening meal," I said.

The next day, Roric returned to Disibodenberg. Hildegard and I spoke at length about the possibility of establishing an anchorage at Rupertsberg. Neither of us could see any good reason to refuse the young monk's request.

"If a men's community can accept an anchor*ess*, why should a women's community not accommodate an anchor*ite*?" Hildegard asked. I could find no basis on which to disagree.

The Chapter meeting the following morning was livelier than it had been for quite some time. There were very firm opinions both for and against the proposal, but the majority did not seem opposed to the idea.

"Surely, it could only enhance the reputation of our community," said Sister Clementia. "It is a very special type of service to God."

Most people murmured agreement.

Brother Arnold raised his hand tentatively. "May I speak, my lady?" he asked Hildegard.

"Of course, Brother Arnold," Hildegard replied with a broad smile. "We would welcome the benefit of your views on the matter."

Brother Arnold stood up and cleared his throat. "I have known Roric – that is, *Brother* Roric – since he was 12 years old. Although I have not seen him since he entered Disibodenberg, I knew him to be a devout and sincere young man, and I believe that his desire to serve God in this way, here at Rupertsberg, is genuine and to be encouraged. That is all." He sat down quickly and examined his feet.

Brother Arnold was a much-loved member of our community, and hardly ever expressed his views in public. I got the impression that his short but heart-felt speech gave the naysayers pause for thought, as there were no more objections voiced at the meeting that day.

"I would like to give people some time to think and pray about this," Hildegard said. "We will vote at tomorrow's meeting."

In the end, it was not even a close-run thing. Only two members of the community voted against the proposal to accept Brother Roric as an anchorite at Rupertsberg. The overwhelming majority were in favour of the idea, and Hildegard announced her plans for the building of the anchorite's small cell.

"Brother Arnold?" Hildegard said, smiling. "Perhaps you would like to take charge of the construction of the cell?"

Brother Arnold smiled broadly. He stood up and bowed to Hildegard. "It will be both an honour and a pleasure," he said.

Hildegard, Brother Arnold and I surveyed our grounds to choose the best place to build the anchorage. We decided upon a small patch of garden at the south end of the cemetery and close to the church, so that Brother Roric might hear, and take part in, the singing of the daily Offices.

The building was completed in about a month, and on 1 October 1166, Brother Roric was entombed in his cell with the same ritual that had so fascinated and appalled me half a century earlier.

Chapter 26

arly in 1167, Hildegard's health began to deteriorate. She started moving about the convent more slowly, and with less energy and enthusiasm than previously. She even stopped singing as she walked around the cloister and the gardens. This was definitely a bad sign.

For most of that year, she managed to perform all of her duties as spiritual leader of our community, but it became increasingly difficult for her to continue. Finally, just after Christmas, she took to her bed.

For several weeks, well into the new year, Hildegard was barely conscious. As on previous such occasions, I ensured that there were two sisters with her at all times, to assist her with eating, drinking and other bodily requirements, and to watch for any signs that her health was deteriorating further. Mostly, she slept.

This continued for some time. Around Easter, she sat up abruptly while I was sitting with her and praying.

"I have just had the most amazing vision!" she said. These were her first words in nearly six months.

"Do not exert yourself," I said, startled but delighted at this sudden revival. "Lie back and rest."

"I cannot," she replied, grasping my hand, her eyes bright with excitement. "I must tell you of this vision!"

"Very well," I said, laughing now, "but do lie down and tell it to me. Bring her some water, please," I said to a young nun who was hovering nearby, open-mouthed.

Hildegard lay back down and closed her eyes briefly, before beginning.

"This was unlike any vision I have ever had," she told me. "It was so full of secrets that I was shaken in my inmost being, and I was out of my body and in a trance." She paused for a moment while she drank some of the water brought to her. "This time, my consciousness was changed in such a way that I felt as if I did not know myself anymore. Just like the gentle drops of rain, the Spirit of God entered my soul and taught me every word of the Gospel written by John the Evangelist, which speaks of the work of God from the beginning, and I felt able to expound it to all." She began to sit up, excited. "And I saw that this explanation would have to be the beginning of another writing which has not yet been revealed. In it, many questions of the divine and mystery-laden creation will be examined." Exhausted, her head flopped back onto the pillow, and she closed her eyes, breathing heavily.

Another major work, I thought, but it sounded fascinating rather than burdensome. I had been sitting listening, wide-eyed. This was, indeed, an extraordinary vision, more so even than Hildegard's previous visions.

The next day, Hildegard seemed feverish. Her face was red, and her forehead was beaded with perspiration, even though it was not a warm day. I instructed the sisters to cool her face with moistened cloths. This did seem to reduce her fever somewhat, but she was barely conscious.

I prayed that she was just exhausted from her efforts the previous day and would soon recover, but this was not to be. She remained in this feverish, semi-conscious state for the next six months, and I doubted that she would ever return to us. Pairs of sisters again sat with her at all times and attended to her needs. I sat with her for part of every day, praying for her, talking to her, *begging* her to return to us. I felt a dark cloud of gloom hovering above my head, travelling with me wherever I went during that time. I felt sure that I would never again be happy.

Then, in late September 1168, one of the young sisters whose turn it was to sit with Hildegard came rushing out of the bedchamber, shrieking.

"She is awake! Our blessed Mother is awake!"

I was in the scriptorium when I heard these words. I dropped the parchment I had been examining, and ran towards the bedchamber.

When I got to the door, I stopped abruptly, uncertain what I would find within. My uncertainty must have showed as I entered the room.

"Come in, dear Volmar," Hildegard said. "Do not be concerned." She was sitting up, smiling at me. I could not decide whether to laugh or cry, so I did both. The tears rolled down my cheeks as I advanced towards the bed, sat next to Hildegard and took her hand, something I almost never did.

"It is *so* good to find you awake, dear Mother Hildegard," I said.

She continued to smile, squeezed my hand, then withdrew hers gently.

"What has ailed you for so long?" I asked as I wiped my cheeks with the sleeve of my robe.

Still upright, Hildegard leaned back against her pillow as she considered my question.

"This illness was blown into me by a blast of the south wind, whereby my body was ground down by such sufferings that my soul could scarcely bear it," she began. "For half a year the blast so went through my body that I was in as great an agony as if my soul were about to quit this life." I winced at this. Hildegard paused and swallowed hard before continuing.

"Then there came another blast of moist wind which mingled itself with this heat in such a way that my flesh was somewhat cooled, otherwise it would have been utterly burnt up." She paused again.

"I wondered many times whether you would ever recover," I said, my voice catching in my throat. "It has been such a long time."

Hildegard brightened a little. "I knew that I would recover," she said. "I saw in true vision that my life had not yet done with its earthly course, but was to be prolonged for some time yet."

"For that, we give thanks to God," I said, smiling.

Hildegard rested for a few days, but was fully awake and able to eat, drink, and walk slowly around the room. After this brief respite, she became keen to know what had been happening during her illness. While, for the most part, there was little to tell, we had recently received news of two matters that I knew would be of considerable interest to her. I was not completely certain that she was well enough to hear about these things – one matter, in particular, would anger her greatly - but I knew that she wanted to be kept informed. I braced myself and began to tell her what had transpired.

Chapter 27

The first of these matters concerned the ongoing papal schism. News had reached us that the second antipope, Paschal III, had died on 20 September. While this could, and should, have been the end of the schism, a *third* antipope, to be known as Callixtus III, had been elected almost immediately after Paschal's death.

I told Hildegard of this development tentatively, fearing an eruption of outrage that would not be good for her health.

"Has the emperor endorsed this election?" she asked after a moment's thought.

"Not that we have yet heard," I replied. "It is my understanding that Frederick is attempting to resolve matters with Pope Alexander. If those negotiations succeed, and Frederick supports the true pope, there will be no role for Callixtus to play, presumably."

Hildegard nodded. "We will wait and see," was all that she said.

I was surprised and relieved by the mildness of Hildegard's response to this news. I then told her of the second matter of importance.

"Shortly before your awakening, we received a letter of petition from Gedolf, Abbott of Brauweiler, concerning a certain noble woman, one Sigewize, who has been possessed for some years by a malevolent spirit," I told Hildegard.

She nodded. "Yes. I know of this matter," she said.

My brow furrowed. How could Hildegard possibly know about this?

She smiled at my obvious puzzlement. "While I lay ill, messengers came to me about this woman again and again," she explained. "In a true vision, I saw that God had permitted her to be possessed and overshadowed by a kind of blackness and smoke of a diabolical fog, which oppresses all the senses of her rational soul. So this woman has lost the right use of her senses and action, and constantly shouts out and does unseemly things."

"Yes," I said, amazed. "That is exactly what the abbott says in his letter. He also tells us that the woman's friends, who have been trying to help her for nearly eight years, took her to the abbott for his assistance." Hildegard nodded. "For three months now," I continued, "he has laboured in every way to set the woman free from the menacing enemy, but has made no headway at all." I paused briefly, reluctant to impose so great a burden upon Hildegard when she had been so ill, but knowing I must tell the tale in full. "His hope now rests, after God, in you, because this demon has finally made known to the abbott that the possessed woman can be set free only by your intervention."

Hildegard did not reply immediately. Finally, she said, "I must do all that I can to help this poor soul. First, I will instruct all of the sisters to apply themselves to both public and private prayers for the woman. Next, I will write to the abbott, telling him what must be done."

Hildegard was still too weak to write, so she dictated the instructions to me.

"The abbott must choose seven priests of known good character. After fasts, scourgings, prayers, almsgivings and celebrations of masses, these priests must then, with humble disposition and in priestly vestments and stoles, approach the sufferer. As they stand around her, they must each hold a rod in the likeness of the rod used by Moses in the wilderness," Hildegard began.

She then dictated an elaborate procedure, in which the first priest was to exhort the malevolent spirit to be gone. This must then be followed by all seven priests striking the woman with their rods – not too hard – upon her head, back, chest, navel, kidneys, knees, and feet. After this, the spirit would be summoned and vanquished repeatedly, such summonses to be interspersed with further beatings. I did not say what I was thinking: *if the spirit does not kill her, the beatings surely will!*

The next paragraph that Hildegard spoke amazed me even further. "If, after this procedure, the evil spirit has not yet been expelled, let the second priest along with the other priests standing by him follow the same sequence until God comes to his help."

After an additional, final paragraph, the letter was complete.

"You must take this letter to the abbott and ensure that this procedure is followed," she told me. "When it has been done, recite the final paragraph over the woman."

Brauweiler lies over 100 miles from Rupertsberg, near to Cologne. The journey took me a week of solid riding upon our best rouncey. I decided that travelling by horse would be quicker than sailing, and I did not wish to tackle the Rhine unaccompanied.

I was greeted very warmly by Abbott Gedolf. I explained that Hildegard could not make the journey herself, as she was still recovering from a long illness.

When the abbott had read Hildegard's letter, he immediately sought the required priests and implements.

On a cold November evening, the seven priests, the abbott, most of the brothers, and I gathered in a large chamber where Sigewize lay on her bed. Once we were positioned around the afflicted woman, the abbott nodded to the first priest, who began the elaborate procedure in stentorian tones.

I watched, fascinated and horrified. Although the beatings were gentle, they were so numerous that I feared for the woman's physical wellbeing. I could only hope that they would be beneficial, at least for her spiritual health.

Hildegard had warned me that this particular demon would not easily be expelled. "He will ignore and mock even the cross of the Lord and relics of the saints and other things which pertain to the service of God," she had told me. She was not mistaken.

All seven of the priests had intoned the words and administered the beatings to no obvious effect. I then approached the woman, and read the following in a clear, measured voice.

"I, Hildegard, O blaspheming spirit of mockery, speak to you in the name of that Truth in which I, by the light of Wisdom, have seen and heard these things. I command you by that name Wisdom to depart from this human being, leaving her in a stable condition, and not in the turbulence of your instability."

When I had finished, the foul spirit gave out an almighty roar, and with much caterwauling and screeching came out of the woman, to the utter fright of the bystanders.

When Sigewize realised she had been set free, she reached out her hand and one of the brothers helped her up. She was too weak to do so without such assistance. She then prostrated herself before the altar and gave thanks to God for her liberation.

The abbott and brothers were amazed and overjoyed at this outcome, and gave thanks and praise to God by intoning the hymn *Te Deum laudamus* ('Thee, O God, We Praise"). Then, unfortunately, while all were still celebrating, the evil spirit came back and sought out again the vessel he had just abandoned.

Sigewize began to quake all over, and with a hissing and shouting, raised herself up and started raving more wildly than before. At this, the brothers were terrified. I was overwhelmed by disappointment, at the failure of the elaborate and demanding procedure.

"How can this be?" I asked nobody in particular. Then, to the spirit I said, "How *dare* you return to God's creature in defiance of His command to leave!" Unsurprisingly perhaps, I received no reply.

The following day, everybody again assembled in the chamber, and the procedure was repeated. This time, the spirit snarled and shouted that it would not leave except in the presence of 'the little old hag in the regions of the upper Rhine, Scrumpilgard, the little old crone' herself. All present knew that it was Hildegard to whom he referred, and I was greatly angered at such disrespect, but not greatly surprised. What could one expect from an evil spirit?

"It has told me this before," said Abbott Gedolf. "It seems that it is true to its word."

The next morning, I left the abbey and returned to Rupertsberg, feeling utterly defeated. I knew that Hildegard was not well enough to make the journey to Brauweiler. What, then, was to become of Sigewize?

The cold weather of winter had arrived suddenly, and travel was near to impossible. We heard nothing for weeks. Then, in February of 1169, we received word that the friends of Sigewize were on their way to Rupertsberg with the afflicted woman. They had decided if Hildegard could not come to them, they would come to Hildegard.

When Sigewize and her companions arrived, there was much consternation in the community. What were we to do with, and for, this poor soul?

Sigewize's friends were accommodated in the guest house, while Sigewize herself was placed in the living quarters of the sisters. Most of the sisters were terrified, but none sought to avoid or abandon the woman, in spite of the mocking and foul words of the spirit, and the disgusting blasts of air it produced.

"How can we drive this demon away?" I asked Hildegard one evening, a few days after they had arrived.

Hildegard thought for a moment, as she sipped a cup of mulled wine. "I have observed that the demon suffers torment in three instances. First, when Sigewize is led from one place to another of the saints. Second, when the common folk give alms for her, and third, when it is compelled to depart through the prayers of the spiritual by the grace of God. It is these things we must focus on," she concluded.

So, for several weeks leading up to Holy Saturday, we and our neighbours, both men and women, worked to heal Sigewize with fasts and prayers, and with almsgiving and penances of our bodies.

On Holy Saturday, the Easter Vigil was celebrated as usual. As part of the ritual, our priest, Father Georg, hallowed the baptismal font by sending his breath into it. Sigewize, who was standing in front of the font, stamping at the floor with her feet and emitting frequent blasts of air, was seized by a great fear and began to tremble. At the same time, Hildegard closed her eyes and swayed back and forth, as if she would faint. I steadied her by taking one arm, and Sister Mathilde took the other. Later, Hildegard told me that, at that moment, she had seen and heard in true vision that the power of the Most High spoke to the diabolical fog by which Sigewize was being tormented, saying, "Go forth, Satan, from the tabernacle of this woman's body. Yield place in her to the Holy Spirit!" Then we all saw the unclean spirit withdraw from Sigewize, and she was finally set free. Everyone who was present rejoiced with songs of praise and exhortations of thanksgiving.

Unsurprisingly, after such a dramatic event, Hildegard was again laid low by illness. For the next 40 days, she was feverish and only semi-conscious. Pairs of sisters again took turns to sit with her and attend to her needs.

One morning in late May, Hildegard sat up and asked for food and drink as if nothing had been untoward. When I came to see her a short time later, she told me what she had felt, seen and heard during this latest relapse.

"I felt the blood in my veins and the very marrow in my bones withering, and setting all my entrails in a turmoil. My whole body languished, and I saw that the wicked spirits were laughing at me raucously, saying, 'Aha! She is going to die, and all her friends who helped her rebuff us are going to cry!' But I knew that my soul's departure was not yet near."

"I also saw in a true vision that I must visit certain communities of spiritual people, both men and women, and candidly lay before them the words that God will show me," she told me.

"Another preaching tour?" I asked, shocked. "Surely God cannot expect this of you. You are far too unwell for such an onerous task."

"Wait, dear Volmar," Hildegard replied. "I have more to tell you. After being told to travel and preach, a most beautiful and loving man appeared to me in a vision. He brought with him so great a consolation that I soared with a vast and immeasurable joy. And he commanded those who were afflicting me to depart, saying, 'Be off with you, for I will not have you torment her any longer.' Immediately, the illness left me, and I have recovered my strength. I feel renewed to the very blood in my veins and the marrow in my bones, as if I have been brought back from the dead!"

My face must have revealed my doubts and confusion.

"I am *well*, dear Volmar," she said, laughing. "I feel as well as I ever have in my life!"

I relaxed and smiled, fighting off tears of relief. I knew there would be no point trying to dissuade Hildegard from this proposed tour. Nothing would ever prevent her from obeying a command from God to do His work, wherever that might take her.

Chapter 28

Hildegard decided to wait until the following year, 1170, to embark upon her fourth preaching tour. She had been so unwell for most of the past three years that she was keen to spend some time with her beloved sisters, rather than depart and leave them again immediately. I thought this was a very good idea.

News of Hildegard's triumph over Sigewize's evil spirit travelled far and wide, and quickly. About a month after the departure of Sigewize and her companions, four brothers from Maria Laach arrived at Rupertsberg, bearing a pallet on which lay a woman cruelly troubled by a spirit. The brothers had tried hard to expel the spirit, but without success. When they heard of Hildegard's abilities in this regard, they set off at once.

Hildegard firmly opposed the impudence and arrogance of the demon with words revealed by the Holy Spirit. She continued with prayers and blessings for many hours until, by the grace of God, she set the woman free from the malevolent enemy.

At about the same time, at the cloister of Aschaffenburg, an evil spirit assailed one of the sisters in a variety of ways. It made her confess to crimes she had not committed, and caused her to howl in terror at the names and the sight of certain persons and animals. This sister was sent to Rupertsberg with a letter from her prior, seeking Hildegard's help. Hildegard comforted the troubled nun and set her free from the delusion of this evil spirit.

Early in July, more news reached us concerning the third antipope, Callixtus. We had heard nothing since September of the previous year, so had given the matter little thought. This was about to change. We were now informed that Frederick had, in fact, recently recognised Callixtus as the rightful pope.

As I had been led to believe, Frederick had been negotiating with Alexander for several months, but their discussions had failed to reach a clear resolution. While this was happening, Callixtus had sent delegates to inform Frederick of his election and to seek imperial recognition. Those delegates had, apparently, reached Frederick in June at an imperial diet held in Bamburg. Frederick, perhaps having decided that a resolution with Alexander was unlikely, gave recognition to Callixtus.

Hildegard was even more livid about this than she had been about the recognition of the first two antipopes.

"I cannot believe it!" she said. "Although it seems to have little effect, I feel I must write to Frederick yet again to register my disapproval in the strongest possible terms."

As on previous occasions, Hildegard wrote the letter and then gave it to me to correct any error in the Latin. This letter was even more alarming than the last.

"He-Who-Is speaks," it began. I cringed. "I shall destroy the insolent along with those who despise me," she wrote. "I shall crush them by myself. Pain, pain to this evil of the evils spurning me. Hear this, King, if you wish to live, or I will run you through with my sword."

I made the necessary corrections, sent the letter, then waited for the consequences. I expected them to be dire.

By the end of that year, Hildegard had received no reply from Frederick. I knew that Rupertsberg's Imperial Charter of Protection gave us a measure of immunity from persecution and punishment, but I was astounded that he made no response to the letter's strident threats. It is true that these threats were said to come from God *through* Hildegard, and were not made by Hildegard herself, but I still considered our community to be very fortunate to have passed through this conflict unscathed.

251

Chapter 29

As the Christmas of 1169 approached, Hildegard and I made plans for the forthcoming tour, which we planned to begin in March 1170.

It was also around this time that I began to experience episodes of dizziness and imbalance. Generally, if these occurred when I was near a wall or piece of furniture, I was able to steady myself and remain upright. On a few occasions, I fell to my knees but managed to get myself up without assistance.

I was not overly concerned by these episodes. I was by no means a 'spring lamb' any longer and attributed the unsteadiness to my advancing years. It did not occur to me for a moment that I would be unable to travel with Hildegard the following year, but the events of Christmas morning put paid to my plans.

I had never been overly fond of rising in the early hours of the morning to sing the Office of Matins, but I liked it less and less as I got older, particularly during the cold months. On Christmas morning, as I made my way reluctantly to the chapel in response to the summons of the bell, I felt quite unsteady. We had barely begun the first antiphon when the whole church began to spin before my eyes, and I felt myself fall forward.

The next thing I was aware of was the sound of hushed, distant voices. I could feel that I was in bed and assumed that I was back in the cell I shared with Brother Arnold. I felt confused – was I not in the chapel just moments ago?

"Why is his face lopsided?" I heard a familiar, male voice ask. Brother Arnold, I thought.

"I have no idea," I heard Hildegard reply. "Sister Mathilde? Have you seen anything like this before?"

A pause. "Yes, once," Sister Mathilde replied. "An old woman in Bingen suffered the same impairment a few months ago."

"Did she recover?" Hildegard asked, sounding alarmed.

Another pause. "I ... I do not recall the outcome," Sister Mathilde replied, but did not sound convincing.

With all the energy I could muster, I opened my eyes and tried to focus on the worried faces at the foot of my bed which, I now realised, was in the infirmary. All three smiled to see me awake.

"Dear Volmar," Hildegard said, coming closer and taking my hand. "How are you feeling? You have given everyone a fright."

I tried to reply, but could not speak. My tongue felt thick in my mouth, and I had no control over my lips. Strange sounds were all that I could utter.

"Never mind," Hildegard said, darting a glance at Sister Mathilde. "Do not try to speak. Save your strength, rest, and get well."

I was confused and alarmed. Why was my face, apparently, 'lopsided'? Why could I not speak?

These muddled thoughts wearied me. I sighed deeply and closed my eyes.

"We should let him rest now," I heard Sister Mathilde say. "I will make sure he is attended at all times."

I remained in the infirmary until the end of January. By then, I could speak slowly and walk around the room with the aid of a stick. My left arm and leg did not seem to be working properly and I hoped that this would improve over time. I was grateful that my right arm and hand were unaffected, as I could at least return to my work in the scriptorium.

During that month, planning had continued for Hildegard's upcoming preaching tour. I was still hoping to go with her, although, in my more realistic moments, I knew that this was unlikely. Hildegard finally confirmed my fears.

"I do not think you should come on this journey," she said to me one day in early February. "You are not strong enough for such arduous travel, and I fear that you may worsen at a place where adequate help is not available."

I knew she was right, but I was devastated. I nodded in response but could say nothing.

Memories of that first tour, when Brother Arnold had taken my place to navigate the Main River, came flooding back. That had been five months of misery. How long would this tour be? I felt even less able to cope with Hildegard's absence now than I had 12 years earlier, and I had not coped at all well then. I felt old, useless and bereft.

A few days later, when I had prayed and thought about the matter, I felt calmer and more accepting of the situation. *God always knows what is best for us*, I reminded myself. I forced myself to be cheerful and positive about the upcoming journey.

One evening, as we sat in front of the fire in Hildegard's chamber, I asked about her plans for the tour.

"I have asked Sister Clementia to accompany me, now that Sister Hiltrud is at Eibingen," she began. "Brother Arnold has also agreed to come, to sail the boat and provide protection, as he did on my first tour." She smiled sadly at me. "I do wish you were able to come, dear friend, but I do think this is a better arrangement."

I agreed, as I knew I must, but I did feel a pang of sinful envy that it was Brother Arnold, and not I, that was going with the women.

"Have you decided on the places that you will go to?" I asked, hoping to change my train of thought.

Hildegard unrolled a parchment across her lap, on which the tour had been mapped.

"We will head south this time," she began, "along the Rhine and Neckar rivers into the region of Swabia. I have decided to visit the Cistercian abbey at Maulbronn, followed by the Benedictine abbey at Hirsau in the Black Forest." I nodded as I watched her finger move along the rivers and then inland. "After that, we will go to the Benedictine double monastery at Zwiefalten, then the Augustinian canonry in Rodenkirchen. Our final stop will be at Kirchheim, on our way back to Ruperstberg."

Zwiefalten? That was such a long way from Rupertsberg. "How long do you think you will be away?" I asked, dreading the answer, knowing it would be a long time.

Hildegard thought for a moment as she rolled up the parchment. "It will take some months, I think. I will aim to be back by November, before winter arrives. We will need to set off in the next few days if we are to achieve this."

My face must have reflected my dismay. November? Nine months. My heart sank, and I could no longer even pretend to be cheerful.

Hildegard smiled and patted my hand. "The time will pass quickly, dear Volmar," she said. "There is always so much to do here. You will be so busy that you will not even notice my absence."

I could have laughed at her last remark if I had not been so sad. "There *is* much to do," I agreed, "but I doubt that I am able to do many of the things I previously did."

"You must, of course, be careful to take care and allow yourself to return to full health," she said. "Only do what you feel able to do. There are many people here who can assist you or even assume some of your responsibilities."

Three days later, the entire community accompanied Hildegard, Sister Clementia, and Brother Arnold to the riverbank, where our cob was moored. We stood and watched as the boat set off, waving our goodbyes. Most people went back to the abbey quite quickly, but I stayed and watched until the boat rounded a bend and could no longer be seen. Only then did I turn and trudge slowly back up the hill, my left leg threatening to give way as I climbed.

I had decided that Hildegard was quite right. I *must* keep busy to take my mind off the gaping hole in the fabric of our community. I also knew that I was not fully recovered, so I concentrated on tasks that did not require great physical effort.

As Hildegard's secretary, it had always been my responsibility to deal with the often-voluminous correspondence that she received. This did abate slightly while she was away, but at least part of my day was still dedicated to this task.

I also continued to supervise and work in the scriptorium, which I loved doing. The sisters who regularly worked there were a dedicated and talented group, producing beautiful copies of Hildegard's works and also those of other writers. We had recently received a volume of the writings of Bernard of Clairvaux on loan from the monastery at Trier, and so one of our most experienced scribes was copying this to add to our library.

The library at Rupertsberg was growing steadily. Hildegard sometimes sent copies of her writings to the libraries of other monasteries and abbeys, and we, in turn, received books from these and other establishments. Sending and receiving books, and finding the best place to shelve the new books were tasks I enjoyed and was able to cope with physically. It could, however, be something of a trap. I often found that hours passed unnoticed if I became engrossed in reading a newly received volume, and I sometimes missed meals or even one or some of the Offices without meaning to.

By June, I was feeling much better, both physically and in my mood. I had settled into a comfortable routine, and the longer, warm days also helped to lift my spirits. I was still missing Hildegard, of course, but was coping with her absence quite well.

Then I had the dream.

I have very rarely had dreams that I remember the next morning. This one was like no other. It seemed so real that I was convinced that the events had taken place.

In the dream, I was working in the herb garden, which I rarely did anymore, when a messenger arrived from the south.

"Hildegard is dead!" he announced, without any warning of the dreadful news.

I dropped my spade. "No! This cannot be!" I wailed.

"It is true," said the messenger. "She fell from the boat and was swept away. Her body was found miles down the river."

In the dream, I began to weep. In reality, I awoke and sat up, sobbing into my hands.

After a short time, I realised I had been dreaming. While this was a huge relief, I became desperate to know whether Hildegard was, in reality, safe and well, but I had no idea how to discover this.

Fortunately, we received news a few days later that everyone was well and that the tour was proving to be very successful. This eased my fears greatly, but I had, for the first time since meeting Hildegard, become aware of the desolation I would feel when she died.

I had never told Hildegard of my feelings for her. It would have been highly improper to do so, of course, but I did want her to know how much she meant to me, and to everyone here at Rupertsberg. I decided that I would write her a letter.

I spent many hours on this letter, writing a sentence, scraping it off the parchment, then writing a different sentence. It took much writing and scraping before I was content with what I had written.

I told her how privileged we at Rupertsberg were to see her every day with fleshly eyes, to hear her with fleshly ears, and to cling to her daily (as was proper). I went on to say that we also knew that, at some time, she would be taken away from us and that, thereafter, we would no longer see and hear her as now. I told her how, when that time came, our grief would surpass the joy we now feel.

My unanswered questions tumbled onto the parchment.

"Who will give answers to all who seek to understand their condition? Who will provide fresh interpretations of the Scriptures? Who will utter songs never heard before and give voice to that unheard language? Who will deliver new and unheard-of sermons on feast days? Who will give revelations about the spirits of the departed? Who will offer revelations of things past, present, and future? Who will expound the nature of creation in all its diversity?" Hildegard did all of these things for all who came to her, with humility and generosity. Who would do these things once she was no longer here?

The answer, of course, was nobody. Nobody could ever hope to fill the void that would be created upon Hildegard's passing.

I read and re-read what I had written. The parchment was so worn from my erasures that it was nearly translucent in places. Finally, I was satisfied that the letter was heartfelt but not inappropriate or unseemly. I rolled it up and placed it into the small wooden chest I kept in the cell I shared with Brother Arnold. I had decided not to send it to Hildegard while she was away. I would give it to her when she finally returned.

I continued my daily routine of prayer and work, but could not regain the contentment I had felt before that accursed dream. Instead, I counted the days until November, when we were expecting the travellers to arrive home. The time passed like a snail moving through mud.

Finally, on a cold afternoon in mid-November, I heard voices coming up the hill from the river. I rushed to the main gate to see who was approaching. It was Hildegard and her companions!

"They are returned!" I called, as loudly as I could, although my voice was much weaker since my illness. Someone must have heard me and spread the news, because a large and noisy throng formed in the courtyard to welcome the travellers home.

I could see Hildegard was scanning the crowd, looking for someone. When she saw me, she burst into a huge smile and waved. I nearly wept for joy. It was *me* she had been searching for.

This had been our longest separation since Hildegard's first tour in 1158. I had felt unexpectedly nervous about seeing her again, but that smile caused all my uncertainty to vanish completely. She was home, hopefully for good this time.

The travellers had much to tell about their journey. As had become the custom, they told their tales while we ate our evening meal that night, listening with rapt attention. Hildegard, of course, did most of the telling.

"The Cistercians at Maulbronn were very polite and respectful, probably helped by my connection with their founder, Bernard of Clairvaux, I think," she began. "They are in good order – a thriving and industrious community."

"Sadly, the same cannot be said of the Benedictines at either Hirsau or Zweifalten. Both of these communities have grown lax. The community at Hirsau seems to have become despondent. They lack any zeal for their calling or their faith. I tried to rekindle their enthusiasm, but I do not think that community will survive much longer." Gasps were heard around the refectory. This was very sad news.

"Zweifalten is also lax, but instead of despondent, they are disorderly and ill-disciplined. I spoke to them quite harshly about their need to correct their bad behaviour, and they *seemed* to realise the error of their ways. Time will tell if they have truly repented."

Much murmuring and tongue-clicking greeted these remarks. "It is fortunate that you went there, Mother," I said.

"I knew of their need from the many letters I had received from their prior and also several of the nuns," Hildegard replied. "It is not a happy place. We should all pray for them earnestly."

We murmured our agreement with this suggestion.

After a pause for food and wine, Hildegard continued. "Our next stop was a much happier one. The Augustinian canons at Rodenkirchen are a lovely community. I have been friends with their superior, Stefan, for many years. Some of you might remember him from his visits here."

Older members of the community nodded and murmured assent. I also knew Stefan quite well, and was pleased that Hildegard had been able to see him.

"Our last stop, at Kirchheim, was a highlight of this journey," Hildegard continued. "I preached publicly there, to an assembly of priests led by Bishop Werner. My sermon must have moved him greatly, as he has requested a written copy of it. I must write it down soon, while it is fresh in my mind," she said, more to herself than us.

"What did you say to them, Mother?" asked Sister Mathilde.

"I told them what is plain for all to see, that the church in Kirchheim is beset and besieged by enemies, and is neglected by uncaring priests and other servants of God." This produced some murmurs of surprise. Harsh words, indeed. "I implored my listeners to allow the fire of the Holy Spirit to work among them to renew and restore the Church to its full glory."

Hildegard sipped her wine while *these* listeners voiced their agreement with Hildegard's stirring words. I looked around the refectory, at our community gathered together on this joyous occasion. I looked at the eager, devout faces, listening to their leader while eating this marvellous feast. I smiled. Hildegard was home, all was well. It was a moment when I could truly say that I felt completely happy. I savoured the moment, knowing that this, like all things, whether good or evil, would not last forever.

Chapter 30

After only a few days' rest, Hildegard threw herself back into her work as leader of the communities at both Rupertsberg and Eibingen.

On our first boat trip to Eibingen after Hildegard's return, I was witness to another of Hildegard's miraculous healings. As we were pulling into the bank below the sister convent, we were approached by a woman carrying a small child in the crook of her arms.

"Please, blessed lady," the woman was sobbing. "My little girl is blind. I beg you to lay your holy hands on her." The child was staring blankly into the distance, and I could see that her eyes were cloudy.

Hildegard scooped some water from the river with her left hand, and blessed it with her right. When she sprinkled it into the child's eyes, the child blinked rapidly for a moment. Then, she looked directly at her mother with clear, blue eyes and smiled.

"Praise God!" the woman shouted, "and blessed be your holy name, Lady Hildegard." The woman rushed away with the child, and we climbed the hill to the convent in silence. Neither of us felt the need for words.

Hildegard also continued to compose music, and to correspond with people of all ranks to give advice and counsel. She managed all of these tasks while continuing to lead the structured life of all Benedictines, with the observance of the Rule and the singing of the eight daily Offices being of particular importance.

I do not know how or in what 'spare' time, but Hildegard also set to work on the third volume of her visionary writings, to be known as the Book of Divine Works.

"When I first saw this work in my vision two years ago," she said to me one evening in late 1170, "I was uncertain of the form it would take, and only vaguely aware of what its content would be. Since then, all has become clear."

"What will it be?" I asked, sipping the spicy hot mulled wine that helped to banish at least some of the chill at this time of year.

Hildegard finished her wine, and poured herself more. "It will be divided into three parts, reflecting the trinitarian nature of God. The first part will concern the world of humanity, the second part will deal with the world of the hereafter, that is, human destiny, and the third part will deal with the history of salvation."

I was shaking my head and smiling. "This will be your *magnum opus*," I said.

As previously, I assisted Hildegard with scribing, translating, and editing the text of this magnificent work. After a few weeks, Hildegard seemed dissatisfied.

"Something is lacking," she said, frowning. Then she sighed. "It needs visual imagery, to aid in understanding the words."

I nodded. We looked at each other sadly, remembering the beautiful art that Richardis had contributed to Hildegard's first treatise. Then I had an idea.

"She is not *quite* as gifted as Richardis," I began tentatively, "but perhaps we could ask Sister Clementia to work with us? She did an excellent job with the music notation in the *Symphonia*," I continued, "and her illuminated manuscripts are quite beautiful." I finished in a rush, hoping that I had not upset Hildegard with this suggestion.

She thought for a few moments, then nodded, smiling sadly. "Nobody can replace Richardis, of course," she said, "but I think Sister Clementia will do wonderful work for us."

I exhaled with relief and smiled.

Sister Clementia was delighted at the prospect of contributing to this work. "This is such an honour!" she said when I approached her with the suggestion.

So, a new team was formed – Hildegard, Sister Clementia and me. We worked well together, and it was almost like old times. Had it really been 30 years since a slightly different team worked on *Scivias*? The time seemed to have passed quickly, but I was certainly feeling its effects. Although I felt quite well, having recovered from my recent affliction, I grew tired more quickly than previously, and I could only see to write in very good light. "No late-night, candle-lit sessions this time," I said to Hildegard late one afternoon, as the light was beginning to fade.

Hildegard smiled and stood up from the table where we had been working. She stretched her back and groaned quietly.

"No, indeed," she replied with a laugh. "As St Matthew tells us, 'The spirit is willing, but the flesh is weak'. We have done enough for today."

I watched Hildegard as she spoke, and thought that she, too, was beginning to show signs of old age. This should not have surprised me – she was now 72 years old, and had endured much illness in her life. I thought again of the letter I had written in her absence. I had decided not to give her the letter, for the time being at least. While it was certain that our time together would come to an end, instead of dwelling on the inevitability of this loss, I resolved to give thanks to

God for the many years that we had already shared, and to
cherish whatever time was left to us.

265

Chapter 31

The year 1171 began with distressing news from abroad. A young Englishman staying in our guest house, named Edward, was on pilgrimage to Rome because his spirit was sorely grieved by an event he had recently witnessed. He begged an audience with Hildegard, and I also attended for the sake of propriety.

"What is troubling you, my child?" Hildegard asked gently.

"I... I have seen the foulest of murders, my lady, and it haunts me by day and night," he began.

"Do the authorities know of this crime?" Hildegard asked.

"Yes, my lady. It is well-known in all of England."

Hildegard raised her eyebrows at me. "Tell me what you saw, Edward," she said. "It will ease your burden to speak of it."

Edward swallowed, then began. "It was in Canterbury, in the cathedral, a few days after Christmas," he said. "The archbishop was in the cathedral, near where the monks were chanting Vespers. Four men entered, and told the archbishop that he must go to Winchester to give an account of himself to King Henry. When the archbishop refused to do so, the men rushed at the archbishop with their swords and ... they *killed* him, my lady! I could not believe what I was seeing."

Hildegard cried out. "No! This cannot be!" I felt dizzy, as if I might faint.

"It is true, my lady," Edward replied. "It was horrible. I tried to intervene, but one of the men sliced my arm, and I fell away." Edward rolled up his sleeve to reveal a heavily bandaged arm. The bandage looked torn and dirty.

"You must have that seen to by Sister Mathilde," I said to the young man, who was quivering all over. "Come. I will take you to the infirmarian."

"Wait, Volmar," Hildegard said. She had regained some composure, and came to stand in front of the young pilgrim. She placed her hand on his head. "May God bless you for your bravery, and heal you in both body and spirit."

Edward stopped quivering, and looked up at Hildegard with a look of wonder in his eyes. "Thank you, my lady." He smiled, as I helped him to his feet and took him to see Sister Mathilde.

When I returned, Hildegard was on her knees, praying. I did likewise, and we prayed together for some time. Finally, Hildegard rose from her *prie-dieu* and sat in a chair, looking pale and tired.

"Such wickedness is beyond my comprehension," she said.

I nodded my agreement. "This is even worse than Archbishop Arnold being killed in *front* of a church," I said. "To commit murder *in* a church must be the worst of all sins."

"Why on earth would anyone do this?" Hildegard asked, presumably knowing that I could not answer this question.

I just shook my head sadly. "No doubt we will hear more of this," I said.

About a month later, a messenger arrived from the Diocese of Mainz, informing us officially of the murder of Archbishop Thomas Becket.

The reason, we were told, was that Thomas had fallen out of favour with King Henry II, even though they had previously been friends. When Henry made the mistake of complaining about Thomas, four of the king's loyal knights took it upon themselves to 'fix' the problem by eradicating Thomas.

"What could Henry possibly have said to warrant such a response?" I asked.

"Wait a minute," the messenger said. "They *did* tell me." He looked at the ceiling, as if the answer might be found there. He closed his eyes before reciting, "What miserable drones and traitors have I nourished and brought up in my household, who let their lord be treated with such shameful contempt by a low-born cleric?" He opened his eyes and looked at us, blinking. "I think that was it," he said.

Hildegard and I exchanged looks of astonishment, at both the mode of delivery and the content of this pronouncement. "The knights would have taken that as criticism of them*selves*," I said. "They must have assumed *they* were the 'traitors and drones' the king was referring to. They obviously thought they could restore their reputations by eliminating the king's 'problem'."

"Yes, but surely Henry did not *mean* for them to take such drastic action," Hildegard said.

"No, I am certain he did not," I replied.

The community mourned for the slain archbishop for many days, and prayed for his soul most ardently. Hildegard was subdued for several weeks, but the busyness of life at Rupertsberg soon overtook her once again, and we continued with our lives of service to God, while always remembering those who had died in the course of such service.

Chapter 32

The next two years were happy and productive ones for Hildegard and me. The community at Rupertsberg was also settled and orderly, and our sister community at Eibingen grew and prospered.

Hildegard was now visiting the Eibingen convent less frequently, but made the trip across the river at least once a month. We were also kept informed of the events and activities at Eibingen by their leader, Sister Hiltrud. She would attend a Chapter meeting at Rupertsberg once a fortnight, and was always full of news and stories.

It was around this time that we became aware of a certain philosopher, reputed for his wealth, who was publicly casting doubts on Hildegard's visions and miraculous feats of healing. He was a man of some influence, and so it was concerning that he was spreading such negative views of Hildegard. Hildegard decided to take a proactive approach.

"I will invite him to come and stay here at Rupertsberg," she told me one evening in early spring. "Perhaps if we can talk face to face, and he can observe our work here, he will adopt a more favourable outlook."

I thought for a moment, then nodded. "That is a good idea," I said. "It certainly cannot hurt, and, as you say, it will probably help." I had no doubt that this man would change his mind about Hildegard if he came to Rupertsberg. I was convinced that nobody who ever met her could be anything other than awestruck.

In mid-April, the philosopher arrived and took up temporary residence in the guest house. He and Hildegard spent many hours in animated conversation on a wide range of subjects. I attended some of these sessions, but rarely managed to insert my own views into the proceedings. Nonetheless, I found the discussions both fascinating and instructive.

I was quite surprised that the philosopher took a keen interest in all aspects of our work at Rupertsberg. I took him to the scriptorium, and showed him one of the illuminated manuscripts that Sister Clementia was working on.

He picked up a finished parchment that was decorated in exquisite colours. He looked at it for some time. "This is of rare and outstanding beauty," he finally said, carefully placing it on a table. He looked at Sister Clementia. "Your gift comes straight from God," he said. She blushed and lowered her eyes while thanking him for the compliment.

I also showed him our library. "It is small," I said, "but we are adding to it whenever possible."

He looked around for a few moments, picking up, opening, then putting down several volumes. "It is a fine collection," he said. "Perhaps I could contribute some works on philosophy to your shelves."

"That would be greatly appreciated," I said. We smiled at each other. I liked this man far more than I had expected to.

Hildegard seemed to have made some progress in persuading the philosopher to accept at least some of her ideas, but his last night at Rupertsberg expelled any doubts he might have had regarding her special relationship with God.

We were all in the refectory, enjoying our evening meal, when a young novice named Hedwig came rushing in and headed straight to Hildegard.

"My lady, please come at once!" Hedwig gasped.

"What has happened, child?" Hildegard asked.

"It is the hermit. I think he has gone mad!" Hedwig said.

Hildegard, Sister Mathilde and I got up and hurried to the anchorage. Hedwig ran ahead of us, leading the way. From outside, we could hear Brother Roric wailing and could see him thrashing about.

"I ... I came to give him his meal," the young novice explained, "but he would not answer me." She turned and ran back towards the kitchen.

Hildegard possessed the only key to the stout padlock securing the door to the anchorage. Fortunately, she carried this with her other keys at all times. She produced the key, opened the lock, and the three of us entered the cell.

Roric was on the ground, tossing and ranting. His face was red and wet with perspiration. Sister Mathilde knelt beside him and felt his forehead and pulse points.

"This is a very severe fever," she said. "I will fetch my remedies, although I fear that I may be too late." She raced from the cell into the gathering dusk.

Hildegard looked concerned but not panicked. She came over to the frantic young man, knelt beside him, and blessed him with the sign of the Cross. He immediately stopped writhing about, and his breathing began to slow. By the time Sister Mathilde returned, he was sitting up and sipping water, while Hildegard dried his face with the sleeve of her gown.

In our haste to attend to Roric, none of us had realised that the philosopher had followed us to the anchorage. He was standing outside the door, but with a clear view of the cell's interior, and his mouth was open like a gaping fish. He came into the cell and prostrated himself before Hildegard.

"Blessed lady," he sobbed. "Forgive me, an ignorant sinner, for ever doubting your abilities."

Hildegard reached down and touched the top of his head. "Please get up, good sir. I do not deserve this adoration. This is God's doing - I am merely his conduit."

The next morning, as we gathered to bid the philosopher farewell, he knelt before Hildegard and asked for her blessing, which, of course, she gladly gave him.

In due course, we heard that the philosopher was now singing Hildegard's praises far and wide, and that many were astonished at the change in him. He also endowed our place with buildings and properties and other gifts. As a final indication of his respect for Hildegard and her community, he petitioned to be allowed burial with us when his time came. This was agreed to unanimously by the Chapter, so that the learned man would be able to spend eternity near to the blessed lady he had come to so admire.

Chapter 33

By the beginning of 1172, Hildegard, Sister Clementia and I had made good progress on the Book of Divine Works. Hildegard also continued to send and receive large numbers of letters, which gave rise to another major undertaking.

"I have been thinking for some time of compiling my letters into an orderly collection," Hildegard said to me one evening in early 1172. "At the moment, as you know, they are piled in the order they arrived, and could be bound in that way, but this may not be the best way to preserve them. Perhaps you could give some thought to this and compile them for me?"

"I would be happy to," I replied. "This will be an interesting task." While I had already seen most of this correspondence, I was not always shown Hildegard's outgoing missives.

I knew where Hildegard's correspondence, both incoming and outgoing, was stored. The room in which she wrote, composed, and conducted the business of the abbey was lined with tall shelves. The parchments were placed here when they had been dealt with.

I knew where they were, but I had never really examined them closely. My heart sank slightly when I did so. There were hundreds of them! This would be no small task.

I started by skimming through the contents of the first few shelves, and noticed that the letters were written by people from a variety of 'ranks', both religious and secular. There were letters from laypeople, priests, monks, abbotts, and even archbishops and members of the nobility. Perhaps I could group the letters on this basis, so, for example, all the letters from laypeople were grouped together, all those from monks and nuns placed in another group, and so on.

Hildegard was pleased with this suggestion, so I began the process of sorting. When I had finished, the letters were arranged by 'rank' of the person writing to Hildegard, and I had also paired each incoming letter with a copy of Hildegard's reply.

It takes but a moment to write of this undertaking, but the actual doing of the task took many months, interspersed as it was between other duties and activities. It was not until early in 1173 that the piles were in the desired order. Next came the task of editing and binding.

I did not, of course, alter the content or form of any of Hildegard's letters. Indeed, I had already been closely involved in the preparation of the more important of these, so I would have been editing my own editing! I did, however, need to transcribe some of the incoming letters, especially those written by laypeople. In some cases, these were poorly written and difficult to comprehend.

I debated whether to retain these poorly written originals, or just the transcriptions and Hildegard's replies. I decided on the latter. The volumes were substantial enough without such duplications. It was, after all, meant to be a collection of *Hildegard's* writings.

One afternoon towards the end of February 1173, I was attending to Hildegard's current correspondence when I happened to glance at the empty shelves. I smiled, feeling pleased that I had finally managed to sort the huge backlog, when I noticed a small piece of parchment on an otherwise empty upper shelf. Curious, I went to look more closely and realised that a parchment had somehow fallen down the back of the shelf, with only a corner protruding. I pulled the corner carefully and found a neatly folded letter. I could see at once from the outer side of the letter that it was Hildegard's writing. It was addressed to 'My dear sister' —

whether this was a blood relative or another nun, I could not tell.

The sorted piles had not yet been bound, so I opened this letter to determine which pile it belonged to. I soon realised, however, that this letter was *not* intended for public perusal, and certainly not for my eyes.

After a few preliminary remarks, the letter proceeded as follows.

"As I have told you before, God instructed me to search for someone 'who would run in the path of salvation' with me. As you also know, I found such a man in Volmar, and loved him, knowing that he was a faithful man, working like myself on the work that leads to God. Holding fast to him, I worked with him in great zeal so that God's hidden miracles might be revealed. All this you already know.

"What I have not told you, or any other living person, is that my feelings for this lovely man went well beyond what had been commanded by God. I have loved Volmar since I first met him, some 60 years ago. I have, of course, never acted on these feelings. Neither have I ever, nor will ever, tell him of this. I trust that you will keep this to yourself, but I confess that I feel greatly relieved to have unburdened myself after so many years."

The letter concluded with a few pleasantries that I paid no heed to. I was dumbfounded. My heart was racing, and my face felt as if it were on fire.

I heard footsteps approaching, and looked frantically for somewhere to hide the letter. I quickly folded the parchment, and slid it back behind the shelf where I had found it. As the door opened, I spun around to see who was entering. The room kept spinning, round and around, and I felt myself falling into darkness.

Epilogue

February 1173

As I lie here in the infirmary, the room growing steadily darker, I wish with all my heart that I could have told Hildegard of my feelings for her, and that I now knew of her feelings for me, but once again my mouth refused to work, and I could not speak the words I so desperately wanted to say.

Perhaps it is better that the words remain unspoken. After all, neither Hildegard nor I would ever have acted on our feelings. Our relationship has been one of deep friendship and mutual respect. That is as it should be.

I have been blessed indeed to have served Hildegard as teacher, adviser and scribe, and to have called her 'friend' these past six decades. God knows that I have served her to the very best of my ability in all things. My only regret is that I could not serve her to the end of *her* days, but only to the end of mine.

Now it is time for me to sleep.

Glossary

abbess	Female leader of an abbey of nuns
abbey	Complex of buildings that houses a community of monks and/or nuns
abbott	Male leader of an abbey of monks
Advent	Beginning of the Christian year, the four weeks leading up to Christmas
anchorage	Small cell in which an anchoress or anchorite lived
anchoress	Woman who chooses to withdraw from the world to lead a (usually) solitary life of prayer and contemplation
anchorite	Male anchoress
antiphon	Short sentence sung or recited before or after a psalm or canticle
Apostles	People who had met and followed Jesus and were sent by him to spread the gospel
armarius	Monk in charge of the library and scriptorium in a monastery
Augustinians	Monastic religious order that follows the Rule of St Augustine

Benedictines	Monastic religious order that follows the Rule of St Benedict
canon	Male equivalent of canoness
canoness	Member of a community of women that observes the Rule of St Augustine
canonry	Community of canons and/or canonesses
canticle	song-text from the Bible that is not a psalm
Cathars	Christian heretical group that flourished in Europe during the 12th and 13th centuries
cellarer	Senior monk, responsible for the physical needs of the brothers, such as food, drink and other provisions
Chapter	Administrative body comprising abbott, prior and monks, responsible for the day-to-day running of the monastery
Chapter House	Chamber in which the Chapter met
chamberlain	Monk responsible for the acquisition, repair and distribution of all clothes, shoes and bedding in the monastery
Compline	Final service of the day, held just before bedtime
confessor	Person who confesses faith in and adheres to Christianity, especially in spite of persecution but without suffering martyrdom
consolamentum	The most significant ceremony in Cathar theology, marking the transition from ordinary believer to member of their

	'elect', usually administered just before death
convent	Christian community of nuns, living under monastic vows
count palatinate	'Count of the palace', a nobleman above the rank of an ordinary count
diet	Deliberative body of the Holy Roman Empire
Divine Office	Daily services, usually chanted, marking the hours of each day with prayer, psalms and scripture readings
Extreme Unction	Sacrament of anointing the sick, especially when administered to the dying
the Fall	Adam and Eve's fall from grace in the Garden of Eden
gospel	Literally 'good news', the announcement that Jesus has brought the reign of God to our world through his life, death and resurrection
the Incarnation	Christian doctrine that God took human form in the body of Jesus
infirmarian	Monk/nun responsible for the treatment and care of the sick
infirmary	Building/room/s that served as an institution's hospital, and also as a shelter for the old and the poor
Lauds	First service of the day, beginning at dawn

magister	Leader, teacher
magistra	Female magister
margrave	Member of the German nobility, corresponding in rank to a British marquess
margravine	Wife/widow of a margrave
martyr	Person who is killed because of their religious beliefs
Matins	Night office, beginning at the 8th hour of the night
monastery	Building/s in which monks live and work
monastic rule	Text that lays down the basic organisation of a monastic community, provides guidelines for the abbott and other officeholders, and explains spiritual principles for the monks/nuns
novice	Prospective member of a religious order who is being assessed for admission to the order
oblate	Person offered to the service of a religious order, usually by parents
Office	See above under Divine Office
oratory	Place set aside for divine worship
patriarch	Biblical persons regarded as fathers of the human race, especially Abraham, Isaac and Jacob
prie-dieu	Prayer desk intended for private devotions

prior	Monk in charge of a priory or second in charge of an abbey
priory	Religious house, smaller than an abbey
prioress	Nun in charge of a priory or second in charge of an abbey
prophet	Person regarded as an inspired teacher or proclaimer of the will of God
psalm	Song-text in the Book of Psalms in the Bible
psalter	Book containing psalms
Prime	Service beginning at 6am
provost	Immediate subordinate to an abbott or abbess
responsory	Chant recited or sung after a reading during a service
rouncey	Standard saddle horse
Rule of St Augustine	Short monastic rule, written around 400 CE by St Augustine of Hippo. The oldest monastic rule in the Western church
Rule of St Benedict	Monastic rule, written around 529 CE by St Benedict of Nursia. Much more detailed and prescriptive that the Rule of St Augustine
sacraments	Religious ceremony or ritual regarded as imparting divine grace, including baptism, communion, anointing of the sick and marriage
sacristan	Monk in charge of the contents of the church, such as robes, candles and

chalices

scribe   Monk/nun who made copies of manuscripts

scriptorium   Building/room where scribes performed their work

Sext   Service beginning at midday

synod   Assembly of bishops and other church officials

Terce   Service beginning at 9am

Vespers   Service beginning at 6pm

Wisdom books   Biblical books of Job, Proverbs, Ecclesiastes, Ecclesiasticus and Wisdom - texts that belong to the genre known as 'wisdom literature'

Wisdom literature   Genre common in the ancient Near East, providing teachings regarding divinity and virtue

Further Reading

Bain, Jennifer (editor). *The Cambridge Companion to Hildegard of Bingen*, 2021, Cambridge University Press.

Baird, Joseph L. (translator). *The Personal Correspondence of Hildegard of Bingen*, 2006, Oxford University Press.

Bobko, Jane (editor). *Vision: The Life and Music of Hildegard of Bingen*, 1995, Penguin Books USA, New York.

Flanagan, Sabina. *Hildegard of Bingen: A Visionary Life*, 1990, Routledge, London.

King-Lenzmeier, Anne H. *Hildegard of Bingen: An Integrated Vision*, 2001, The Liturgical Press, Collegeville, Minnesota.

Hart, Mother Columba and Jane Bishop (translators). *Hildegard of Bingen: Scivias*, 1990, Paulist Press, New Jersey.

Kujawa-Holbrook, Dr Sheryl A. (translator and editor). *Hildegard of Bingen: Essential Writings and Chants of a Christian Mystic – Annotated & Explained*, 2016, SkyLight Paths Publishing, Vermont.

Newman, Barbara. *Symphonia: A Critical Edition of the Symphonia armonie celestium revelationum (Symphony of the Harmony of Celestial Revelations)*, 1988, Cornell University Press.

Silvas, Anna. *Jutta & Hildegard: The Biographical Sources*, 1999, The Pennsylvania State University Press.

White, Carolinne (translator and editor). *The Rule of St Benedict*, 2008, Penguin Books Ltd, London.

Author Bio
Andrea Sherko

Andrea lives in Melbourne, Australia, and is currently negotiating her seventh decade of life.

Andrea's two main passions are music and animals. She enjoys composing, singing, playing, and listening to a wide range of music, from medieval to pop, and everything in between. She has also enjoyed sharing her home with a variety of furred, feathered, and finned creatures, including cats, rabbits, guinea pigs, canaries, and goldfish. She currently lives with three rather indulged cats: Tosca, Rufus, and Gizmo.

Andrea also loves learning new things. She has tertiary qualifications in Business, Law, Theology, Music, Training and Assessment, and Editing/Proofreading. Although not studying at present, she has an unfulfilled ambition to obtain a Doctorate, hopefully in Music and/or Theology.

Andrea has had a variety of jobs, having worked as a trombone player, music teacher, shop assistant, commercial laundry hand, government investigator and policy officer, lawyer, library assistant, and receptionist at various times, and for varying lengths of time. She is currently seeking to re-enter the workforce after an extended absence that began with the COVID lockdowns and continued when her elderly mother required full-time care.

Andrea enjoys writing in a variety of genres, including poetry, short stories, and essays. *The Saint and the Scribe* is her first novel, and she has plans for the next one, which will be based on the story of St Guinefort, a heroic greyhound who lived in medieval France. Samples of Andrea's writings can be viewed on her blog, *Persuasive Words*, which can be found at: https://persuasivewordsnet.blogspot.com/

www.ingramcontent.com/pod-product-compliance
Lightning Source LLC
Chambersburg PA
CBHW071421200726
48294CB00002B/473